# SULDRIC'S KING

## BROM GEISTMAN

Lord Daetari's Tower
Eskalon
Ferun Keep
Port Neloor
Imperial City
THE EMPIRE
AETHARA

GOBLIN MOUNTAINS
Forest City
ULTARA ORRALIS
Lirien
Wizard's Council
GREGOR'S FOREST
Redstone
Hearthmere
Edge Hollow
WITCH MOUNTAINS

Published by Geistman Press

BromGeistman.com

Edited by Philip Athans

Proofread by Scott Colby

Cover art by Graphoria

Map illustration by Travis Hasenour

First Edition

ISBN   979-8-9949562-0-5

# 1

The forge had been relentless today, the heat unusually intense—air dry as tinder. For early spring, it was hot enough that the grass had already gone brown. Edric's broad shoulders gleamed with sweat as he wiped his brow, chest rising and falling with the weight of hours worked.

"Hand me that towel, Calen," he said, peeling off his sweat-soaked tunic.

Calen passed him the towel, then wiped his own forehead with a sleeve before pulling off his tunic as well. Helping his father in the smithy was usually a rhythm he could fall into. It was steady, careful work he took pride in. But the heat today dragged at him, turning his grip uncertain and his breath uneven. Edric didn't slow once; sweat poured off him, but the heat hadn't taken any strength from his swing.

The plowshare still glowed in the forge, sullen and red, waiting for another round of hammer blows. They'd been at it since morning. The metal had refused them—warped and unwilling, bent at an ugly angle after striking a buried boulder in a newly broken field.

"Bet you're wishing you'd gone with your grandmother to Rosewick after all. A long ride and talk of herbs would've been easier than this," Edric teased.

He grasped the glowing plowshare with heavy iron tongs, muscles shifting under his skin as he lifted. Calen moved to the other side, guiding the stubborn metal to the waiting anvil. Edric raised his hammer high and brought it down hard.

Sparks burst as steel met steel, the sharp ring still hanging in the air when a shout—close, urgent—made them both flinch and turn. Edric's hammer hovered mid-swing.

"Come on!" came a yell. "It's too hot! Let's go swimming!"

Toby stood there, naked and grinning wide, waving like he thought this was the best idea he'd ever had.

Edric groaned, rubbing a soot-stained hand over his face. "By the gods."

He glared at Toby. "Calen, get some pants on that boy before your mother sees him." He turned back to the anvil and brought the hammer down hard.

Edric didn't look especially bothered. He never did. Boys were boys, but Calen knew that tone. If his mother saw Toby streaking around the forge again, they'd all get an earful.

Calen didn't need a reminder of how his mother felt about appearances.

She already hated the way the town looked at them.

They were seen as rough-handed and wild—blacksmiths living on the outskirts of town. And with townsfolk always showing up unannounced to drop off tools or ask for repairs...it wasn't worth the risk. But it was more than that.

People stared at his father.

Men, women—it didn't seem to matter. Calen had seen it: the way they lingered too long at the forge, the way their eyes followed Edric when he worked shirtless in the summer heat.

Some of them giggled and whispered. Even as a kid, Calen hadn't liked it, and his mother liked it even less. A naked Toby wouldn't help.

"Oh! She's not even here!" Toby yelled. "She went down to the market to get more goop for Grandma Mira's smelly ointments."

Edric frowned. "You're overheated. Go cool off and get your brother inside before a customer—or your mother—sees him."

"Whatever you say," Calen replied, forcing a grin and offering a mock bow as he stripped off his trousers and tossed them at his father's feet.

Edric tilted his head. "You know that's not what I meant."

Calen bolted after his brother, bare legs flashing in the glare.

"Last one to the river's a troll!"

***

Edric sighed and turned back to the anvil, adjusting his grip on the tongs.

The boys' laughter rang through the clearing—loud, naked, and half-feral.

Truth be told, he'd have gone with them.

River water on bare skin, sun through the trees—it sounded a hell of a lot better than sweating over stubborn iron.

But someone had to keep the heat, and someone had to finish the work.

That was his job.

Their job was to run. To shout. To be loud and free and shirtless and shameless.

He continued hammering out the plowshare.

***

The boys crashed through the underbrush, stumbling down dusty paths, bare feet thudding against the warm, fir needle-covered ground. Running helped; the breeze on his sweat-soaked back and legs felt like the first relief he'd had all day. Twigs snapped. Insects scattered. Their laughter echoed through the trees.

"You run like a chicken!" Toby shouted over his shoulder.

"You smell like one!" Calen fired back.

"You're just mad 'cause I'm faster!"

"I'm mad 'cause I've got your butt in my face!"

They burst onto the riverbank in a final sprint, skidding to a stop on the edge—only to be greeted by silence.

The small river wasn't a river anymore.

A few thin trickles slid between sunbaked stones, barely deep enough to keep the water moving. The air shimmered with heat. The only sound was the buzzing of flies.

"What happened to the river?" Toby said, frowning at it.

"It looks like it died," Calen said, his eyes tracing the dry riverbed from bend to bend.

Toby let out a shout and spun in a circle. "Then I'm going to the pond!"

"That's thirty minutes in the other direction!" Calen shouted after him, but Toby was already charging into the brush.

Calen wasn't worried. The pond was over in the neighbor's back pasture. It was all boys over there too, and old Merrick didn't care—he was probably in there already himself.

Calen looked around, squinting into the sun. The heat pressed down on him, thick and stifling.

With Toby gone and the river bone-dry, there wasn't much left to do.

He sighed, scratched the back of his leg, and wandered a few steps toward the trees. He had to take a leak anyway.

Calen stepped into the trees and pissed; nothing beat doing it outside. Just as he was finishing, the forest went quiet. The insects stopped first, then the birds, until all he could hear was the quiet trickle of water. The hair on the back of his neck stood up. For half a heartbeat, he was sure there was something in the riverbed—something big.

He froze, one hand still at his side, eyes fixed on the rocks, and turned slowly. Nothing moved. No bear. No beast. Just stone, scrub, and silence.

Stepping down the riverbank, he crossed the dry bed toward the spot where he thought he'd seen movement. Half-buried in the rocky earth, jutting out at an angle, was a strange stone—not shaped like a normal one. Its corners were sharp, its sides flat, the edges only slightly weathered. He worked it loose from the mud and turned it over in the sun. Dark, almost black, it shimmered with faint gold markings when tilted just right—lines of writing or symbols, delicate and intentional.

He held it in both hands, turning it slowly, letting the sun play across the vanishing etchings. Then something shifted—not the stone, but the way it felt. It was warmer than it should have been. He stood still, frowning. The air was hot, but he wasn't; no sweat, no sting of sun in his eyes. The dryness in his throat was gone. Out of habit, he licked his lips. He wasn't thirsty anymore.

The sun still hung high—bright, harsh, close to noon—but he didn't feel it. It was like standing in the shadow of a great wall. A chill worked its way into his stomach. Maybe I should put this thing back, he thought.

He crouched and set the stone where he'd found it, nestling it back into the rocks, and stepped away. Another step, and the heat returned like a wave—first on his shoulders, then on the back of his neck. The thirst came next, followed by the sting of sweat in his eyes. He turned back.

The stone lay exactly where he'd left it.

"You've got to be kidding," he whispered.

He stepped forward and picked it up again. Nothing happened at first. But after a few seconds, the sun was dimmer. The heat eased. His thirst began to fade.

"All right," he said. "Guess you're coming with me."

He turned back to the trees and started up the narrow path leading home.

Calen moved through the trees quietly, the strange stone cradled in his hand, its weight both comforting and strange. The woods weren't hot anymore. The air was perfect—cool, still, with a breeze that felt peaceful on his skin.

This was real magic.

He'd never seen or felt anything like this before.

He'd grown up hearing Grandma Mira talk about magic—the kind that lived in the roots and stones and whispered in the trees. He'd always thought it was just stories and poems, pretty things she believed in because...well, she was old. But now he could feel it in the stone.

He couldn't tell Dad. Dad would think it was dangerous, probably take it straight to the regional council. The thought made his jaw clench. No, he thought. Not yet.

He caught his foot on a thick root and instinctively braced for the fall, but the root split cleanly under his step and he barely lost his balance—no stumble, no pain, not even a scratch. That was the stone.

He looked down at it in his hand. He wasn't giving it up.

*** 

By the time he reached the edge of the clearing, the sun still blazed overhead, casting short, sharp shadows beneath the trees. The clearing shimmered in the heat, but he barely felt it.

He paused at the tree line, eyes sweeping the space between the smithy and the main house. The clearing was quiet—no voices, no sign of Toby, no sign of his mother.

The forge sat still, the embers low and glowing in the pit. The anvil loomed where it always did, half in sun, half in shadow. A bucket of water steamed faintly beside it.

He crept around the back of the smithy, staying low. His clothes were there—folded neatly on the bench, his boots beside them.

He bent to grab his pants.

"At least you're finally starting to look like a man. Scrawny, but it's a start."

Calen flinched and spun. Edric stood in the doorway, arms crossed, a soot-stained rag hanging from one hand.

"Thought you boys were off swimming," he added. "Didn't expect you back till tonight."

Calen kept his eyes down as he pulled on his trousers.

"Where is your brother?"

"He went to Merrick's."

Edric grunted, already turning back toward the forge. "Well, let's hope he doesn't come back smelling like pond muck. If your mother has to scrub him, she'll raise hell—and if she doesn't, you're the one sharing the bed."

Calen moved quickly to slide the stone into the pouch on his belt. It settled there easily, unnoticed.

Edric didn't turn around.

"Well," Calen said, taking a step back toward the house. "Grandma'll be back soon, mixing up her herbs—and with a smell like that, who's going to notice pond muck anyway?"

Edric huffed a laugh without turning. "Fair point. I might sleep out here tonight."

Calen didn't wait for more. He turned and made his way to the house.

***

The house was quiet as Calen stepped inside.

The entryway was dim and stifling, the air thick with settled heat. It was just wide enough for a bench, some boots, and a few hooks. Beyond it, the main room opened in all directions—kitchen to the left, dining table in the center, the main bedroom door tucked to the right.

He didn't linger. He crossed straight to the far wall where the ladder rose to the loft, wedged beside the door to the washroom. His feet barely made a sound on the rungs as he climbed.

The loft was small and airless, the low ceiling trapping the heat of the day.

The bed he shared with Toby was little more than a lumpy mattress stuffed with straw, but right now, it was perfect for hiding something.

He knelt and lifted the blanket, then tugged back the edge of the mattress. There—a gap between the slats and the wall. His space for hiding coins, an arrowhead—once, a frog. He slid the stone into place. It fit snugly, like it belonged.

The ladder creaked softly as Calen climbed down.

The air was different.

Cool and clean.

The heat was gone. The light through the windows had softened. Even the buzz of insects outside felt far away.

Before he could decide how he felt about that, the front door swung open behind him.

"Calen?" Gwen's voice floated in ahead of her, "Oh! It's nice in here, I was coming in to open up the windows—but this is lovely."

She stepped inside, arms full—two canvas sacks and a bundle wrapped in cloth. Her cheeks were flushed from the sun, hair damp at the temples.

She kicked the door shut with her heel, then paused, breathing in.

"Huh. That's strange. It's actually cool in here."

Calen grabbed the water cup off the counter just to keep his hands busy, "Hey, Mom."

"Feels like the breeze found its way in. Did you open something?"

He shook his head. "No, just got back from the river—it's all dried up."

She gave him a tired smile and dropped the bundles on the kitchen table. "Well, whatever's going on in this house, I hope it lasts. I was ready to stick my head in the well!"

She brushed a hand over her forehead, then glanced out the front window.

"Well, I don't think you'll have to worry about the river for long, it looks like a storm might be blowing in. I could see clouds coming up from the west out across the plains on the way up—dark ones, too. I hope your grandmother makes it back before it breaks. She wasn't expecting rain, I don't think she took her slicker."

She turned to the bundles on the table, untying one of the sacks and revealing a handful of carrots, a bunch of onions, and a wrapped wedge of cheese. In the second, tucked neatly inside, were several blocks of beeswax and a large jar of lard.

"Take these two down to the cellar for me, will you? She'll want them when she gets in."

Calen nodded, lifting the supplies. They were heavier than they looked, but his arms were used to hauling iron, and he took the narrow stairs down into the cool cellar with ease. The stone walls kept the space dim and quiet, and the scent of dried herbs, earth, and the old wood hung thick in the air. He set the items down where Mira worked—square in the center of the table, just as she'd expect them. Back upstairs, Gwen was already unpacking the rest of the groceries. She looked up.

"Grandma's going to be up late tonight, mixing her ointments," she said, wiping her hands on a dish towel. "If those herbs start to lose their potency overnight, she'll throw a fit. And she'll be sleeping like a stone all day tomorrow, so don't go stomping around. I'll need both you and your brother helping with chores."

"Speaking of," she added, straightening up and glancing at the door, "where *is* your brother?"

"He went to Merrick's," Calen said, "after he saw the river was too dry to play in."

Gwen let out a low groan. "Of course he did. Which means he'll be running around half-naked all day with those wild Merrick boys."

"Fully naked," Calen muttered under his breath.

"What?"

"Nothing."

She shook her head and turned back to the vegetables. "Men. Living with a house full of men. Just go see if the water's warm enough in the tub. We'll have to scrub the mud off that child when he gets back."

Calen had just turned toward the side room when the front door banged open again. Toby burst inside, still wet and grinning, streaked with mud from shoulder to knee—and not a scrap of clothing in sight.

"Hi, Mom!" he shouted, totally unfazed.

Gwen nearly dropped the onion in her hand. "Have you been *naked* this whole time?"

Toby looked down at himself like he hadn't noticed. "Uh…"

"Answer me, young man! Have you been marching through the village like that!?"

"You don't go through the village to get to Merrick's," Toby offered.

Gwen blinked at him, her social nightmare momentarily eclipsing everything else.

"You're muddy, you stink, and you're naked. Go with your brother and get in the tub. *Now.*"

Toby snorted with laughter and bolted to the washroom, leaving a trail of dusty footprints and flaking mud behind him.

"Make sure he uses soap!" their mother shouted after Calen as she waved him off.

"I'll take care of it," Calen said, already following Toby.

The washroom wasn't much—just a plank-floored nook off the side of the house with a half barrel tub and a small window that let in the light. The water was lukewarm at best, but Toby didn't seem to care. He stood grinning in the tub, arms outstretched like he was expecting royal treatment.

Calen began scrubbing.

After a while, Toby said, "You missed a spot," pointing to his butt with a grin.

Calen rolled his eyes and dunked the cloth back in the bucket. "You've got moss behind your ears, and I'm pretty sure that's an actual slug."

Toby squealed and thrashed. "Get it off!"

From the front of the house, the door creaked open.

Calen heard Edric's boots on the floorboards and the low thud as the door closed behind him. Gwen's voice followed almost immediately, sharp and full of steam.

"I swear, Edric, even after all these years, I'm *still* not used to living with boys."

Edric's voice rumbled something in response, too low to make out.

"I was raised in a house with *girls*," Gwen said proudly. "Three sisters, and not one of us ever tracked mud indoors, or ran through the house naked, or hollered like a wild animal, or caught frogs! We were clean. We were *refined*. We had *manners*."

In the washroom, Toby tried to stifle a laugh and failed. Calen dunked the cloth again and started scrubbing at the dried dirt on his brother's arms.

"I married a blacksmith," Gwen continued, voice raising, "a big, loud, shirtless blacksmith—and now I've got two smaller blacksmiths running around like feral goats! Honestly, Edric, *you* are the man of the house. You need to keep your boys in line."

"You hear that?" Calen whispered to Toby. "You're a feral goat."

Toby bleated loudly and splashed water over the edge of the tub and on Calen's sleeve. Calen glared and removed his own shirt to prevent it from getting even wetter.

"Quit it, or I'll leave the slug behind your ears."

At that moment, Edric leaned in through the doorway, arms crossed and a crooked grin tugging at his beard.

"You two don't even *know* what you're doing to me," he said in a low voice. "One more stunt like this, and your mother's going to start locking me out of the bedroom—again."

Calen's lips thinned. He raised a skeptical eyebrow.

"If I'm in *your* bed, you're out in the hay!" Edric glared. "Just get your brother clean, and *keep* him clean—at least until your mother has calmed down a bit," he said, looking over his shoulder.

The rest of the bath passed in a blur of splashing, scrubbing, and quiet grumbling.

By the time they were both dry and dressed in oversized sleep shirts, the afternoon sun was still high, filtering warm light through the kitchen window.

Dinner was simple. Edric had cleaned up the dusty footprints.

It was just past dinner when the front door opened with a gentle creak. The air shifted as if the house itself recognized someone important had returned.

Gwen looked up from rinsing dishes. "That you, Mother?"

Grandma Mira stepped in with the same steady composure she always carried, her slate-gray cloak still clasped neatly at the neck. She dusted one boot against the threshold before stepping inside, a heavy woven basket looped over her arm, packed tight with bundled herbs and waxed cloth parcels.

"I made it back just in time," she said, glancing toward the window. "Saw lightning out on the plains. Should hit soon."

Gwen paused, frowning slightly. "Really? I haven't heard a thing, but the clouds were dark earlier."

Edric stood quickly, crossing the room to take the basket from his mother's arm. He glanced outside, eyes narrowing. "That's coming in fast now."

He reached for his boots. "I'll batten down the smithy before it hits, and put the horses away."

"The horses are already taken care of, love," Mira replied, shrugging off her cloak. "Didn't want them spooked and tearing through the fences. Got them settled just in time."

Edric froze mid-lace, confused. "I didn't even hear you come up. I would've helped."

Mira waved a hand. "Well, you were all busy. No harm done."

Edric shook his head and went out the door.

Mira was already headed for the cellar. "I need to start processing these herbs tonight before they lose their strength. I'll be down in the cellar for a while."

"There's food waiting down there for you," Gwen called after her, "just in case you forget to eat—*again*."

"Thank you, dear," Mira said with a grateful smile, and she stepped down the stairs.

The front door blew open a moment later, and Edric rushed inside, brushing dampness from his sleeves. "By Dae, it's really coming down out there!" The rush of heavy rain coming in, he shut the door behind him. Water dripped from his hair.

Gwen glanced at the loft ladder. "Calen, you know how Toby gets with storms..."

Edric nodded. "Best to get him settled now, before it gets any worse."

Calen nodded and gently led Toby to the ladder. The boys clambered up to the loft, where Toby immediately flopped into bed and sprawled out like a cat. Calen lay beside him, not quite ready to sleep. His thoughts were on the hidden stone.

# 2

T he pounding started just after sunrise.

At first it was distant—like a knock caught in a dream–then sharper, faster. Urgent. Someone was beating on the front door, shouting, and from the other side of the house came more voices—raised, frantic, calling Mira's name.

Edric was already up, moving fast. He shoved open the bedroom door, barefoot and bare-chested, still wearing the linen under-breeches he slept in. Gwen's voice called out behind him, startled, but he didn't stop.

He flung open the front door, half expecting fire or bandits—but it was worse in its own way. Four or five disheveled villagers stood on the porch and in the yard, soaked with sweat and mud, eyes wide with panic.

"Where's Mira?" one of them gasped. "Edric—your mother—we need her. Now!"

Another man clutched a bleeding arm, shirt torn and hanging loose. A woman behind him sobbed openly, her dress streaked with ash.

"She's here!" another voice shouted from the far side of the yard.

Edric turned just in time to see Mira emerging from the cellar, still in the same clothes she'd worn the night before, streaked with herbs and wax. She moved with purpose toward the crowd, desperation in their eyes.

Sandra, the glassblower's wife, was the first to reach her. "Mira, please—it's bad down there. Regg is still trying to pull his apprentice out of the rubble!"

Thom Vellor stood nearby, pressing a linen-wrapped arm to his side, blood soaking through. "I think the wall came down on the Gorrin girl," he said, barely above a whisper. "She's not waking up..."

Behind them, Devrin Gorrin stood pale and still, his fists clenched tight. "She was closing up the coop when it hit. She didn't even make it back to the door."

The villagers hurried down the open cellar stairs after Mira, disappearing into the dim space below. From inside came the sounds of clinking jars, rustling cloth, and Mira's sharp voice commanding them. "Careful with that jar—no, the salve bundles go in the burlap, not the crate. Those are on the top shelf—yes, all of them!"

One by one, the villagers reemerged, arms full of boxes and jars, bundles and wrapped satchels, and hauled Mira's supplies to the cart waiting near the fence. The wheels groaned under the growing weight.

Edric stood by the front step, watching it all with a furrowed brow. None of this made sense.

The night before had been quiet after he came in. No wind, no crashes, not even a flicker of lightning through the shutters. Just a steady drizzle, lightly tapping the roof.

But the yard said otherwise.

Leaves and debris covered everything. Large branches lay scattered across the grass. The smithy's roof had buckled at one corner, a few shingles were missing entirely, and water still pooled near the doorway where it had flooded inside. The stacked firewood had half collapsed into a mess.

Behind him, Calen and Toby stepped outside still in their night shirts, hair tousled, faces pinched with confusion.

"What happened?" Calen asked, blinking at the wreckage.

"Was there a storm?" Toby added, rubbing one eye.

Before Edric could answer, Gwen stepped out behind the boys, fully dressed.

She took stock of her sons, pantless and barefoot, her husband in his under-breeches, and the entire decimated yard.

"Of course," she said. "Why is it that every time something happens around here, someone is half naked?"

Edric shot her a look and headed inside to get dressed as she scanned the mess.

***

"What happened here?" she asked, more to herself than anyone else. "We slept through all of this?"

Gwen wandered slowly into the yard, her eyes scanning the branches and puddles, the overturned market cart. Her brows furrowed, lips pursed in a tight line turning slowly in place, trying to piece together what little memory she had of the night before.

Her gaze landed on the open cellar doors.

She made her way over and paused at the top of the steps. The cool air from below drifted up from the cellar and carried a thick, pungent scent—earthy and bitter, with sharp notes of dried roots, wax, and something rancid under it all.

She bent down and pulled the cellar doors shut with a solid thud, sliding the latch into place.

Edric strode out, fully dressed, looking like a man who already knew what he was going to find—and hated it.

He didn't glance at Gwen. He just started walking.

She fell into step behind him without a word, but after a few paces, she paused and turned back.

"You stay here," she said to Calen. "Watch your brother."

Calen started to speak, but she cut him off with a look.

"If you want to help, check the animals and clean up the yard. We'll be back as soon as we can."

Then she turned again and followed her husband down the road, the muddy path swallowing their footsteps as the morning settled into a strange, heavy quiet.

***

As soon as their parents disappeared down the road, Toby clapped his hands together and grinned.

"Hooray! There's probably water in the river now!"

Calen didn't respond right away. He just stood there, eyes trailing over the yard—the broken limbs, the half-collapsed smithy, the muddy tracks leading off in every direction.

"Be quiet," he said finally, not harsh, just distant. The words came out flat, hollow.

Toby blinked at him, confused, but didn't argue.

Calen let out a long breath and turned to the house.

"Come on," he said. "We need to get dressed."

Calen started to go back inside, surveying his home. It looked perfect. No puddles against the house; the windows were spotless. The herbs strung up on the porch to dry were hanging neatly, untouched.

Inside, Calen tossed a clean tunic and breeches to Toby. "Get changed," he said. "You're going to clean up the yard while I figure something out."

Toby groaned but didn't argue. Once he was dressed and fed, Calen nudged him toward the door.

"Restack the woodpile," he said, "and don't leave the yard. I mean it."

Toby saluted dramatically and marched outside with exaggerated importance.

Calen shook his head. Then he turned to the ladder.

He hadn't thought of the stone—not since last night. He climbed up into the loft and retrieved it.

The yard was wrecked. The smithy was half ruined. But the house—

The house was perfect.

Because of *this*.

Then—

A scream. Toby's.

Calen jolted to his feet, the stone nearly slipping from his hands as he scrambled to get out of the loft.

"Toby?"

He didn't wait for an answer. He jumped down, heart hammering in his chest, and burst out the front door.

Toby was on the ground near the woodpile, curled on his side, sobbing and clutching his leg. A thick, splintered branch lay beside him, the kind that would take two grown men to move.

"Toby!"

Calen dropped to his knees beside him. His brother's shin was bent at an unnatural angle, and blood had already begun to soak through the fabric of his breeches.

"I didn't see it," Toby gasped, his face pale. "I didn't see it fall."

Calen's mind raced. Mira. He needed Mira.

He looked down the road—empty. His parents were long gone.

"I'm taking you to town," he said. "Just hold on."

Calen grabbed a blanket from indoors and wrapped it around his brother. He adjusted the stone in his belt pouch, picked up his brother as gently as he could, and started walking to town.

The road stretched ahead, cutting clean through the open fields between the forest and town. Calen had walked it his whole life, but never like this—never with Toby in his arms, blood soaking through a blanket.

He moved fast, eyes fixed on the distant rooftops rushing past the edge of the plain. Even from here, he could see the signs: broken trees, scattered debris, a dark smear where someone's barn used to be.

Toby whimpered and shifted, and Calen tightened his grip.

The boy should've felt heavier. His arms should've been aching by now, but they weren't.

He didn't think about it. He just kept walking.

The town came into view just as Calen crested the last rise of the plain. From a distance, it still looked familiar—clusters of wooden buildings, a few stone chimneys, rooftops pitched and simple. But as he got closer, the damage came into focus.

Walls had collapsed. Shingles were scattered in the mud. One building near the edge of town had lost an entire side, and Calen could see straight into what had once been someone's kitchen.

People moved through the wreckage in small, frantic groups. Some carried buckets, other blankets or boards. Smoke rose from a smoldering roof across the square. A cart lay overturned, wheels half buried in the mud.

In the center of town, the village square had been turned into a rough recovery area. Blankets had been laid out in a broad circle, most of them occupied. A handful of people sat or lay wounded—bandaged limbs, bruised faces, splints hastily tied with scraps of cloth.

Off to one side, under a long awning, the bodies were laid out. Blankets covered each one. Calen tried not to notice them.

He spotted Mira near the middle of the village square, kneeling beside a woman with a wrapped head wound. She moved quickly, speaking softly, hands steady. A few villagers helped her, passing jars and cloths back and forth.

His parents were nowhere in sight. They were probably helping others away from the square.

Calen didn't slow. He tightened his grip on Toby and stepped into the chaos.

Calen stepped on the green, careful not to jostle Toby as he wove between villagers and wounded.

Mira knelt over a man with a gash running across his forehead, speaking low as she smeared something across the wound—a thick salve the color of moss. Calen had seen it a hundred times before. She'd used it on him more than once, muttering her usual prayers as she worked.

But this time, it *glowed*.

Not brightly—just a soft green light at the tips of her fingers, winding through the ointment as she spread it. Calen froze.

Had it always done that?

The glow faded as quickly as it came, the salve already bandaged in place. Mira moved on to the next patient without missing a beat.

Calen adjusted his hold and moved closer, eyes still locked on Mira's hands. Something had changed.

"Grandma!"

His voice cracked across the open square, sharp and desperate.

Mira looked up from her patient, eyes narrowing for a split second before widening in recognition.

"Calen?" she breathed, already rising to her feet.

She rushed to him, skirts brushing the grass, her sleeves still smeared with salve and blood.

"What happened?" she asked, reaching for Toby as Calen knelt down to lay him gently on a nearby blanket.

"A branch," Calen said, breath catching. "It fell. His leg—look."

Mira didn't hesitate. Her hands were already moving, her eyes scanning the injury—quick, practiced, but tired. Exhausted.

"It's broken," she said, brushing blood away with trembling fingers. "Badly."

She turned to a lady that had been assisting her. Calen didn't recognize her. "I need the violet flask. Small leather pouch, front of the supply cart. Go."

The unknown lady took off running without question.

Calen hovered nearby, watching her, heart hammering in his throat.

She hadn't even looked at him properly—not yet. But as her eyes landed on his, something in her expression shifted. A second of hesitation. Confusion? Recognition? Then it was gone.

The runner returned, breathless, and handed her the flask.

Mira uncorked it with her teeth and drank.

Her hands steadied almost instantly.

She reached down, placing one hand above Toby's knee and the other below the break.

"Don't speak," she said. "And whatever you do, don't touch me."

Her eyes fluttered closed. Her lips moved—no louder than a whisper—and her hands began to glow. Not soft this time. Not gentle.

Green fire this time. Bright and sudden.

The air around them rippled. Calen felt the hair on his arms raise. The scent of burning herbs hit his nose.

Toby screamed—but only for a second.

Then it was done.

The light vanished. Mira sagged forward, catching herself on her hands, panting.

Calen stared.

The leg was whole.

Mira pushed herself upright with a low groan and wiped the sweat from her brow. She glanced over at Toby, then landed on Calen.

She studied him for a long moment. Not his clothes, not looking for cuts or scrapes. *Him.*

When she spoke, her voice was low but clear.

"Now...how about you tell me what's going on with you?"

Calen's mouth opened, but nothing came out. His hand drifted toward the pouch at his hip, thumb brushing the edge of the stone through the fabric.

"I...I should go find my parents," he said. "They might need my help."

"Calen..."

But he was already jogging away.

"I'll come right back!" he promised over his shoulder, and he slipped into the crowd before she could stop him.

Time blurred after that.

Calen moved through the village in a daze—helping where he could, fetching blankets, handing out water. He saw buildings cracked wide open, roofs caved in like crushed tin, and a cart split in two where a tree had fallen. Faces he knew looked back at him, hollow-eyed and smeared with ash.

At some point, he found his parents. Gwen had taken charge of organizing supplies, her voice sharp and focused. Edric had helped clear a blocked alley, lifting the charred beams like they were kindling.

In the days that followed, everyone stayed busy. There was always something—branches to clear, carts to right, shingles to rehang. People didn't dwell on the storm. They patched what they could and got on with it.

Calen did the same.

But each night, after the house had gone still and the lamps were out, he'd take the stone from his pouch and hide it under the floorboard. And every morning, before anyone else was awake, he'd slip it back into his pouch.

He hadn't meant to keep it from Mira.

But the moment never felt quite right.

The longer he waited, the easier it was to wait a little more.

# 3

Around three weeks later, Mira stepped into the yard, her traveling cloak clinging to her shoulders. The sun was high, the road quiet behind her, and the house was untouched. The storm had flattened half the village—but here, the wood shone clean, the windows sparkled, and even the porch herbs had grown fuller, as if the rain did nothing but nourish.

She paused, frowning faintly, but didn't linger on it. The familiar ring of metal on metal drifted from the smithy in the side yard. She followed it.

Inside, the heat of the forge had long faded, leaving only the faint tang of soot and oil. Edric stood with a cloth in one hand, wiping down one of the workbenches. Calen was stacking lengths of scrap into a barrel nearby, lips pursed in concentration.

Edric looked up first. "Well, look who finally escaped the town."

Mira let out a low breath and offered a tired smile. "They were very kind to me. Too kind. But it's good to be home."

"You're sure?" Edric said, grinning. "They didn't offer to build you your own house downtown?"

"They tried," she said dryly. "I told them healers don't need houses, just sleep."

Calen glanced up, gave his grandmother a small smile, and kept working.

But Mira didn't look away from him. Her eyes lingered—longer than Edric noticed. There was something there. Something she'd sensed before in the town square.

Her smile faded.

"Edric," she said gently, never taking her eyes off Calen, "would you excuse us for a moment?"

He blinked. "What?"

"I just need a word with your son. Alone."

Edric looked between the two but settled on Calen. "What did you do?"

"Nothing," Mira said. "Go on inside. We'll be just a minute."

Edric gave Calen an accusing look, but wiped his hands and left without protest, disappearing into the yard.

Mira waited until he was out of earshot.

Then she turned to Calen, eyes sharp now. All the weariness had left her face.

"You want to tell me why you're coated in magic?"

Calen blinked. "What?"

Mira didn't flinch. "If I closed my eyes right now, I'd swear I was standing in the same room as a wizard. Now why is that?"

Calen didn't answer. His hand went to his belt pouch, fingers brushing the flap, hesitating just for a second–then he reached in and drew it out.

A stone.

He held it out to her, eyes lowered. "This," he said quietly. "It started when I found this."

Calen handed her the stone, dull and unremarkable, like something pried from an old fence or the base of a forgotten well.

Mira turned it over in her palm, suspicious.

She brought it closer to her face, angling it toward the light.

Then she looked back at Calen, sharper now.

"Where did you find this?"

Calen seemed a bit awestruck, and she knew he'd never seen his grandmother this way. He likely thought her magical ramblings were just her..."personality," but she was intentionally deliberate now, methodical. This wasn't a story—this was real magic, and the stone had her full attention.

"I found it in the riverbed north of here."

Mira turned the stone over in her hand once more. "Just sitting there?"

"No..." pondered Calen. "I felt like there was something big standing in the river, but when I went to look, it was just this—half buried in the mud."

"When?" she asked, patiently.

Calen thought about it a moment. "The night before the storm," he said at last.

Mira looked up as if she could see the sky through the roof of the smithy. "An oddly timed springtime drought, you find *this*, and then a storm..."

She turned her attention to the stone, then spoke to it. "Don't hide from me," she commanded. "What are you?"

The stone warmed in her hands—subtle at first. The surface began to change; it became deeper somehow, and the golden runes surfaced faintly across its face.

Mira didn't flinch. "There you are."

She adjusted her grip slightly, then knelt on the floor, closing her eyes. Listening.

Her lips moved, not in words Calen would recognize—maybe not words at all.

The runes on the stone pulsed several times.

Mira slowly opened her eyes.

She looked at the stone again, calm and unreadable. Then, softly, she said, "Thank you."

She stood, quiet in her movements, and paced around the room, contemplating.

Eventually, she placed the warm stone back in Calen's hand.

"Best not to mention this to anyone. You two will keep each other safe for now, while I think of what to do," she said and walked back to the house.

***

Calen took a step after her—then stopped.

He glanced down at the warm stone in his hand, then at the house.

"What in the gods just happened?" he wondered aloud.

The forge snapped behind him. The stone was quiet.

Calen decided he should probably be in the house as well. He popped the stone back in its usual pouch and crossed the yard.

As he stepped into the house, Edric was at the table, hunched over a cup of tea. He didn't look up.

"What did you do?" he asked flatly.

Calen blinked. "What? Nothing! She just—"

Edric glanced up, gave him a once-over, then went back to his tea.

"Uh-huh."

Calen turned and walked back out the door. Maybe inside wasn't the best place to be right now.

# 4

The morning sun filtered through the trees, already high enough to cast long lines of light across the clearing. The air was crisp and felt clean in Calen's lungs. He stepped out into the yard, boots damp with dew, axe balanced over one shoulder. He'd split three logs already, stacking them neatly by the side of the shed, when the sound of soft footsteps behind him made him pause.

"Calen, come with me, will you?" Mira's voice was calm, but there was a weight behind it.

He wiped the back of his hand across his brow, stealing a glance over his shoulder. Mira stood at the edge of the clearing in her traveling cloak, a small satchel slung across her body.

"Now?" he asked.

She nodded. "Now."

Calen set the axe against the stump and dusted off his hands. Mira didn't wait for him to catch up—she turned and walked into the woods with the same steady pace she always used, the one that made her seem like she was simply part of the forest, not walking through it. He jogged a few steps to fall in behind her, the morning light catching in the silver threads of her braid.

They moved deeper into the trees, past familiar glades and old stumps he recognized, until they gave way to undergrowth he couldn't name. The light shifted gradually, the canopy thickening overhead, turning the air cooler, damper. Calen hesitated, confused. "I've never been out this way before…"

Mira turned slightly giving him a faint smile. "I know."

Calen stopped short, turning in a circle, mouth slightly open in disbelief. "Wait—no, I've been through this area. I've hunted rabbits in this stretch. There's no way I missed all…this…"

Mira didn't stop walking, "Then perhaps it wasn't here to be seen."

He hurried to catch up, voice low and urgent. "No, seriously—Grandma, I *know* these woods. I could walk them blindfolded. That clearing back there doesn't exist."

Mira didn't slow. "And neither does the one coming up."

They pushed through the curtain of low branches, and the forest opened up around them. A clearing lay ahead, silent and circular, a thick bed of moss underfoot and a stone altar rising gently at its center—weathered, ancient, half swallowed by the earth, like it had been waiting a very long time to be found.

Mira stepped to the side and gestured for Calen to continue.

He stepped forward, his eyes locked on the altar. The air felt different here—still and watchful, like the trees themselves were holding their breath.

Calen swallowed. "What is this place?"

Mira stepped beside him, her voice softer than before. "It's as old as the forest. Not many people know it's here, and fewer still could find it if they did. For now, I use it as a meeting place. It's...well hidden."

A flicker of movement caught his eye—something bright like the morning light reflecting off a droplet of water. Then, with a sudden flutter, she appeared.

She was no taller than a candle, suspended on thin, transparent wings that shimmered like oil on water. Her skin glowed faintly, a soft lavender hue, and her hair—if it was hair—shifted like curling smoke. She hovered for a moment, then floated down, landing gracefully on the edge of the moss-covered altar stone.

Calen froze.

This wasn't a clever trick of the light or a forest insect. This was...a fairy. An actual fairy. His heart stuttered. He blinked once, then again, hoping the vision would resolve into something explainable. But it didn't. She was still there.

She tilted her head and smiled, the expression both familiar and impossible, like something from a storybook.

Calen's mouth opened, but nothing came out.

"Calen," Mira said softly, her voice grounding. "Meet an old friend."

He didn't move. He couldn't. He was still trying to believe what his eyes were telling him.

"You're not real," he finally whispered.

The fairy laughed. It was the sound of bells, distant and strange.

"I get that a lot."

Calen's breath had barely returned to normal when Mira stepped forward, voice calm.

"She's here to help us," she said. "And to help *you,* Calen."

The fairy's wings flickered as she crossed her legs on the altar stone, watching him curiously.

"Hey, kid!" She nodded. "I've been keeping an eye on you. You're more interesting than you know."

Calen opened his mouth, closed it again. "I—I don't understand."

"You will," Mira said, nodding. "But first, you need to know what you've been carrying."

He glanced down at the waist pouch where the stone lay resting. "The stone?"

The fairy chuckled. "It's not a stone. It's part of a castle."

"An enchanted castle," Mira continued, "hidden deep in the northern forest and full of forces that don't take kindly to visitors."

Calen frowned. "Why are you telling me this?"

"Because," Mira said gently, "we need your help."

The fairy leaned in, smiling like someone about to share a secret. "We want you to put it back."

"But not inside," Mira clarified. "Not through the gate. You'll approach quietly, from the east side. You'll find a crack in the wall—there are many. Pick any one. The stone will fit in any of them."

She continued cautiously, "Then, once it's placed, you'll go down the hill behind the castle. There's a path that goes down to the river. Where the trail meets the water—" She nodded at the fairy. "—she'll be waiting for you."

Calen stared at them, stunned. "Wait. I—I'm going alone?"

"You'll be safer this way," the fairy said. "Too many questions if Mira goes. Too much attention. But you? You're just a boy on a walk."

He was quiet for a long moment.

The wind stirred the trees around them, but Calen didn't move. "But why me?" he asked again.

"I can't take it," Mira said, lowering her voice, "and Liri can't carry it..."

"Lirith Sabrinae—that's me," the fairy said, adjusting one wing rather than reminding them she hadn't been introduced. "But my friends call me Liri."

"Oh, hush, Liri," Mira said, a note of tension in her voice. "You know this isn't easy for me."

Mira exhaled and turned to him fully. "This stone is part of a dangerous castle in a dangerous place. We need to return it. Quietly. Without fanfare. Without anyone noticing it's been gone."

Calen shifted. "So, you want me to just...activate the stone. It will take me to a dangerous castle, and I just walk over to it and stick the magic stone in one of the cracks in its side?"

Liri shrugged. Picking a bit of moss off the altar, she gestured to Calen and said to Mira, "See? He gets it."

Mira gave her a look, then turned back to Calen. "You won't be alone. Liri will be just down the hill. Then she'll lead you back home."

Calen frowned.

Mira continued, "The stone has been gathering energy for decades. It has enough power to get you there. But you can't use it to return—not that you'd be returning with it to begin with..." Mira wrung her hands. Calen had never seen his grandmother this troubled.

"But I don't know how to activate the stone..." Calen began.

Liri stretched her arms overhead. "Well, that's because you haven't woken up your magic yet!"

"Liri..." Mira warned.

Calen blinked. "Woken up my—?"

Before he could finish, Liri flew upward in a blur of light and batted him on the nose.

Calen flinched, hand flying to his face. "What in the—?"

A pulse.

Calen looked around. The forest around him seemed to sharpen—the chirp of birds louder, the breeze cooler, the stone suddenly more present in his pouch at his waist.

Liri looked different—less like a dream, more like a person. Her glow had dimmed, not vanished, but softened into something skin-deep. The shimmer of her wings was there, but now he could see the weight of her posture, the slight tension in her shoulders, the way her feet curled naturally over the altar's edge. She was still small, still strange—but suddenly real in a way that made his chest tighten.

Even the altar beneath her looked changed. Faint lines ran along its surface, not glowing but etched, as if time had worn stories into its skin. The moss below him shimmered with dew he was sure hadn't been there before.

Mira had gone silent.

For a moment, she didn't blink, didn't breathe. Her face had drained of color, mouth slightly parted.

"No..." she whispered—so softly Calen wasn't sure he'd heard it.

Liri turned her head slightly, wings lifting behind her in a slow sweep. "He needed it," she said, not apologetic, just certain.

Mira's eyes snapped to the fairy. "Liri, what have you done?"

Calen looked between them, heart still pounding.

Mira took a threatening step closer to Liri. She looked as if she was about to squash her.

"He's marked now; they'll feel him! It's why I couldn't go!"

Liri crossed her arms, wings folding neatly behind her. "And what would you have done instead? Sent him in blind? This way he'll be even faster."

Mira's voice shook when she said, "You don't understand, Liri. You've stripped him of his camouflage. That was the one thing keeping him safe."

Liri crossed her arms, wings folding tightly. "Safe? Or hidden? Because there's a difference. You wanted him to grow old pretending to be something he's not."

Mira's eyes flashed. "I wanted him to live."

Calen stared at them. "Safe from what?"

"Enough of this!" cried Mira, stepping in between them. "Enough! We will continue on as planned, and we can address the rest later."

"Very well," Liri chirped, fluttering away. A faint trail of fading light lingered behind her.

Mira handed him her pack, the weight of it catching him off guard. "I've packed enough for five days," she said, her voice calm but tinged with urgency. She looked older, frailer. "You shouldn't need that much though. You should be back in three with Liri's guidance. Fairies can travel quite fast with company."

Calen adjusted the strap over his shoulder, eyes fixed on Mira, who was guiding him back from the altar.

Calen glanced down at his palm. "So, just tell it I'm ready?"

Mira nodded once. "It will know."

He looked at her, uncertain.

"You'll know," she said softly, her face unreadable.

Calen took a slow step back, and then another. The stone pulsed faintly in his palm, warm and steady.

He tightened his grip.

"Okay," he whispered, "I'm ready."

The air seemed to shift around him, and static gripped his hair. The birdsong faded, and even the leaves stilled.

The light dimmed.

Calen glanced up. The sun was gone.

He turned. The clearing was empty.

No altar, no trees he recognized. No Mira.

Just shadows on unfamiliar trunks, shorter and broader than the pines near his home. The underbrush was thicker, the air—much warmer. Even the scent had changed. Earthy, dense, full of damp leaves and distant flowers he couldn't name.

Calen looked around, trying to orient himself.

The light caught him first. Not the slant of midmorning sun he'd left behind, but the faint golden edge of dawn rising over the trees.

Dawn. Again?

He blinked hard, as if that might explain it. But the shadows were long, the air damp with night, and the world hadn't woken up yet.

Calen looked around, instinct pulling at him before the thought could catch up. The sunrise—that was the first thing. He'd already felt it warming his back earlier, climbing toward midmorning. But here, now, it was just cresting on the horizon again. He squinted at the soft light filtering through the canopy. The sun was in the wrong place. Or he was.

The trees were wrong too. No more pines towering in tight lines. These were broad-limbed oaks and maples, their leaves wide and rustling in a looser pattern. He crouched low, fingertips brushing the forest floor. No moss. No ferns. Just dry, unfamiliar leaves and brittle twigs.

Just then, the thought occurred to him—the stone.

He lifted it from his palm, holding it up to the light.

Cold. Dull. Lifeless.

The faint warmth that had pulsed against his skin was gone. No sense of presence, no whisper at the edge of thought. Just a stone now—gray and inert, as if whatever had lived inside it had burnt itself out.

Calen felt suddenly vulnerable and more alone than he had ever been. The forest around him was still wrapped in shadow, the faintest hints of dawn coloring the horizon. He took a slow, steadying breath, trying to calm his racing thoughts. Mira said he'd arrive east of the castle, which meant if he moved west, he'd find it. He glanced upward, eyeing a sturdy tree nearby. Climbing it would give him a better view once the sun rose, so he tucked the stone back in its pouch and made his way up the tree.

The bark felt rough and unfamiliar under his hands as he climbed, the branches thick enough to hold his weight easily. Settling into a sturdy perch, he drew out the provisions Mira had packed, unwrapping a small loaf of bread and cheese as he waited. He peered carefully into the shadows around him, eyes straining to discern shapes in the dim pre-dawn gloom. The forest felt denser here, crowded with branches that reached out in twisted patterns unlike the tall, straight pines he knew from home. Every rustle or faint shift in the underbrush below drew his attention, though nothing revealed itself. He chewed slowly, alert and uneasy, waiting for the daylight to reveal where he'd found himself. He remembered Mira's fearful words, how his camouflage had been stripped away, leaving him easy to detect by forces he couldn't yet imagine. The thought made him shiver, and he instinctively pressed closer against the rough bark, careful to stay silent and hidden. Whatever she'd meant, he wasn't about to take any chances.

As the sky brightened to a pale, rosy hue, Calen realized the thick leaves above obscured his view more than he'd anticipated. He shifted carefully, dropping back to the forest floor with a soft thump, the dead leaves rustling quietly under his feet. Orienting himself briefly with the sun rising at his back, he began moving forward, heading west, certain the castle couldn't be far.

He moved swiftly but cautiously through the trees, his heart lifting slightly as the thinning woods ahead seemed to hint at a clearing. A low ridge rose gently in front of him, covered with thick shrubs and fallen logs, forcing him to climb carefully over and around the debris. At the top of the ridge, Calen paused, breath catching in surprise. Open plains stretched as far as the eye could see, an endless expanse of rolling grass and scattered clumps of trees. There was no castle. Not even a hill or mound large enough to conceal one.

Closer, maybe three or four hundred yards ahead, ran a broad road bustling with activity. A large cart rattled northward, its driver casually flicking the reins at the two sturdy horses. To the south, three travelers chatted as they walked, baskets swinging at their sides, and farther along, several solitary figures hurried about, each absorbed in their own errands.

Calen stood rooted to the spot, confusion settling heavily in his chest. This wasn't right. Not right at all.

# 5

Calen hesitated at the forest's edge, glancing down at the road again. He wasn't supposed to talk to or be seen by anyone, but these were not the dark, dangerous, magically enchanted woods he'd imagined or expected.

He stepped cautiously from the bushes, boots crunching softly on dried grass. He paused at the edge of the road, watching as travelers hurried past—farmers, merchants, women with baskets. No one seemed to pay him any attention, all occupied with their own journeys.

Then he saw her: a girl, close to his own age, walking alone and humming softly to herself. Her hair was pulled back loosely, and a small satchel hung from her shoulder, swaying as she walked.

He swallowed nervously, then called out, "Excuse me?"

She halted immediately, spinning toward him, eyes widening slightly in surprise. She looked him up and down curiously, unafraid. "Hello?"

Calen stepped forward, trying to look less out of place than he felt. "Sorry, I...I seem to be a bit lost. Could you point me toward the castle?"

Her brow arched. "Castle? You mean the Imperial Palace? That's over two thousand miles west, clear on the coast."

Calen blinked, startled. "Two thousand—no, I meant..." He paused, realizing how strange it would sound to ask someone about a castle that, apparently, no one even knew existed.

"Actually, maybe I am mixed up. I'm not a spy, if that's what you were thinking."

Her eyes narrowed slightly, though amusement tugged at the corner of her mouth. "That's exactly what a spy would say. Especially one with an accent like that. I've never heard anyone speak like you before."

Calen laughed awkwardly, looking back at the forest.

"I'm not used to seeing trees in that direction. It's a bit confusing."

"What do you mean?" the girl asked. "The forest is always to the east."

Calen thought for a moment. "Where I'm from, the forest is always to the west."

She stared at him, expression shifting from suspicious to one of outright fascination. "The west? You're telling me you traveled through the whole forest and you came out alive?"

He hesitated, suddenly aware of how impossible his claim sounded. There was a trade route at the southern edge of the forest, near the mountains, but it was tightly controlled by the Vashari traders, easily identified by their intricate facial tattoos. No outsider would dare imitate them.

"I didn't exactly go through the whole forest," he said slowly. "I just ended up here."

The girl raised an eyebrow, clearly skeptical. "'Ended up here?'"

Calen hesitated, trying to think of plausible explanations. He couldn't exactly mention teleportation and fairies.

"I got lost," he finally offered. "Really, really lost."

She studied him another moment, then shook her head, a half-smile forming on her lips. "Well, let's get you into town, our little wandering forest prince, and we'll sort things out from there."

She turned and started down the road, beckoning him to follow. Calen quickly caught up, falling into step beside her.

"I'm Lyra," she said, glancing sideways at him. "What's your name, mysterious traveler?"

"Calen," he replied, feeling slightly relieved. "And thanks for helping me. I didn't realize how lost I was—"

"Clearly," Lyra laughed. "People don't exactly wander through the forest and stumble onto the road every day—at least not like you. So—where exactly are you from?"

Calen hesitated, but this girl seemed nice—beautiful, actually. He'd never seen anyone with golden hair before. Everyone in his village had black hair, like his own, or brown.

"Edge Hollow, just east of the forest."

Lyra's eyes widened. "East? You really came through the forest? I mean, people talk about all sorts of things living there—creatures, magic, monsters. Honestly, you're lucky to be alive." Lyra paused thoughtfully. "Does everyone there, uh, look like...you?"

Calen managed a small laugh. "Magic? Monsters? I've spent my whole life there, and I've never seen anything like that." He realized suddenly that that wasn't true.

Calen's mind fluttered. That answer had been true a few weeks ago. His whole life. He hadn't wrapped his head around everything that had happened yet.

Lyra gave him an intrigued look. "Really? Huh. Maybe the stories are just to keep kids from running off."

"Could be," Calen agreed. "My grandmother is always telling stories. What about you? Have you lived here your whole life?"

"Born and raised," Lyra said with a sigh, her voice carrying the tone of someone who longed for someplace more exciting. "My family's been in Hearthmere for generations. You'll see soon enough. It's not a castle, but it's home."

They walked on quietly for a few moments, the gentle crunch of gravel under their feet filling the silence. Calen found himself stealing occasional looks at Lyra, wondering how much he could tell her—and how soon she'd notice there was more to him than being lost.

The road curved gently. The heat was rising with the sun, warm enough that sweat clung to the back of his neck. Cicadas buzzed from the tall grass, and black birds darted overhead. He wiped his palms on his trousers, suddenly aware of how out of place he looked—clothes a bit too rugged, hair unbrushed, boots dusty with forest soil.

Lyra didn't seem to notice. "We'll be there in a minute," she said. "The gates always surprise people the first time."

Calen frowned. "Gates?" He pictured houses all lined up with perfect little gates in their yards.

Lyra nodded. "The town is walled in. The empire's been pushing east for years—always sniffing around, claiming it's for trade routes or our own protection. But everyone knows they want to take over. 'The wall's a message.' That's what my dad says."

The path faded wide, and they were at the edge of a wide clearing, the forest to the east, like a dark curtain. Small houses with farmyards dotted the area, but the road led up to the gate.

The wall stood massive before him—weathered timber fitted so tightly together it might as well have been carved from a single tree. Three stories high at its center, where a heavy iron-bound gate stood open, flanked by two squat towers with slitted windows and sharp-eyed men watching from within. The wall stretched out far in either direction, vanishing into the haze of the morning.

He had never seen something so deliberate, so immense.

Calen stopped cold.

"Wait...this isn't—this isn't a castle, is it?"

Lyra gave him a sideways look. "Uh, no. It's just a city!"

But his chest was tight. "Because I was told..." He swept his eyes over the wooden walls, the towers. "It's just the walls—they're huge!"

"Yeah, well, we like our privacy."

She obviously meant it as a joke, but Calen didn't laugh. His eyes were wide, searching the wall like it might lurch to life and swallow him whole.

Lyra's smile faltered.

She studied him for a long moment, and something in her expression shifted—the pieces finally clicking.

"You really *are* from the east," she said. Not in disbelief this time, but from wonder. "You've never seen anything like this before."

Calen shook his head slowly. "It's all wood. The castle was supposed to be stone. I don't...I don't even know where I am."

Lyra's eyes softened. She stepped a little closer, her voice gentler than before. "Hey," she said, "it's okay. You're not in any trouble. You just got turned around, that's all. Happens to traders and hunters sometimes too."

He didn't answer right away. His gaze was fixed on the gate towers, where two armored men stood like statues, spears in hand, bows on their backs, eyes scanning the road.

"Are those...soldiers?" he asked.

Lyra followed his line of sight and nodded. "Sort of. City guards. They keep things orderly."

Calen stared. The gleam of their polished bracers, and...he didn't know what they were called. Tall axes on poles... He only knew they looked dangerous catching the morning light.

"I've never seen armor before," he whispered nervously. "Or weapons like that. Or men who look like they're ready to kill someone." Calen had made plenty of farm equipment with his father, but never weapons.

Lyra snorted. "Those two?"

She tipped her chin toward the guards. "The tall one on the left is Bran—he once screamed like a child because a spider crawled up his collar during guard duty. And the other one, Jory, fell into a pig trough last week. Took days to get the smell off him."

Calen balked. "Seriously?"

"Dead serious." Lyra grinned. "They act all tough up there, but they're as soft as baked pears. Don't worry—they're harmless. Bran is friends with my brother. I'll introduce you to him later."

And with that, they passed through the gate without incident.

# 6

The city unfolded before them, alive with motion and sound. The road spilled into a wide thoroughfare paved with compacted earth and edged in flagstones. On either side, timber-framed buildings stood shoulder to shoulder, their shutters thrown open, spilling warm light and morning smells into the street.

Ahead, the road sloped gently toward a large market square already stirring to life. Merchants rolled open canvas stalls while children darted between barrels, chasing each other through tangles of crates and carts. Beyond the square, a broad, stone-faced building loomed—part storehouse, part meeting hall, judging by its size and the clamor of voices already echoing from inside.

To the left, a narrow path led to what looked like barracks, a row of squat, uniform buildings marked by banners and the clink of armor being tended. Off to the right, a two-story structure with a carved overhang and tall windows suggested something more official—an administrator's office, perhaps.

Calen took it all in like a man trying to read a book at a glance. He had never seen so many people moving with so much purpose. A boy walked past, leading two goats on a rope. A woman shouted over her shoulder as she balanced a basket on her hip.

It felt overwhelming and alive in a way that Edge Hollow never had. Everything was louder, closer—people brushing past him, voices layered in the air, color and motion packed into every narrow space.

Lyra glanced down at her bag. "I had to run to the dairy just north of town. Mama forgot to put her order in yesterday, and if I didn't go get it myself, we'd have nothing for breakfast."

She thought for a moment, then said, "Okay, so...bringing a strange boy home at dawn would probably earn me more questions than I feel like answering. Especially after my sister—"

Calen blinked, feeling abandoned. "I'm not dangerous, you know."

"I know," she said quickly, then smirked. "But my mother's mind doesn't always work like that. Look, just hang out in the market here. I live two streets over. I'll drop this off and be right back."

He nodded. "All right."

She jogged off with an easy confidence, disappearing into a narrow street between two squat buildings. Calen turned, eyeing the square.

The city was truly awake now. Merchants rolled carts into place. Stall awnings were being tied off. Someone carried a basket of steaming bread past him, the scent trailing in its wake and making his mouth water. Two children chased one another, yelling and giggling as a woman called after them. The noise, the closeness, the rhythm of it all—it was overwhelming. None of this was like home. Where he came from, people lived far apart and spoke quietly. Here, everything pressed in, voices overlapped, and the world moved quickly.

He drifted toward the fountain at the square's center and leaned against a stone ledge, trying not to look too lost. A few curious glances and a couple smiles slid his way, but no one approached him.

Lyra returned not long after, her arms free now. "I told you I'd be back," she said, slightly breathless, voice raised above the noise of the crowd. She took his hand. Before Calen had time to blush, she said, "C'mon. Let me show you around!"

They wove through the square, Lyra pointing out the bakery. "Best morning buns in the world, and I'm not exaggerating."

A cobbler's shop, a small chapel to some god Calen didn't recognize.

"Oh! This should be interesting!" Lyra exclaimed.

They crossed the square toward a row of quieter storefronts tucked beneath an arched walkway, leading him to a small stone shop with a stained-glass window set into the front wall. As they entered, a bell over the door announced their arrival.

The air inside was dry, smelling of ink and beeswax, leather bindings and old smoke. Lyra strode to the counter and called out, her tone easy and familiar. The shopkeeper looked up with a smile that said he knew her well.

"Luthor," she began, "I'd like to introduce you to my new friend, Calen. He's not from here."

"It's a pleasure," the man said warmly. "How can I be of service?"

"We're trying to find a map that shows where he's from," she said, glancing around the room as if the answer might be hanging on the walls.

"Well," Luthor replied, still smiling, "you've come to the right place. I've got the best maps in the region. And since we aren't under the Empire's thumb, mine aren't restricted."

He looked Calen up and down. "Now, where did you say you were from, young man?"

"Edge Hollow," Calen said, stepping up to the counter.

Luthor frowned slightly. "Hmm. I've never heard of it. Where's that located?"

"On the other side of the forest," Calen replied simply.

The man paused, blinking. "Well, you—" He stopped himself, then stammered, "W-We don't get many travelers from the—the other side of the forest." After a beat, he added, "Ah—yes. I have one here."

He crossed to the far side of the room, climbed a small ladder, and pulled down a midsized leather scroll. Bringing it back to the counter, he unrolled it and weighed the corners down with polished glass stones.

The map showed a vast forest to the west, stretching the full length of the parchment from north to south. There was a sharp hook where the forest widened, a great lake to the north, and a sprawling city on the far eastern coast.

"All right, son," Luthor said. "Does any of this look familiar?"

Calen studied the parchment. He'd never seen the land drawn this way before, but the shape of the forest tugged at recognition—the hook of it. His town had been right along that curve. He pointed quickly, touching the page, then drew back his hand, embarrassed.

"Ah," the mapmaker said with a nod. "Yes, well—that's quite a ways off. Fifteen hundred miles east of here, give or take a hundred." He admired the map, still nodding.

Fifteen hundred miles, Calen thought. That would take months of travel.

"Oh—and," Calen said, hesitating, "I was looking for a castle. It might be...rumored to be enchanted?"

Luthor's eyes lifted toward the shelves. "Well," he said thoughtfully, "there's supposed to be a castle far to the north that the wizards use. Not much is known about it, but it's even farther north than you are west from here." He said, pointing at the place on the map Calen had identified.

"So—over fifteen hundred more miles north?"

"Oh yes," Luthor said confidently. "Probably even double that."

Calen felt his blood run cold. How could he be so far off? Why had he ended up here? If he tried to reach the castle, it might take a year or more.

"Are you all right, son?" Luthor asked kindly. "You look a bit pale."

Calen's eyes stayed fixed on the place he'd pointed to.

Lyra touched his arm gently. "Calen, are you okay?"

His head turned toward her, though his eyes stayed on the map for a long moment before he finally met her gaze.

"I think I'm very lost," he said quietly.

"Well, you're not lost," Lyra said, hand still on his arm. "You know where you are, and you know where you're trying to go. You just need a plan to get there."

She smiled at him, and warmth spread through his chest. For a moment, it felt like there was still hope in the world—if only in her smile.

Lyra gave Luthor a final thank you, her hand still lightly on Calen's arm as she guided him to the door. The bell chimed behind them, and the clamor of the morning market swept back in—bright and loud. Calen blinked hard, thinking he'd actually felt better back in the shop. He had never seen so many people in one place before.

She didn't speak as she guided him a few paces off the main walk, toward the covered wall of a building that held a sliver of shade. A single shoe sat on the ledge there, cracked at the heel.

"So...thinking." She looked at her hands, as if trying to measure the distance. "What would it take to get you to your mystery castle? It's near the twin cities, isn't it? That's seven, maybe eight months from here. Even if you left today, you wouldn't reach it until autumn."

Calen lurched forward and swept the shoe from the ledge. It flew end over end and slammed into the cobbles, startling a few locals, who drew back.

"Eight months?" His voice broke into a shout. "I'm supposed to walk for eight months?" He stared at her now, eyes wide. "That's impossible."

Lyra jerked back, her shoulder striking the wall.

"Why am I here?" he shouted, not caring who heard. The heat rose sharp in his chest. "It was that fai—" His jaw snapped shut. He looked at her. "It's not fair."

She took a step closer to him. "Then don't walk it," she said. "But you can't stand here and burn over it, either."

His jaw clenched and unclenched, but he said nothing. She had a point.

"All right," she said, "first thing—you need somewhere to sleep." She looked him over. "Supplies. Food, coin, boots that won't fall apart. You can't leave with nothing and expect to last eight months."

Calen nodded.

"So...where do we put you?" she said, glancing over the street as if searching for a place. "You can't sleep with me—" She stopped, color rushing to her face. "I mean, not at my house."

Calen's eyes dropped, unsure where to rest, and stopped on her chest. Heat surged through him. He looked away sharply.

"You don't have coin, do you?" she asked.

He shook his head.

"Right. No inn, then." She drew in a steady breath. "Well...the barracks will take any man who's willing to work."

"The barracks?" he said. "With the soldiers?"

"Yes. The soldiers," she said. "They're...mostly decent. It'll get you settled until we can make a real plan. And they pay. You can start saving."

Calen thought about it. He had worked beside his father, but he'd never been paid. The idea of having his own coin... He liked the thought of it.

Lyra stepped back into the flow of the street, and Calen followed without a word.

The market thinned as they headed for the front gate. Stalls gave way to plain stone buildings, then a wider road. The noise shifted—less shouting vendors, more clatter of metal, boots on dirt.

Up ahead, the outer wall rose above the rooftops. The barracks sat against it, long and square, built of timber and grey stone. Even at a distance, Calen could see movement in the yard—men with spears, shirts hanging loose, steel flashing in the sun.

He slowed, suddenly feeling young and weak.

Lyra didn't wait for him. She crossed the road toward the open yard, and Calen forced himself to follow.

A man near the water trough straightened, wiping sweat from his neck with the back of his arm. He grinned when he saw her.

"Well, look who's wandered back. Didn't bring us milk this time?"

Lyra didn't slow.

"Milk suits you. Everyone remembers what happened when you tried beer."

A roar of laughter broke through the yard.

"Seen any spiders today?" she added.

That drew an even louder howl. The man scrubbed a hand over his face. "Enough, Lyra…"

She lifted a brow. "You started it, Bran."

She nodded toward him, glancing at Calen. "This is Bran. Quartermaster's son. His mouth is bigger than his courage."

Bran gave her an understanding grimace before turning his attention to Calen. "Who's the boy?" he asked, looking him over.

"This is Calen. I found him wandering this morning. He needs a place to stay."

"Ah, ever the little stewardess," he said appraising her. "Very well—we can take him in, but you—go away. We don't need your inspecting eye all over us. You make the boys nervous." He gave Lyra a look that was half warning, half grin. "I'll take care of your little friend."

Lyra's jaw tightened, but she didn't argue. She gave Calen a single nod and stepped back. "I'll see you later. You're in good hands." She turned and walked out of the courtyard.

The men closed in slowly. One reached out and gave Calen's forearm a testing grip. Another slapped his shoulder as if greeting an old friend. Fingers ran along muscle, measuring. One younger guard, lanky and quick, pushed a weighted ball into his hands.

"You ever sparred?" the lanky one asked, grinning.

Calen shook his head. The ball weighed heavy in his palms. He tossed it back—harder than it had come.

An approving whistle rose from the circle.

"Got arms on you," someone said, and a rough hand clamped his bicep before another tugged his shoulder pack away. Fingers caught his collar, pulling his tunic over his head.

Cold air hit his skin.

"He's a fit one," another voice called.

Calen's heart pounded. Bodies pressed close. He didn't know where to look—faces, hands, steel. No space to move. No space to run. Panic crawled up his throat.

One man tried to wrench his arm for wrestling. Another shoved a practice sword at him. Hands crashed against his shoulders, appraising. A palm cupped his backside to roars of laughter.

He opened his mouth to speak, to shove someone back—

"Easy!" Bran barked, forcing his way in. "Easy there, boys. Give the man some room. "Back to it!" Bran shoved a few shoulders as the men laughed their way off. "You'll get your turn later."

A chorus of jeers and insults followed, but they peeled away one by one, returning to drills and weights.

Bran stooped, grabbed Calen's tunic and pack, and tossed the tunic back into his arms.

"Cover yourself," he said, not unkindly. "Come on. You'll breathe better away from them."

He led Calen to the stables, away from the groping hands and eyes.

Inside, the air was warm with hay and horses. Bran motioned to an empty stall cleared of tack.

"I hope you do not mind this for now," he said. "Everyone begins here. It's tradition."

He set Calen's pack onto the straw.

"In time, you'll move up. You will have a proper bed. A better place. But you must earn it."

"I'm okay with that," Calen said, picking up his pack. "I've slept in the hay many nights."

Bran nodded. "Good. Then you will do well here. Have you mucked out stalls?"

Calen glanced at the horses, then back at Bran.

"Yes, sir," he said, quieter now.

"Then start there," Bran said. "Shovel, water, feed. We will see you fed after."

Bran left him with a shovel, a water pail, and a row of stalls that stretched farther than Calen had expected. The horses only snorted and shifted as he worked, hooves thudding against wood while he dragged out matted hay and dung, one barrowload at a time.

It was slow work. Not hard—he had done worse with his father—but there was no rhythm here. No voice telling him what came next. Just filth, flies, and the scrape of iron on stone. By noon, his shirt was soaked through. By afternoon, his arms were shaking from hauling water buckets across the yard.

No one spoke to him.

Men came and went, stepping over the troughs he carried, laughing at jokes he did not hear. Once, a pair of them walked past with bowls of stew and bread. One of them nodded at Calen's labor and said, "New blood." The other spat and kept walking.

When the mess bell rang, Calen followed the crowd to the long tables under the overhang. A pot slammed down at the end of the bench, slopping out more grey stew and a chunk of bread. Beer was poured from a shared jug. Calen tasted it once and nearly gagged—bitter, sour, nothing like the cider back at home. The stew was worse. He forced two bites, then left it and returned to the stables.

He sat in the straw and tore a strip of ham from his pack. He chewed slowly, staring at the wall, knowing it would only last him a few days.

Night fell. The neighboring barracks filled with noise—snoring, coughing, arguments muffled through walls. Every now and then, men, alone or in a group, would stumble out and piss in the courtyard. Someone else was singing off-key. Calen lay on his side, eyes open.

He could not stay here long.

Calen woke to the sound of someone grunting.

At first he thought it was a man lifting weight—but then the smell hit him. He pushed himself up on one elbow. Just beyond the stall wall, a soldier was crouched over the latrine trench, bare-backed and unconcerned, pissing and shitting in the open air as he scratched his ribs.

Calen looked away. The man didn't.

"Hey, you're the new boy!" he called, far too cheerfully.

Calen felt heat rise in his face.

"What are they having you do today?" the man asked.

"Um..." Calen kept his eyes on the straw. "I'm not sure yet."

"No worries," the man called back. "I'm sure Bran will find something for you to do!" He stood, hitched up his trousers, and wandered off, whistling.

Calen stayed where he was long after the man left, knees drawn up, unsure whether to move or stay hidden in the straw. He had never felt smaller. He could not name what he had done wrong, only that he must have done something. He quickly took the stone out of his pouch to see if it had woken back up—maybe it could get him out of here. But it was still cold and dark.

When he finally stepped back into the yard, the sun was higher. Men were already drilling, shouting, laughing. No one looked for him.

He almost turned back to the stables—when he saw Lyra leaning over the far gate. She was scanning the yard. She had come looking for him.

She spotted him and came to meet him halfway across the yard. There was no smile this time.

"Calen…" she said quietly. "What have they done to you?"

He didn't answer. He couldn't.

She studied his face—the dirt, the hollow under his eyes, the way he stood as if expecting another shove.

She reached him, eyes running over the filth and fatigue clinging to him.

"Hmm," she said. "Maybe this is not your kind of work."

Calen swallowed but said nothing.

"You have any skills?" she asked.

He hesitated. "I…worked in a forge. With my father."

Lyra's expression sharpened. "A blacksmith?"

He nodded once.

"Calen," she said, breath catching with sudden purpose, "Dean has been begging for an assistant for years."

"Who's Dean?" Calen asked, his voice rough.

Lyra's brow lifted above a faint, almost relieved smile.

"He runs the city forge. Old as iron and twice as stubborn. He has been shouting for an apprentice since I was twelve."

She nodded toward the gate. "Come on. If you can swing a hammer, he will feed you." She paused. "He is...a bit grumpy."

Calen looked at her.

"As long as he doesn't shit in open troughs, I'll be fine."

Lyra blinked. "What?"

"Never mind." He pulled the gate open for her.

Lyra led him back through the market and then west, where the streets grew quieter. Calen followed in silence, one hand on his pack, the sounds of the barracks still in his ears.

The road curved past a stone structure, smoke rising in the plumes from a chimney and the rhythmic *clang* of iron echoing out from within. A line of horses tied at a wooden pole. Calen felt a surge of relief. Finally, something felt like home.

"That's the smithy, and the farrier," Lyra said, slowing, "Old Dean runs it—grumpiest man in town. But his partner, Ronan, is nice enough, and he does all the shoes for the horses—that's why they're all lined up here."

Calen stopped walking.

Lyra turned, eyebrows raised. "What?"

He was staring into the open workspace, where a heavyset man pounded a glowing bar of iron against an anvil. "My dad is a blacksmith," Calen said wistfully. "I helped in the forge almost every day."

The man inside—gray-bearded, barrel chested—glanced up and scowled. "You loiterin' or lookin' for work?" he barked.

Calen stammered but didn't get any words out.

"He's new in town, Dean. He's actually a blacksmith's apprentice!"

Dean grunted. "That so? Got a busted shovel back here nobody's been able to reshape without cracking it. You any good?"

Calen stepped forward. "Yeah. Not weapons, but farm tools I can do."

The forge was familiar. The heat on his skin felt like home. Calen took off his traveling coat and peeled off his shirt. Dean handed him the warped shovel and stepped back, arms folded. Calen set to work.

In less time than should have been possible, the shovel lay set, reshaped with smooth precision.

Dean inspected his work, clearly impressed. "Well," he said, "looks like the boy knows what he's doing!"

He squinted. "You got a place to stay, son?"

"No," Calen admitted.

"Then you're staying here! Help me with the forge, I'll feed you and get you a bed upstairs. You'll be sharing with my business partner's son, Reeve. He's a nice lad. Can't find good hands these days—not ones who know the craft! Everyone wants to be in business nowadays—buy and sell and trade—and *do nothing*!" He laughed with joy. "Oh, I'm happy to have you, son!"

Calen didn't hesitate—this was leagues better than the barracks. "I'd appreciate that."

"Wonderful!" the old man cried. "Let's get you set up!"

Lyra leaned in. She seemed to be admiring Calen's lean, bare upper body. "Show off!"

Calen caught the look and flushed, but said nothing.

"Let's get to work. I have a backlog. If we finish early, we can celebrate!" Dean called from the back.

Calen laughed, shrugging. "I guess I have a job—and a place to stay!" He rubbed the back of his neck. "Thanks for rescuing me"

She nodded. "I'll stop by tomorrow. We'll try those buns I was telling you about!"

She gave a little wave, turned, paused, then looked back and smiled before disappearing into the growing bustle of the street.

# 7

Dean wasted no time in putting Calen to work. The smithy bustled with heat and hammering as Dean introduced him to the forge layout, the bellows, the various racks of iron and steel, and the work orders stacked neatly in a carved wooden box by the front counter. Calen listened carefully, nodding at each explanation. Much of it mirrored the layout of his father's forge, though more organized and far more expansive.

"This rack here is for custom orders," Dean said, tapping a heavy iron hook with a pair of tongs. "That bin's for wagon repairs, and in that corner—" He gestured toward a rack of hoof picks and horseshoes. "—Ronan comes by for those. We keep extra for the farrier trade."

As if on cue, Ronan ducked his head into the smithy. A light-haired man with streaks of soot along his muscular arms, he gave Calen a long look. "A new lad?" He strode over and inspected Calen, running his hand down his arm, checking for muscle.

"Calen," Dean answered for him. "Hard worker, and good with a hammer. Might even give your son a run for his coin."

Ronan chuckled. "That'll be the day." He glanced over his shoulder. "Reeve's been dying for someone to complain to besides me."

Reeve himself appeared behind his father, a year or so older than Calen with unruly, dark blond hair and a wry expression. "Oh, new guy? Finally, someone to talk to besides my dad."

Calen thought perhaps Ronan had been joking, but maybe it was true.

The workday was busy but satisfying. They repaired two wagon axles, reshaped a dozen horseshoes, and forged new hinges for a merchant's barn doors. Dean seemed to grow more energetic with each hour, clearly thriving in the rhythm of clanging metal and rising steam.

As the sun dipped lower and the last customer left with a wheelbarrow full of iron fittings, Dean clapped soot-streaked hands together. "Right then! Now for the real magic. Come on, boys. You too, Calen."

He led them to the side of the building and behind a wall, where a small outbuilding stood. Pipes ran to and from the smithy, its door thick with steam. Inside, to Calen's astonishment, was a tiled shower room. Stone floors sloped gently toward a central drain, copper pipes twisted along the wall, and a large iron tank at the back hissed with heat.

"Custom job," Dean said proudly, stripping off his outer layer. "Boiler feeds through a stove I rigged under the forge heat. One of my finer inventions. Beats freezing in a trough—and you can use it year-round, even in the snow!"

Calen laughed, eyes wide as he stepped inside. Ronan and Reeve followed, already half out of their pants. The room filled with warmth and camaraderie as they scrubbed away the grime of the day, steam curling around them like a private reward. It was a kind of comfort Calen had never known—a small luxury shared with strangers who already felt like something more.

Afterward, they dressed in fresh tunics. They lent Calen one of Reeve's.

Dean explained, "Wash lady comes every morning, so put whatever you want cleaned in that basket. I put it out every morning. She's right around the corner. All the jobs that require boilers or burners are all in this area."

The living quarters were attached to the back of the forge, warm and welcoming with polished wood floors and a long dining table. A back door opened onto a modest garden, well-tended and fragrant with herbs and flowering vines.

Dinner was simple but hearty, paired with cider poured into metal cups Dean had forged himself. He raised a toast. "To full bellies and good hands."

Ronan chuckled. "And to wives who cooked better than we ever will."

"May they rest in peace and never see the state of our pantry," Dean replied.

Calen smiled but said little, absorbing the atmosphere—the quiet understanding between old friends, the ease of shared work and shared grief. These men had built something together, and now, somehow, Calen was part of it.

During dinner, Ronan set his cup down with a sigh. "Bit of excitement in Thistlebrook today."

Dean raised an eyebrow. "Yeah? What happened?"

"Imperial troops came through," Ronan said. "Claimed they were there for trade route inspections, but by midday, they were in full skirmish mode. Tried to take the city, but the locals pushed them back."

Dean grunted. "It's only a matter of time before they try that here." Looking at Calen, he said, "Thank the gods we thought to build that wall. None of the other local cities have anything like that."

"They had mages with them too," Ronan said, his tone serious.

Dean glanced up. "Real ones?"

"Tactical mages from the palace, is what I heard."

Dean gave a low whistle, then grumbled, "I always get mages and wizards mixed up."

Ronan chuckled. "You're not the only one who's confused. A mage's just someone trained up in magic—usually for fighting. The Empire's got schools for it. Heard the program's nasty...starts with boys barely old enough to walk." He shook his head. "Now, a wizard? That's different. You won't find any in the Empire. To be called a wizard, you've got to work magic for a hundred years straight. Supposedly, you don't just get the title after that—you stop aging." He took a swig of beer. "That's what the chronicles say, anyway. Who's lived long enough to check a wizard's birth record?" He laughed and waved a hand. "Mages, on the other hand? They die like the rest of us."

Calen stayed quiet. He wasn't sure before now wizards even existed. It seemed like more and more of Mira's tales were coming true. Maybe all of them were.

After dinner, Dean gave him a quick tour: the washroom was at the end of the hall, a simple chamber with a window that opened to the garden. Upstairs, he showed Calen the sleeping quarters. They had been divided up for more privacy with Dean and Ronan having their own living spaces and bedrooms.

A spare room in the middle was Reeve's. "We'll get you a cot until we can build you something better," Reeve said.

Calen nodded. "I don't mind sharing a bed, actually. At home, I sleep with my brother every night. He's young still."

Reeve thought about it. "I haven't had to share a bed before... Didn't think I'd want to, but you seem nice enough."

Just before they settled in for the night, Calen checked on the stone. It was still cold.

While they were laying there, Reeve asked, "Hey, where are you from? You've got an accent I've never heard, and your hair is so dark. Everyone around here has lighter hair."

Calen paused. No one had thought to ask him this before now, and Lyra was the only one who knew his identity. It felt too crazy to say. Calen could barely believe it himself.

"I'm from the east side of the forest. I got smuggled by Vashari traders. I—uh, I don't like to talk about it..." Calen hated lying.

"No way!" whispered Reeve. "That's crazy. My mom and Dean's wife and son were all traveling back from Allenguard when they were ambushed by bandits... They were all killed. There's lots of bandits on the roads lately. That's why the Empire wants to put soldiers here..."

Calen lay quietly staring at the ceiling. No wonder this city had walls.

8

Morning crept in slow and quiet, light sifting through the edge of the curtain and casting soft shapes across the room. The air was warm, the kind that clung even before the sun was fully up, and sometime during the night, the sheets had slipped down to the foot of the bed.

Calen blinked the sleep from his eyes and stretched carefully. Reeve lay beside him, face down and completely uncovered, one arm flung over his pillow. At some point, he must've kicked off his shirt too—he was bare now, the line of his back trailing down into a surprisingly furry bottom, fuzzy like the start of a peach.

Calen's mouth twisted into a smile. It was kind of cute, honestly.

He shifted closer without really meaning to, breathing in. Reeve smelled faintly of pine and clean earth, like sun-warmed needles and forest air. It seemed impossible, considering how he worked with horses all day, but it reminded Calen of home—of mornings that were quiet and safe, lying next to his brother in the loft. The thought settled warm and steady in his chest.

On impulse, he pulled off his own shirt—just so they were even. He glanced down at himself—still smooth, apart from a bit under his arms and a faint shadow trailing down below his belly button. He wondered if he'd end up like his dad, whose chest and arms were quite hairy, besides from what had been singed away.

Reeve gave a sleepy grunt and shifted. Calen rolled gently to the edge of the bed and swung his legs over, running a hand through his hair.

"Morning," Reeve mumbled, voice thick with sleep.

Calen grunted in reply, then stood, gathering yesterday's clothes from where they'd been tossed. Reeve sat up slowly, stretching with a yawn before tugging on clean breeches. He looked over to Calen. "You need clothes," he concluded. He went into some drawers and tossed them to Calen, then padded out of the room to allow him to get dressed. He stopped at the door and sniffed. "You smell good." he said, frowning slightly, then walked down the hall. Calen lifted his arm and sniffed, pondering.

So do you, he thought, smiling to himself.

Calen joined Reeve in the hall, put on his boots, and grabbed the laundry. At the side gate, he dropped it into the basket Dean mentioned the night before. The area of town still smelled faintly of ash from the previous day, and somewhere in the back, water was heating in a kettle.

"Ready?" Calen asked.

Reeve nodded, running a hand through his hair. "Let's go see what kind of a mood Lyra's in today."

The morning sun had warmed the cobbles by the time they reached the bakery. The door was propped open, letting the smell of yeast and sugar spill into the street. Lyra leaned against the wall beside it, arms crossed.

"You're late," she said, grinning. "I was about to eat your share."

Calen shrugged. "Had to wake up first."

Reeve murmured "It's our day off..."

Inside, the bakery was cozy and lit by the morning light. There was a long wooden counter and shelves stacked high with crusty loaves and braided rolls. A heavyset woman with flour on her cheeks looked up as they entered.

"Well now," she said, squinting and then smiling at Calen. "You're new!"

"He's with me," Lyra said cheerily.

The baker's eyes lingered on Calen—not suspicious, just soft, like she was seeing something sweet. "First one's always free for newcomers," she said, reaching behind the counter. Then she paused, plucked a second bun from the tray, and added it to the wax paper wrap. "Here. You look like you could use extra."

Calen blinked. "Thank you."

The buns were warm and sticky with glaze. He held them carefully as Lyra and Reeve paid for theirs, and they stepped outside again into the sunlight and the open seating area and sat down.

"She's never given me two," Lyra said, tone casual but eyes sharp.

"Maybe she's just nice," Calen offered.

"She isn't," Reeve muttered, already chewing.

The square was beginning to fill with the morning bustle.

"So," Lyra said excitedly, "how do you like them?"

Calen was in heaven. He'd never had dessert bread before. Lots of puddings and custards, but not this. It was amazing and chewy, soft and sweet.

"Oh, this is amazing..." he cooed, taking another bite.

After splitting the extra roll between the three of them, Lyra asked, "Where to next?"

The tailor shop sat right next to the bakery, its front window crowded with lace-trimmed shirts and vests displayed on elegant mannequins. Calen had never seen glass windows this big before. A brass bell jingled overhead as Lyra pushed open the door.

Inside, the air was cooler, scented with pressed linen and cedar. Bolts of fabric lined the walls, and a curtain swayed gently at the back of the room. A tall man with silver-threaded hair and pinched spectacles looked up from his measuring tape.

"Lyra," he said smoothly, "and company."

"This is Calen," she said. "He's new to town and an apprentice at the forge."

The tailor's eyes swept over him with immediate, attentive interest. "That explains the shoulders," he said, thoughtfully taking him in. He looked down his nose. "And the soot under the nails."

Calen shifted awkwardly, putting his hands behind his back "Sorry..."

"No, no, it suits you," the man said, brightening. "Rough edges. Very rustic. Stay still."

Without permission, he stepped forward and tugged gently at Calen's sleeve, straightening the seam as though picturing him in something finer. Then, without hesitation, he circled around, talking to himself about structure and posture. He ran both hands across Calen's seat, making it seem natural, but he was clearly feeling what was underneath. He then slipped two fingers deep under the waistband of his pants and gave a light tug to check the fit.

The tailor chuckled and paused in front of him, lifting a swatch of dark blue linen and holding it against his chest. "Hmm," he said. "Yes. This or green. Something cool to contrast with your tone."

He stepped back slightly and tilted his head. "You're a rare coloring for this town. Everyone's light and fair. And those eyes...brown but not muddy. There's warmth in them. Like coffee or varnished wood."

Reeve made a quiet choking sound behind him.

"I'm not looking for clothes," Calen said.

"Of course not," the tailor said, finally releasing him. "But when you are, come to me. You're going to want something nice for when you're courting young ladies," he said, eyeing Lyra. "First fitting's free."

The bell jingled again as they stepped out into the square.

Reeve cleared his throat. "He touched your ass."

Calen looked between them, not quite understanding the concern. "Friendly people?"

Lyra giggled, looking him over. It seemed like she was still picturing him in nicer clothes as well.

They cut diagonally through the square. Bran sat on a stoop with another soldier, half in shade.

"Hey—look who's back," Bran called.

Calen recognized the broad jaw and that same careless grin from earlier. The other man lounged with a bottle balanced on his thigh.

"You ditch the yard for the forge, pretty boy?" the second one said. "Figures you'd be more useful polishing tools."

Bran snorted. "Yeah, on your knees for Dean, huh? Bet the old man tips in nails."

Calen hadn't planned to stop. He didn't owe them anything. But he turned his head anyway.

Bran's grin held, but something behind it slackened, like his mind had wandered somewhere it shouldn't have. The other soldier looked Calen over again, slower this time.

"Hell," the second man said, a bit too loudly. "If that's what you're after, we've got better back with us—"

He grabbed his balls through his trousers, still grinning—then froze, breath catching like he'd surprised himself.

Reeve laughed. "Is that your weapon today?"

Bran's grin fell. He reached over and yanked the bottle out of the man's hand. "What the hell are you drinking?"

Luckily, Lyra was far enough ahead to have missed the exchange. They caught up to her, blending back into the moving crowd as if nothing had happened.

The sun was climbing now, and the square was busier—traders selling trinkets, children running between carts, dogs barking at pigeons. The air was thick with motion and sound. An old woman with a basket paused in front of them, leaning on a carved wooden cane. Her eyes landed on Calen, and her face lit up.

"Oh, my stars," she said, beaming. "A new face. And such a handsome one, too."

Calen gave a polite smile. "Good morning."

"You remind me of my husband," she said, stepping closer. "He was tall like you. Kind eyes, too. You *look* kind."

Before Calen could respond, she was already digging through her basket.

"Here," she said, pressing a pale yellow handkerchief into his hand. It was soft, embroidered with little green leaves. "For luck."

"Thank you," Calen said, surprised.

She reached up and patted his chest twice with a gentle hand. "You're going to do something important. I can feel it." And with that, she hobbled off into the crowd.

They stood there for a moment, watching her leave.

"She gave you a handkerchief," Reeve said flatly. "Did she *bless* you?"

"She was being so weird," Lyra said, eyeing the woman's retreating figure. "That's Marda. She doesn't *give* anything. She once charged me for a rotten pear."

"Why would you want a rotten pear?" asked Reeve, disgusted.

"Well, it wasn't all bad, I just—"

"Hey! New boy!" A voice called across the square.

A girl about their age was striding toward them, braids swinging, hands dusted with flour. She wore a smock over a pale dress and moved like someone who wasn't used to being ignored. "You just move here?" she asked, stopping in front of Calen.

"Uh...yeah. A few days ago," he replied, looking to Lyra to help him out.

The girl gave him a quick once-over and smiled. "Well, welcome. You've got good hands. Ever work a cider press?"

Calen blinked. "No, I haven't."

"Pity," she said. Then, after a pause, she reached out and ran a fingertip down his forearm. "You'd be good at it."

Reeve made a noise somewhere between a cough and a groan.

Lyra stepped in smoothly. "He's already apprenticed. No side jobs."

The girl lifted her hands, still smiling. "All right. Just being friendly."

She gave Calen a wink and turned to head back to the bakery.

They stood in silence.

Reeve glanced sideways. "Okay, that's enough."

Lyra crossed her arms. "I've lived here my whole life, and people aren't like this."

Calen looked between them, visibly rattled. "Did I do something?"

"No," said Reeve. "That's the problem."

Something cold fluttered low in Calen's chest. Liri had unlocked something inside him. His grandmother was upset about it. She had said he'd lost his camouflage, that he would be noticed. Is this what she meant?

Calen looked down at the handkerchief still curled in his fingers.

"We should go somewhere else," he said, quietly. "Somewhere with fewer people."

"Yes, please," Reeve said, already leading them away from the crowd.

Lyra fell in behind the boys. "There's a spot up the hill, just behind the grain stores. No one goes there during midday. It's quiet."

They walked without speaking for a while, the noise of the square fading behind them with every step. Calen didn't look back.

Lyra took the lead, winding their way up a narrow path behind the grain stores and up a hill until the noise of the square faded to birdsong and wind.

Calen sank down on the slope and stared at the handkerchief in his hands. He didn't speak.

Reeve flopped beside him with a grunt. "All right," he said, "what the hell is going on with you?"

Calen took a deep breath. "I don't know... People keep acting strange around me. I'm not doing anything."

"You said you were kidnapped," Reeve said, watching him. "Dragged here or something."

Calen hesitated.

Lyra, still standing, arms folded, gave quite a snort. "That's not true."

Reeve glanced at her.

"I met him yesterday," she said. "In the woods north of town. He just...walked out. Alone."

Reeve sat thoughtfully. "Seriously?"

Calen exhaled through his nose. "I panicked. I didn't know what to say. Everything felt too big. We were going to bed. I didn't want to start with something that sounded insane. I don't even know why I'm here or what's going on."

"And 'I was kidnapped' seemed like a better story?" Reeve said, glaring at him.

Calen shrugged.

Lyra lowered herself on the grass beside them. "You really didn't plan on coming here, did you?"

Calen shook his head, on the verge of tears. "No, I was supposed to go somewhere else. Somewhere specific. But—but I got sent—" he sniffed. "It sent me the wrong way."

"To a castle..." Lyra said softly, almost to herself.

Calen nodded.

Reeve leaned forward, resting his arms on his knees. "So, you came out of the forest," he said. He looked over his shoulder to the dark wall of forest across the way. "That's where all the weird stuff is."

Lyra gave him a look. "Weird stuff?"

"You know what I mean," Reeve said, starting to get a bit excited. "Magic things. Cursed things. Elves and purple dragons and—all that stuff!" He turned to Calen in mock suspicion. "Are you a purple dragon?"

Calen blinked a few times, startled, and then huffed a quiet laugh. The tension in his shoulders eased slightly.

"Definitely not," he said. "But if I turn into one, I'll let you know."

Reeve leaned back with a shrug. "Well, you do smell nice."

Lyra studied Calen, then sniffed at him. "It's true," she admitted, softly.

"Maybe he is magic, and he just doesn't know it," Reeve suggested. "Maybe he's some sort of fairy creature from the forest, and he just thinks he's human."

Calen tilted his head. "I am *not* a fairy creature. I come from a small town on the other side of the forest is all. It's not as...built up as all this. It's just small houses and fields."

"See?" Lyra said. "He's not magic; he's just rural."

"I always thought of rural people as smelling bad," Reeve countered.

"Uh, Reeve!" Lyra scolded. "Don't be rude."

She paused, searching Calen's face with a faint frown.

"He does seem to have an effect though, so maybe there is *something* to it..."

Calen looked down, brushing a thumb along the edge of the handkerchief. "So, what am I supposed to do? Just...never talk to anyone again?"

Lyra shook her head. "You can't hide. That's not fair to you. But if this thing keeps affecting people...it could become a problem."

Reeve grunted. "Yeah, if the wrong person falls head over heels and starts offering up land deeds or marriage proposals..." he said, looking at Lyra. She glared back.

"I don't want that," Calen said. "I don't want people doing things they don't mean. I don't even *like* being noticed like this. I'm used to being alone in the forest—these crowds make me..."

Lyra gave a sympathetic smile. "It's not your fault. But it's also not *nothing*."

Reeve scratched his jaw. "I mean, it's kind of like walking around with a leaking love potion. You're not pouring it, but you're dripping it everywhere."

Calen made a face. "Thanks."

Reeve chuckled, thinking out loud. "Well, it might not be all bad. Think about it. You could probably get free buns every morning. Discounts. Better rooms. Skip every line in the market. I bet you could ask someone for their boots, and they'd hand them over with a smile."

Lyra frowned. "Yeah, but...what if you couldn't stop? What if it's too easy to use it? You wouldn't even notice you're doing it anymore. Just—turn it on whenever you wanted something."

She glanced at Calen and then Reeve. "That's how good people go bad."

The words were heavier than she seemed to have expected.

They all went still.

The wind stirred the grass around them. A bird called in the distance, high and brief, then silence.

Reeve exhaled. "Okay. That just got dark."

Calen stared at the ground, lips pressed together. "But she's not wrong."

Lyra brushed her fingers through the grass beside her. "I think we should stop for now. Think about this before we do anything else."

Reeve looked like he wanted to protest, but just nodded.

"We can meet again soon," Lyra added. "Talk more. Just...figure it all out together."

There wasn't much more to say. They rose quietly and made their way down the hill.

# 9

The market was still busy, and overly kind strangers smiled at Calen, offering him meat, clothes, jewelry, or just a gentle nod. All of it benign. All of it oddly consistent.

Lunch was simple. They ate at a sunny table by the window in a local place, sharing a platter of cold roast chicken, fresh sourdough bread, and sliced melon drizzled with honey.

After they ate, Lyra brushed crumbs from her skirt and stood.

"I've got some things to do with my family this afternoon," she said. "But let's talk again soon, all right?"

Reeve gave her a short wave. "Don't get enchanted on your way home."

She rolled her eyes but smiled faintly, then walked off down the road, braid swinging behind her.

Reeve and Calen wandered the town a while longer, exploring the streets they hadn't seen yet, stopping to look at the trinkets and tools and whatever caught their eye, and headed back home for dinner at sunset.

Dinner was quiet, and by the time the dishes were cleared and the sun dipped below the rooftops, the air had cooled enough to draw a breeze through the open windows.

Reeve stretched and stood. "Shower?"

Calen nodded. The two of them stepped into the yard and into the custom bathing room, turning on the showerheads. "I'm pretty sure even the mayor doesn't have a shower this nice," Reeve bragged. "It's a custom job. Dean did it all himself. He was tired of walking all the way to the public baths every day after work."

"It's amazing." Calen grinned, letting the water pour down on him. He'd only ever had baths before this.

"I've been thinking," Reeve said, a bit mischievously. "If you're going to learn about this enchantment of yours, we need to test it."

"Test it?" Calen repeated.

Reeve turned. "Yeah. Carefully. Can you turn it on and off, or is it passive—like a scent you're wearing?"

Calen tilted his head under the stream, letting the water soak his hair. He wasn't sure he wanted to admit this yet.

"I think...both? I can feel it now. Like a ball of light near my face, and when I focus, it gets stronger—especially when I'm looking into someone's eyes... I was kind of playing with it today at the market after Lyra left."

Reeve turned his head, water still dripping from his hair. "You were? On who?"

Calen turned to face the wall. "E-everyone we met."

Reeve blinked. "Wait—everyone?" He scrubbed a hand down his face. "Gods, no wonder we got those free pastries."

Calen looked over his shoulder. "Well, I haven't had pastries before. They don't have bread like that where I'm from—they're really delicious."

Reeve gave him a look. "So, your first moral compromise was over dessert?"

Calen shrugged, perhaps a bit guilty. "They were really good."

Reeve shut off the water and reached for the towels, handing one to Calen and rubbing his through his hair. "Have you been able to tone it down? Or turn it off yet?"

Calen frowned slightly, water still running down his back. "Well...if I do the opposite of how I turn it on, I *should* be able to shut it off. But I haven't practiced. I'm not sure I can. Not completely."

Reeve grinned. "Okay, well—we're testing it tomorrow."

Calen looked over, startled. "Tomorrow? How?"

"On customers, of course," Reeve said, like it was the most obvious thing in the world.

Calen let out a short, incredulous laugh. "Really? You're insane. What if it goes wrong?"

"Then, I dunno, they buy more than they meant to, and we make more coin..." Reeve replied, shrugging it off. "Things are so boring here. At least it'll make the day interesting."

They finished drying off and headed inside, still joking about all the ridiculous things that might happen the next day.

***

The forge was already warm by the time Calen and Reeve arrived, sun just beginning to filter in through the high windows. The scent of coal and iron lingered in the air, but the coals hadn't been stoked yet. Dean and Ronan hadn't come out from breakfast, which gave them a window to experiment.

Reeve dropped a crate beside the worktable. "All right. Test Day. Are you ready?"

Calen gave him a skeptical look. "Define ready."

"Too late." Reeve grinned. "We're starting with pricing."

"Wait," Calen asked suspiciously, "you already have a list of things you want to test?"

"Of course," Reeve replied.

Calen felt a bit used, but he was curious too, and he hadn't put as much thought into it. He was game to try.

They didn't have to wait long.

The first customer of the day was an older man in need of two replacement horseshoes. He was a regular—came in twice a month, always paid in exact coin, and *always* grumbled about prices.

Calen stepped forward with the practiced charm of a shop boy. "Two shoes, right? That will be eight silver."

Reeve coughed. That was well over double the usual price.

The man blinked, looked at his horse, and nodded. "Fair enough, but only if you do them yourself!" He handed over the coin without blinking.

Once he was gone, Reeve turned to Calen, eyes wide. "*Okay. Prices: confirmed.*"

Calen laughed, looking after the man. "That was terrifying."

The next few interactions came like clockwork.

Test Two: Upselling.

A middle-aged man came in for a standard hinge bracket. Calen chatted while fetching it, then casually gestured to a set of polished brass bolts. "These would go great with that."

The man hesitated, then nodded. "All right, throw in a dozen."

He didn't even ask the price.

Reeve leaned in after he left. "Two for two. You're a menace."

Test Three: Customer Returns.

Not long after, a laborer passed by the open stall and stepped in. "I'd like to return these doorknobs. The job I had lined up canceled last minute."

Calen looked at him. "Surely, you'll have new work soon. Isn't it better to keep them for that?"

"I suppose you're right," the man agreed. "I'll just keep them on hand." He smiled warmly and left.

The boys nodded to each other knowingly.

Test Four: Attracting New Customers.

Two well-dressed women strolled into the stall, which was entirely unusual—they were clearly on their way somewhere nicer, with gloves in hand and embroidered shawls. They stepped past the main stall and paused as if genuinely curious.

"Oh," one of them said, her voice light with amusement, "I've never been in a blacksmith's shop before."

The other tilted her head, eyes drifting to Calen. "Whatever are you working on?"

Reeve glanced up from the anvil, clearly surprised. "Uh, hinges today. Brackets too."

"Hinges," the first one repeated, like it was an exotic word.

"And what is it that *you* do here?" she asked, greedily looking Calen over.

"Oh, just about everything," he replied, sticking out his chin like he owned the place.

The lofty ladies exchanged an amused look, shared a laugh, and slowly wandered back to the street, whispering to each other.

Calen turned to Reeve. "Did *that* count? That one lady was really pretty."

Reeve looked dazed watching them stroll down the street. "I've been working here my whole life, and I've never seen a lady here!" He thought for a moment, then turned to Calen. "How is it feeling?" he asked.

Calen thought about it for a moment. "Natural, I guess. Kind of like flexing a muscle I didn't know I had."

"How hard have you been trying?" Reeve asked, looking him over.

"Not too hard..." Calen reflected.

"Okay then," Reeve said with intention. "This time I want you to really go for it. Give it everything you've got! Flex that muscle as hard as you can—really crush it."

Calen looked at him, eyes wide. He smiled, excited, and said, "Okay!"

A moment later, a man stepped into the open stall—older, but still fit, broad-shouldered with thick hands and the kind of no-nonsense stride that said he knew exactly what he needed.

He dropped a canvas pouch on the counter. "Need a hundred six-inch nails."

Calen stepped forward.

This time, he didn't just let the warmth float from him—he focused. Let it gather in his mind like heat behind his eyes. Then he pushed it forward as he met the man's eyes—forced his will inside him.

"One hundred?" Calen said, voice smoothly. "That many? What are you building, a fortress?"

The man blinked. He seemed to be falling into a daze.

Calen turned to fetch the nails, bending slightly as scooped them from the crate. When he turned back, the man was still staring.

He was completely still. Mouth slightly pursed. Arms limp at his side.

And beneath the loose hem of his tunic, it was unmistakable. A distinct shape rising, tenting the fabric, growing firmer by the second.

Calen froze. "Oh no."

Reeve made a strangled, gasping noise from his throat. "Uh—yeah, you got him. Maybe turn that off now."

"I am," Calen said sideways. He closed his eyes and did what he'd practiced: pulling the light back, making it cold.

The effect was immediate.

The man sucked in a sharp breath and blinked as if awakened from a dream. His gaze dropped below his belt, following Calen and Reeve's eyes.

His face flushed dark red.

"Heh," he said. He looked up and then back and forth between them.

"You know how it is..." he said, shrugging. "The wife's not...you know...as she used to..."

The boys just smiled and nodded.

They wrapped up the transaction, and the man hurried off.

They stood there in silence.

Reeve turned to Calen, mouth open. "You gave that man a *boner*. In public!"

Calen buried his face in his hands. "I didn't mean to."

"But you *did*. Like—instantly. He was *ready to go!*" Reeve crowed emphatically.

Calen turned his back to the counter and looked up at the ceiling. "The good thing is: I think...I figured out how to turn it off now."

"Good!" Reeve cheered. "See? We're getting somewhere!"

Reeve broke into full-blown laughter. Calen joined him.

"What are you boys laughing about over here?" Ronan stepped out from behind a stack of barrels, a raised eyebrow and a suspicious smirk on his face. He had a half-oiled rag in his hand and a belt slung over his shoulder.

Calen cleared his throat, trying to wipe the grin off his face. "Nothing. Just—uh...funny customer."

"That's not an answer," Ronan said, wanting to be in on the joke.

Before Reeve could answer, Dean's voice rang out from the back.

"Whatever it is, bottle it!" He emerged with an armful of scrap. "We haven't seen foot traffic like this in years. Calen, you must be a lucky charm."

He gave a rare grin—broad and honest—as he set the metal down. "Keep it up. We'll be swimming in coin by week's end."

Reeve glanced sideways at Calen and mouthed, *Lucky Charm?*

Calen gave him a guilty smile and whispered, "Don't even."

# 10

Dean and Ronan had finished up their showers, voices fading as they left the custom bathing room behind. Calen and Reeve lingered for privacy, toweling off in the warm steam.

"I *still* can't believe you did *that*," Reeve whispered scandalously, barely containing his excitement.

"I'm just glad I figured out how to dial it back!" Calen said, handing him a towel. "If Dean had seen...well—*that*..."

"Ha!" Reeve giggled. "*Poor* Mr. Innith..."

Calen blinked. "Oh! Is that his name?"

"Yeah..." Reeve said, trying not to giggle. "And now we know what he's packing. His wife is a teacher."

Calen winced. "Sorry."

"No!" Reeve cheered. "It was fun..." He paused, a thought striking him. "Hey! Do it to me!"

Calen turned to him, confused. "What?"

"The thing—the charm... Hit me with it! I want to know what it feels like," Reeve said, bouncing up and down like he was in a boxing match.

Calen shook his head. "No. That's a terrible idea."

"Now you've got control. We *have* to test it," Reeve pushed.

Calen hesitated. "But what if you...?"

"It's fine!" Reeve assured him. "It could be fun!"

Calen looked him over. It was a strange request, but he was curious.

"Fine." He exhaled. "All right, but don't say I didn't warn you."

They faced each other wrapped in towels, feet on damp tile. Calen met Reeve's eyes, drew the light up near his face, and pushed.

Reeve's expression shifted instantly—his breath caught, his eyes went wide. "Okay! Stop! Stop! Stop!" he yelped, clutching his towel.

Calen reeled it back in.

Reeve staggered back and braced himself against the wall, still gripping the cloth. "Wow. That works. Way too well."

He paused, then jerked his head toward the door. "Can you...?"

Calen blushed and nodded, already moving. "Yep. Got it."

***

That night, after the forge had gone still and the lights were out, they lay side by side in the soft dark. Calen had been able to keep his aura tight all evening. They had run out for a quick treat after dinner, and no one had been affected.

Reeve groaned. "Ugh."

Calen turned his head on the pillow. "What now?"

"You smell nice again," Reeve admitted. "It's like it's back."

Calen sighed. "Hold on."

He focused for just a moment, drawing the warmth away, cooling himself down from the inside out like snuffing a flame.

"Try now."

Reeve rolled over and stuck his nose in Calen's armpit. "Ugh. Pit. Yep. That's armpit."

He rolled back over with a dramatic sigh. "I've never been so relieved to smell armpit in my life. I don't think I could take another hit of that again tonight. That aura of yours is something else."

They both chuckled in the dark.

Calen smiled faintly to himself. "Good night, Reeve."

***

The weeks slipped by like warm honey, slow and golden. Calen had never imagined he'd feel so at home in a city full of strangers. With his charm power under control, life had settled into something steady. Customers no longer swooned, conversations stayed normal, and he'd even managed to tuck away a bit of gold. Dean respected his work, and he and Reeve still shared a room, though Calen had finally earned a bed of his own.

He missed his family—his dad, his mother, his grandmother. But it was his brother he thought about the most. They'd been a team. He used to watch out for him, keep him from doing anything too stupid. Now he was here, and his brother there, without him.

The heat was worse than anything back home. What had passed for a sweltering day there now felt mild compared to this. Some afternoons, it was like standing next to a bonfire, the kind that left your skin flushed and your shirt soaked through before noon.

And now, rumors churned. Not about him, thankfully, but of the Empire—trouble brewing out west. Random skirmishes and broken treaties, rising tensions. Most people dismissed it as gossip, but others whispered in worry.

One morning, after Reeve had already left the room, Calen lay back on the bed, staring at the ceiling while the morning light spilled faintly across the floorboards. He hadn't checked the stone in days. It wasn't a habit anymore. Life had felt almost normal.

Curiosity stirred. He reached under the mattress for the belt pouch, more out of habit than hope, fingers finding the familiar weight. He drew it out, meaning to glance at it once and put it away again—but stopped.

It should have been cold.

It had been under his bed for weeks, untouched, forgotten. But the stone was warm against his palm, as if it had been sitting in the sun.

He turned it over in his hand and noticed the familiar gold strings of writing, visible only where it caught the light.

His heart started pounding in his chest, his throat tightening. "It's awake."

He began to panic. What do I do?

"Hello?" he said, voice tight. "Can you hear me? Are you there?"

Nothing.

He looked at it for a long moment, thumb tracing its edges. "I guess you're coming with me again."

He stood quietly, still puzzling, and began to dress, securing the pouch to his belt for the first time since arriving in the city.

When he finished, he let out a long breath.

He hadn't realized how alone he'd felt. The people here were kind, and the work was steady. Reeve was a good friend. But this—this quiet warmth at his side—was different. It was something he'd had before he was stranded here.

Maybe he could figure out how to speak with it, as his grandmother once had. Maybe it could tell him how to get back or how to finish his mission.

But he didn't have time now. Lyra would be waiting.

For a moment, he thought about staying, to investigate further, but the thought of Lyra waiting in the market tugged harder. She had a way of doing that.

Whatever the stone wanted, whatever it meant, it could wait a little longer.

One of the highlights of these weeks had been the time Calen spent with Lyra. She always seemed to find him—pausing in the doorway of the smithy with a quick smile, catching him on his way to deliver a finished order, or falling into step beside him in the market. She was vague about where she lived but spoke often of her large family and, more often still, of her father. As he made his way through the streets now, he caught himself smiling, thinking about her.

"Father says the Empire's rule leaves no room for the liberty of smaller states," she'd told him one afternoon as they strolled past the bread stalls. "Their punishments are swift, and their control absolute. He believes our safety lies in unity and vigilance."

Calen didn't pretend to understand all the politics. To him, the Empire just sounded big, powerful, and bossy—not a place where people were free to choose their own way.

He found himself looking forward to her visits in a way he didn't quite understand. He liked the way she laughed, the way her eyes brightened when she talked about something that mattered to her, even the way she tilted her head when she was waiting for him to answer. At sixteen, he'd never felt much of anything like this before—a restless warmth in his chest that made him want to keep her talking, to keep her close. It was strange, and it made no sense, but he didn't mind the feeling.

A few days ago, he and Reeve had been in the smithy, working side by side, when Lyra stopped by with a basket from the fruit stand. She'd handed Calen a pear—*why is she so obsessed with pears*—laughing at the soot on his face. Reeve had said nothing at first, just kept hammering at the glowing iron until she left. Only then did he glance over and say, "You two seem to be seeing a lot of each other."

His tone had been light enough, but he hadn't looked up from his work. Calen had only shrugged, not thinking much of it at the time, though the memory had a way of coming back to him now, uninvited. He figured Reeve was just worried he'd spend less time with him if he started hanging around Lyra.

He pushed the thought aside as the noise of the market swelled ahead, bright and loud in the morning air. The market buzzed with its usual energy—voices calling over one another, clinking wares, and the smell of fried dough and roasted corn thick in the air.

Calen spotted Reeve and Lyra near the spice stall, already deep in an argument about whether dried pepper flakes were a requirement on some dish he'd never heard of. He smiled and waved them over, and they wandered slowly through the maze of stalls.

It was nice to be able to walk anonymously again, without the charm drawing too much attention. The stone at his side pulsed faintly, its power wrapping him in cool air that made the crowd's heat bearable.

Then Calen noticed.

A small stand, just a table, off to the side in the middle of the square. Crates from other vendors surrounded him, but no signs, no wares, nothing being advertised. Just a noble looking man in dark, regal clothing seated quietly, arms folded. He wasn't calling out like the others. He wasn't working his stall. His eyes moved over the crowd like he was studying something only he could see.

Calen slowed.

"Morning," he offered.

The man flinched and sat up abruptly, as though caught doing something he shouldn't have been. For a moment, his composure slipped, eyes wide, mouth parted in stunned expression. Then, just as quickly, he pulled himself together. He straightened his cuffs and smoothed his expression, then offered a thin, practiced smile—one that didn't reach his eyes.

"Oh," he said, voice a touch too bright. "Well, good morning."

"I haven't seen you here before," Calen said, stopping a few feet from the stall. "I've been coming here to the market a while now. Thought I knew all the vendors."

The man blinked, smiling and twitching a bit nervously. "Yes, well. I don't always set up in the same spot."

Calen glanced at the empty table. "What are you selling?"

The man's gaze drifted slowly down to the table as if he was looking to see himself, only just now realizing how little he had brought. "Ah, yes." He cleared his throat, patting his jacket down searching. Then, with a flourish far more dramatic than necessary, he drew a long, curved knife from a sheath in his belt.

"This knife," he declared, setting it on the table with ceremony. "Very sharp."

Calen looked at it. Then at him.

The man nodded, solemn. "One of a kind."

Calen nodded slowly, still watching him. "Oh, well..."

His eyes drifted to the man's hand, where it rested casually near the knife.

A ring.

It caught the light oddly—neither metal nor stone exactly. Dark as obsidian, but not opaque. It shimmered faintly, like smoke swirling just under glass. At first glance, it looked solid, but the longer Calen stared, the less sure he was about its composition. It reminded him a bit of Liri's hair.

It wasn't decorated. No crest, no setting. Just a smooth band—perfectly formed and unsettling in its simplicity.

The man followed Calen's gaze.

"Oh," Calen said, eyes still on the man's hand. "That's a really interesting ring."

The man's eyes widened. He sat up very straight. His fingers twitched—just once—before he tucked the hand under his other arm as if it had been resting there the whole time.

"Is it?" he replied, voice cracking. Then, more smoothly, he said, "I suppose I don't think about it much. Family heirloom."

Calen opened his mouth to respond, but it was only then that he noticed his friends standing with him.

The man's gaze shifted to them briefly. Whatever flicker of discomfort he'd shown before vanished, replaced with the same polished veneer.

"Well," he said, brushing invisible dust from his sleeve, "if you're not planning to buy the knife, I suppose I should see to my other customers." He gestured vaguely at the otherwise oblivious crowd.

Calen gave a polite nod. "Right—of course."

He turned, Reeve and Lyra falling into step beside him as they drifted back into the main market path.

After a few paces, Calen muttered, "Did you guys see that ring?"

Reeve frowned. "What ring?"

Lyra shook her head. "He wasn't wearing a ring. No wonder he gave you that look when you asked. He must have thought you were insane."

Calen looked back to where the man had been sitting. He was gone.

# 11

Weeks passed. Orders came in. Steel was hammered. Calen's coin pouch was getting heavier, and his shoulders stronger. He had spent any alone time he could get trying to find a way to communicate with the stone, but without any success.

One morning over breakfast, Dean took a swig from a clay cup, then grimaced.

"This milk tastes like ass," he muttered, sniffing the rim.

Calen wiped his hands on a cloth, glancing over. "Lyra mentioned a dairy just outside the north gate. Said it's the best milk she's ever had."

Dean grunted. "Outside the gate? I know it. Expensive..."

Calen nodded.

Dean scratched his beard. "Well, we're not starving these days. Go ahead, take the morning, bring back a few jugs. Gold's in the drawer."

On his way out, Calen flagged down one of the runners that wandered up and down the street to send word to Lyra that he'd be in the square after breakfast.

Somehow, she was there before him, standing at the edge of the crowd with that quick smile of hers, a milk satchel slung over one shoulder and a sweet bun halfway gone in her hand.

"Morning," she said, brushing a crumb from her lip as she tore off another bite of the sweet bun. "So, you're running errands for the forge now?"

He gave a half-smile. "And it's an excuse to see you again."

Her eyes softened at that, the smile lingering a fraction too long before she looked away.

"You'll like this place. They keep the cows happy, and the milk's sweet."

They passed through the north gate, nodding to the guards. The air was already warm, heat rising off the stone in shimmering waves. Beyond the wall, the city fell away into open country—golden plains dotted with wildflowers, a sky so wide it seemed to swallow the horizon. Narrow paths curled between the fields, and the air smelled faintly of clover.

Calen walked with his arms loose, gaze drifting. It felt strange to be out here again, beyond the press of the city. Freer, somehow.

"You all right?" Lyra asked, watching him from the corner of her eye.

"Yeah," he said, "just thinking. I haven't been back out here since..."

"Since we met," she finished for him, her voice quieter now.

"I couldn't even tell you where I came out," he admitted, scanning the endless line of trees.

"Oh, it was just over there." She pointed toward a break in the bush. Her tone was casual, but the way her eyes lingered on the hill, she seemed to be remembering fondly.

The dairy lay in a shallow green dip, its red-tiled roof warm in the sun, the barn buzzing with flies. Calves blinked lazily as they crossed the yard.

Inside, a broad-shouldered woman with sleeves rolled high handed off two tall jugs and insisted they sample a chilled cup while she wrapped the rest in damp cloth. The milk was so cold it made Calen's teeth ache. Lyra laughed when he winced.

"You come back next week," the woman told him, patting his arm. "You've got a good face. I trust you."

Back outside, Lyra's smile turned sly. "Was that the charm?"

Calen gave a short laugh. "No," he said.

"Ah," she grinned, "then she wants you to marry her niece."

He rolled his eyes. "Do I look like I'm ready for in-laws?"

"With that face?" she said, stepping close to take one of the jugs from him. Her fingers lingered against his. "You're halfway to an arranged marriage already."

They both paused. She didn't move away, and neither did he. There was a stillness between them now, the sounds of the yard falling distant. Calen found himself noticing the way the sunlight caught her hair, how her eyes seemed to be studying his face like she was memorizing it.

A strange heat rose in his chest. He wasn't sure what it meant, only that he didn't want to break whatever was happening. His gaze dropped for the briefest moment to her mouth, and when he looked back up, she was watching him like she knew.

The space between them seemed smaller than it had a heartbeat ago.

He felt himself leaning in without meaning to, his pulse loud in his ears.

Then a sharp whinny broke the moment. Both of them flinched, and the sound of hooves carried over the rise.

Lyra laughed softly, but there was something in her eyes now—something that made Calen's stomach twist. "We should get back," she said, though she didn't step away immediately.

When they finally started walking, she fell in beside him, close enough that their arms brushed now and then. He didn't move away.

They crested the rise, the sun high above them—and that's when they saw the horses.

The road curved gently down toward a cluster of carts and wagons stopped along the path, a minor bottleneck just south of the dairy. At first glance, it seemed innocent enough, but then Calen saw the armor.

Six men. Four remained on horseback, watching the road and the fields with easy confidence. Two more were on foot, methodically pulling apart the contents of a merchant's cart while its owner stood by, arms folded tight, lips pressed into a thin line. Canvas bags were opened, crates lifted and set aside, jars examined and put back with less care than they'd been packed.

And to the side, slightly apart from the others, sat a rider cloaked in red. His armor was lighter, more ornate. His horse was still—eerily still, as though frozen in place by more than training.

"Imperials," Lyra muttered, her jaw tight. "The one on the horse—that's a battle mage. He could burn everyone where they stand before anyone had a chance to run."

Calen slowed, eyes fixed on the rider.

"We should turn back," Calen said nervously, already slowing. "Or cut through the forest. I know how to move in it—we can skirt the road. They'll never see us."

Lyra's jaw tightened. "I'm not going to slink off like a criminal," she said, voice proud. "This is my home."

Lyra didn't slow. In fact, Calen thought maybe she sped up a little. Shoulders square and steps measured, like someone approaching a problem she already planned to scold. Calen followed half a step behind, trying not to glance too often at the armed men ahead. They were nearly at the carts now. The men on horseback looked down with idle interest, one nudging the other with a half-smile as Lyra approached.

One of the foot soldiers stepped forward, blocking their path with a raised hand.

"Morning," he said. "Routine inspection. You'll need to open your pack."

Lyra came to a halt. "We're just coming back from the dairy," she said, voice even. "All we have is milk."

"Even better," the soldier replied, jerking his chin toward Calen's satchel. "Then it won't take long."

Another soldier hopped down from his horse and headed for Calen.

"Oh, there's no need to search me," Calen said, turning on the charm.

The soldiers stopped, looked him over, and turned back.

The battle mage turned in his saddle, gaze sharp under his red hood. His eyes landed on Lyra, and something shifted in his posture.

"You," he said, voice cutting through the noise of the road. "I know you."

Lyra stood defiant.

"That face..." the mage went on, reining his horse around. "Mayor Haldan's daughter, aren't you?"

Lyra didn't answer. She lifted her chin.

Calen paused. *The mayor?*

The mage smiled, slow and pleased. "Well. That's a surprise. A very valuable one."

Two of the soldiers on horseback began to circle around, closing off the path behind them.

Calen felt his heart sink. His hand shifted subtly to his side, fingers brushing the stone in his pouch. He didn't reach for it—just knowing it was there made him feel steadier.

He looked up at the circling riders. "You don't want trouble," he said gently, gazing at each one in turn. He pushed his will forward. "We're just going home. Nothing worth your time."

The effect was instant. The two men flanking them relaxed in their saddles, brows relaxing. One of them gave a little shrug. "He's right. We're not here for peasants."

They started to turn their horses. Already their attention was back on the large merchant cart they had been disassembling prior to their arrival.

"What are you doing?" the mage yelled, trotting his horse between them.

The charm hadn't seemed to work on him.

The mage's horse reared as he wheeled it around. "You—" He jabbed a gloved finger at Calen. "What did you just do?"

Calen took a step back. "Nothing, I—"

The mage didn't wait. His hand came up, blue runes flaring into existence above his palm.

Instinct took over. Calen's hand dropped to his belt, closing around the stone. It burned against his skin, heat surging up his arm—something ancient and sharp flooding his chest.

The mage leveled his palm, and a jet of frost roared toward him, the air snapping cold, streaked with blue light.

Calen thrust the stone forward. A pulse tore out from it, shattering the spell mid-flight—the frost scattering into a spray of harmless snow.

Everyone went silent.

"A wizard," the red-cloaked man whispered, the word like a curse.

Then he spun his horse and shouted, "Retreat!" and galloped back the way they'd come, the other soldiers scrambling to run, a few screaming in terror.

Calen stood very still, breath shallow, the stone cooling in his hand. And then a voice, an old man... "Get back to the city. We have much to discuss."

It was coming from the stone.

# 12

The silence after the horses faded was deafening, shattered an instant later by a swell of anxious voices. While Calen hid the stone back in his pouch, Lyra stood watching the soldiers retreat for a moment, then turned to Calen, mouth open in confusion.

Her eyes searched his face like she was trying to find someone else underneath.

"You're a wizard," she said finally, her voice thin. "You've been a wizard this whole time."

"No," she continued, shook her head slowly. "No, this doesn't make sense. You were just a boy from a backwater village. You didn't even know how to buy fruit..."

She gave a breathless laugh—half in disbelief, half in exasperation. "You acted like this was all new to you. You said you'd never been in a city before!"

Calen took a step forward. "Lyra, I—"

"And *you* let me parade you around like some wide-eyed little farm boy?" Her voice cracked, loud enough to get voices chattering in the lingering crowd. "I showed you the bakery like it was your first time seeing bread. Was that a joke to you?"

She took another step toward him, eyes bright with fury. Calen stepped back.

"You let me think that I was your friend!"

Then her expression shifted—horror cutting through her rage.

"You used me to get in. I let you in! I brought you through the front gate!" She paused. "I brought danger into the city!"

She turned to the onlookers, voice raising.

"He's been casting spells on us this whole time!"

The crowd gasped. A few faces turned on Calen, eyes wide.

"No wonder *everyone* liked you," Lyra spat. "You *made* us all like you!"

She turned from him and began walking, each step stiff and purposeful, like it was the only way to hold herself together.

Calen followed, not sure if he was supposed to, but too stunned to stay behind.

People began trailing after them, slowly at first, then in growing numbers.

They had walked nearly all the way back to the city before Lyra found her words again.

"Just tell me this isn't what it looks like," she said without turning, her voice carrying more pain than anger now. "Tell me you're not a spy. That you didn't mean to lie. That I wasn't just a mark to you."

"Lyra, I—"

"Was any of this real?" she asked. "Were you ever even really lost? Or was that all part of the plan—befriend the mayor's daughter?"

She wheeled back. Calen almost walked into her.

"You're no better than the Imperial guards!"

And then she turned back, picking up her pace.

"I trusted you," she said, voice thin. "I thought you were just a sweet, shy kid from the forest..." Her voice rose with each word. "Do you know how stupid I feel!"

They began to walk past the outer wall, houses on either side. A woman paused in her garden, trowel still in hand. Two boys stopped playing and stared. The farther they went, the more eyes turned to follow them. Lyra's voice, sharp with emotion, carried easily in the warm summer air.

"You aren't the person you've claimed to be, Calen—if that is your name!" she said loudly now, almost performing for the crowds. "You're a liar. And a spy!"

They were at the gate.

One of the guards on the parapet leaned over the edge. "Everything all right down there?" he called, sounding more amused than concerned. "Having our first lover's spat, Calen?"

Another guard joined him. "Don't worry lad! Just apologize and buy her some flowers!"

"I told you she was too pretty not to be trouble," a third chimed in. "Go on, girl, tell us what he did!"

Lyra didn't even glance up. "We were just attacked by Imperial soldiers on the dairy road!" she shouted, her voice cracking with urgency. "Soldiers and a mage. They were searching carts—harassing people."

The guards quieted.

"He cast on us. He cast on Calen! And Calen stopped it—with magic!"

The hush didn't last. Murmurs spread through the guards, eyes flicking from one man to another. Somewhere in the back, a voice muttered, "No one can stop Imperial magic."

Another followed, lower still: "Only a wizard could."

One of the foot guards stepped up to her and put a hand on her arm, his voice wary. "Lyra, are you being serious right now?"

"I'm not joking," she said.

The hush behind them broke. "I saw it!" someone shouted. "He held out his hand and drove them all away!"

"There was a flash of light!" another called.

More voices joined in, overlapping, each trying to be the one to explain.

"Calen's a wizard!" she said, almost in tears. "He's been spying on us all. Don't let him in. Close the gates."

The guard's eyes went between her and Calen—then he blew hard into a curved horn. The sound rang out, sharp and clear, a call to arms.

Shouts rang out across the fortifications. Armor clattered. Footsteps pounded overhead. Soldiers scrambled to their posts along the ramparts.

Two guards Calen didn't recognize stepped in front of him, hands on their weapons, glaring.

Lyra looked him dead in the eyes, and for a moment her fury turned into heartbreak.

"Wizards belong in towers," she said, her face solemn. "Not in my city."

She backed up a few paces, and the gates slammed shut.

The two guards still outside didn't say a word. One of them was Bran.

"Bran, I—" Calen started.

"That was a mean trick to play on her, old man," he said, glaring at Calen.

The smaller side gate was already open for them. They walked through without a glance back. The door shut behind them with a dull, final thud.

Calen stood frozen, staring at the wall. Sunlight struck the timber, turning it into a blinding sheet of gold.

Old man?

He didn't blink. Didn't breathe.

The gates loomed, silent and sealed. Above them, guards lined the parapet, bows in hand, eyes fixed on him. None moved.

He stepped back, slow and unsteady, then turned to the road.

Empty.

The square was deserted. Carts stood abandoned. A basket of bread lay overturned in the dust, a trail of rolls leading nowhere.

His gaze swept the street, the wagons, the shuttered houses. No one.

Beyond the eastern fields, the tree line waited—still, dark, unchanging.

He ran.

Dry grass whipped at his boots as the fields opened wide around him, dust rising in his wake. The forest drew closer—not like the wall behind him, dead and unyielding, but alive. Breathing.

He reached the trees and slowed, stepping into the cool shade. The forest swallowed him in a few strides. He pressed his back to an ancient trunk, heart hammering, as if it could shield him from all he'd left behind.

Peering around it, he saw the city still in the sunlight—unmoving, indifferent.

He'd hoped for someone. A voice calling his name. A hand reaching after him. Anything to say it was a mistake.

There was no one.

He leaned against the tree, breathing heavily. He peeked once more. Still nothing.

He let out a shaky breath and slumped down, knees drawn up, arms draped over them. He stared ahead, unfocused—his mind as bleak and scattered as the dust he'd kicked up running behind him.

His vision blurred before he understood why. The first sob escaped like a gasp, sudden and sharp. He covered his face, shoulders trembling as the flood broke loose—hot, helpless tears soaking his sleeves. He cried like he hadn't since he was a child, the sound startling him. It was deeper now, rough and jarring. The thin whimper he remembered was gone.

This was foreign.

He couldn't even cry right.

Another sob tore loose, then another. His shoulders shook harder. His fingers dug into the dirt. Everything had been ripped away.

Time passed. How long, he couldn't say.

The sobs came and went in waves until there was nothing left—only the dull throb of a headache, the rawness of his throat.

The forest rustled softly all around him—wind in the branches, birdsong in the distance.

For a long time, Calen didn't move. Then, something shifted.

Not a noise. Not a breeze—just a feeling.

The air didn't move, but the light bent—like heat rising off stone, only gentler, quieter. The light rippled, and she was there.

Liri.

The shimmer of her wings caught the strange curve of light, bending it just enough to announce her presence without disturbing the silence. Her glow was faint in the dim forest, and the smoke-like strands of her hair stirred as if in response to her breath.

Calen didn't stand. He didn't flinch. He just stared at her, his expression unreadable at first—then, slowly, something else surfaced.

His voice was flat. "What did you do to me?"

Liri blinked, wings fluttering once.

"Well, *hi* to you too," she said lightly. "This is the part where you yell at me, isn't it?"

Calen's mouth twisted in anger.

"You think this is funny?"

He stood now, slow and stiff, like someone who'd just remembered how to move.

"I tore through a man's mind. I nearly killed someone who trusted me. My hands—" He looked down at them like they might still be burning. "My soul—feels wrong."

"Calen, I didn't mean for things to—" She stopped, frowning. "Wait. Why didn't you go to the castle?"

Before he could answer, the stone stirred in his pocket, its voice slipping in between them like warm smoke.

"Don't be too hard on her, lad. She only woke up a part of you that was always meant to wake."

Calen reached into the pouch and drew it out.

The stone pulsed faintly in his palm.

He stared at it.

"Oh, *now* you decide to speak," he said, voice rising. "This is just perfect!"

He held it away from him, like it was offensive.

"*All* this magic, *all* these voices, *all* this power—and where were you just now?" His eyes shot daggers at Liri. "Where were *you*?"

She flinched, floating back a little, but then returned.

"Well, I've been looking for you, silly," she said, voice bright. "You vanished! You were supposed to end up at the castle, not—" She glanced around. "—here. Wherever *this* is."

Calen stared at her, his breath still uneven. But the words landed differently than he expected. Not defensive. Not guilty. Just...confused.

"You were looking for me?" he asked, the edge in his voice softening.

Liri nodded, her wings fluttering again.

"Yeah, only this *whole* time."

He looked down at the stone in his palm. Its pulse was steady. Calm. Like it had all of the answers and none of the guilt.

Calen's brow furrowed.

"It was *you*!" The pieces were clicking into place. "*You're* the reason I didn't make it to the castle," he said. "*You* chose this place, chose *all of this*." Calen was ready to throw the stone into the forest.

The stone pulsed once, as if in affirmation. Then it spoke, its voice that of a wise, caring old man—soothing, steady, impossible to shout down.

"The castle was never the right place for you. Not yet. You landed exactly where you needed to be." It paused, then added with gentle pride, "Look at how much you've learned. How much you've grown. You've seen more of the world already than Mira would have ever allowed. And your power... You've awakened your natural-born gift. Would you trade that away?"

"I—" Calen's words caught in his throat.

"Would you have ever made such good friends? Like Reeve? Like Lyra? You've found purpose now—an occupation, a life. Friends. Almost a family. A city that sees you, values you. Would you have had any of that, had you not been brought here?"

A beat of silence followed—thick, heavy.

Then Liri tilted her head, pondering the stone's words. "What power? What gift?"

She floated forward a few inches. "All I did was wake you up to magic. I didn't—" She glanced between them. "I didn't *give* you anything."

Calen looked at her, then back to the stone, and then back to her.

He opened his mouth, hesitated, and then said, "I...I can make people like me...make them do what I tell them to do. Even—" He paused, voice dropping. "—want me. Like, sexually."

Liri floated closer, thinking.

Then it seemed to hit her. She fluttered up in the air.

"Wait. Seriously?"

Calen nodded.

"That makes sense! That's just like your grandfa—"

"Ah, yes!" the stone cut in smoothly, its tone warm and un-hurried. "A curious and unforeseen development! Many magical beings possess a variety of charms or talents. Helping plants to grow, perhaps. Conjuring a small weather event. These things are not uncommon at all!"

Liri's mouth closed. She hovered a little lower, eyes darting at the stone and then away.

Calen hardly noticed.

He was staring at the stone. "So...you're saying this is *normal?*"

"Quite right," encouraged the stone.

"But I'm not a magical being," Calen countered.

"Well," the stone replied, almost amused, "perhaps that's something you *can* blame on Liri."

Calen turned to her, eyes narrowing.

She hovered a little higher, wings twitching.

"Okay, now, hang on—you see, the truth—"

But she stopped. Just for a second.

Something passed behind her eyes—something like fear. Or regret.

She looked away.

"Yeah," she said quietly. "Sorry."

Calen sat quietly. Thinking.

Liri fidgeted in the air, darting between him and the stone. Then she clapped her hands together, making dust.

"Oh! Well. Uh—never mind *all* that," she said, voice snapping back into brightness. "We still have a mission to accomplish, remember?"

She flew in a circle and gestured dramatically.

"I can use my fast-travel and *really* pour it on. We could have that stone back in the castle by sundown, if we really tried. Then, I'll have you home in, what? Two days, tops? Mission complete. Everyone—err—thing handled. You, back in your cozy little bed. Mira, not mad at me. Sound good?"

She nodded and grinned, a little too wide.

"What are you waiting for, handsome? Let's go!"

She flitted across the woods, leaving a pixie dust trail behind her.

Calen's eyes widened. He had never even considered it could be this easy again.

"You mean... we can go? Right now?" he asked.

Liri grinned.

"Of course, dummy! Here we go!"

She shot upward in an excited spiral, her wings catching the light. Tiny sparks shimmered in her wake as the air around her began to bend. Leaves stirred on the ground. The edge of something magical pressed against the air like tension before a storm.

Then the stone spoke, quiet but firm. "Leaving? Just like that?"

Liri stopped her spinning and turned. The spell died.

A pause.

"After everything you've built? The friends you made? The coin still sitting in your room, unused? You would walk away now like it was just a dream?" It paused. "And what of them? Reeve? Lyra? Dean? Ronan? The people who housed you, fed you, believed in you?

"They will remember you as the one who fooled them. The boy who took their trust, their kindness...and left. Not a friend. A painful echo of betrayal. A memory they flinch from."

The stone paused, then softer, almost tenderly, asked, "Don't you want a chance to remedy that, if not for yourself, then for *them*?"

Calen's jaw tightened. He looked down at the stone, voice rising—not in rage, but in helpless anger.

"*Of course* I want that! Of course I do! But you saw what they did."

He raised the stone in the direction of the city, as if to show it directly, eyes burning.

"They locked me out. There are guards all over the wall. There's no way I can get in—no way I can explain it. No way I can *fix* this!"

Liri darted a little closer, voice bright—too bright. "And you don't *have* to," she said dismissively. "There's no point in looking back, right? We can only move forward!"

She looped in the air, wings shimmering. "We get this wrapped up. You get your stone–" She looked over at it, then commented suspiciously. "—chatty guy—where it needs to go, and then you're home! Mira's waiting for you. Your dad, your mom, your brother—*all* of them, just waiting for you to come back."

She smiled, wide and eager. "Let's get that done right now!"

Calen was quiet for a long moment. Then he nodded just once.

"I don't like it," he said. "And I'm probably going to regret it. Maybe forever."

He didn't look back. Didn't need to. Everything behind him felt impossibly far away already.

He only looked at Liri.

"But the point is—it's time to go."

And with that, he took a step toward her.

"Excuse me," came a formal voice from behind him. "I don't mean to interrupt your conversation with...no one," the voice continued, carefully polite, "but I'd like to introduce myself."

Calen froze.

Slowly, he looked over his shoulder, eyes wide, and slipped the stone back into its pouch.

Behind him stood a man, dressed in formal—no, luxurious—clothing: a gold trimmed jacket that gleamed faintly in the dappled light, polished boots, and a posture that suggested he practiced it in mirrors. Two soldiers flanked him, standing just a step behind, silent but clearly at attention.

The man smiled as if he and Calen were old friends meeting at a garden party.

"Well met," he said brightly. "I do hope I'm not interrupting anything *important*."

Calen glanced around. Liri was gone.

The man stepped forward, with poise. One hand swept to his chest, the other extended outward like a host welcoming a guest to an opera.

"My *deepest* apologies," he said, voice like velvet stretched over amusement. "There appears to have been some...*confusion* earlier."

He smiled quickly—unnaturally. Teeth perfect. "Guards panicking, gates slamming, people shouting—yes, well, we've all had days like that, haven't we?"

He chuckled lightly, as if it were all terribly inconvenient but ultimately, *charming*. "A complete misunderstanding, of course. Emotions were high, protocols were... *flung to the wind*."

He bowed deeply, his golden curls catching the light. "But now, let us begin again."

Rising with a gleam in his eye, he said warmly, "Mayor Haldan, at your service. And I daresay, you've made *quite* the impression." He turned slightly and gestured to the soldier on his left. "We've also brought...this."

The guard stepped forward, holding out a slightly scuffed satchel.

"It appears in your earlier *exit*, you left it behind." Haldan's smile twitched just a bit wider.

Calen took the satchel quietly.

"We took the liberty of retaining it. I do hope your—what was it?—*milk* survived the journey." The soldier beside him nodded at Calen encouragingly.

Calen said nothing.

He couldn't.

A moment ago, he had been ready to leave it all behind—to vanish into myth, into fairy stories. Now, here he stood, milk in hand, facing a polished mayor and two city guards like some strange ceremony had already begun without him.

He didn't move. Just blinked, still catching up.

"I would greatly appreciate it," said the mayor, with a respectful dip of his head, "if you wouldn't mind coming back with me to the city."

"The events of today," he continued, "must be discussed. And I can think of no better place to do so than in the quiet of my humble office."

He nodded. "You would, of course, be my honored guest."

Calen nodded back, fixing the satchel over his shoulder. He glanced around again for Liri, but she was nowhere to be seen.

"All right," he said quietly.

It was all he could manage.

"Splendid," Haldan said, the wind tugging at the hem of his coat. "You've done us a great service, truly. Not just in what you stopped—but in what you represent."

He glanced over at Calen with something like quiet admiration. "There hasn't been a wizard in Hearthmere in a very long time."

# 13

They progressed across the field at a steady pace, guards in tow. The city slowly rose up before him as the forest had just moments before.

"I can't quite recall the last time a wizard walked through our gates," Haldan said, gesturing ahead. "I was a boy. I remember seeing him. He wore green robes—I think. Long white beard. He only stayed a day—long enough to fix something or other. I don't recall him doing any tricks..."

He smiled faintly, as if recalling something curious rather than fond.

"My father was mayor then. I remember how quiet the streets became when the wizard passed. People didn't know whether to bow or—"

He caught himself and smiled wide, slipping back into his polished charm.

They continued on, the grass whispering under their boots. The city loomed larger now, its walls reflecting the harsh summer light.

"I must say," Haldan added with a sidelong glance, "your sense of restraint is admirable."

He gestured lightly. "Most men of your talents might have made a great spectacle of it. Flames, or perhaps a speech—thunder from the sky." He gave a theatrical flutter with his fingers, then chuckled. "But you just...retreated to the forest. I suppose that is your domain."

He said it with a curious tilt of his head, as if still trying to reevaluate a piece of art he thought he understood.

As they approached the gate, the scene could hardly have been more different than the last time Calen had seen it.

Where empty streets had stretched in silence, now a crowd had gathered—rows deep on either side. Banners had been raised, the city's colors fluttering from the poles that hadn't been there minutes before.

*Where did these come from?* Calen thought, his steps slowing for a moment.

It was like the city had reinvented itself while he wasn't looking.

It felt like walking back into a memory someone had rearranged.

When they reached the gate, the full scale of the welcome revealed itself.

Two long rows of guards stood at rigid attention on either side of the main road—six, maybe eight deep—armor polished to a mirror sheen. Their spears were upright, their gazes fixed ahead, unmoving. They didn't bow, didn't speak, didn't even blink.

Somewhere in the crowd beyond, someone began to clap. Another followed. Then more. Cheering now.

Calen's mouth fell open, but no words formed. He just kept walking...

And then, familiar ground.

He knew exactly where he was now. The gate behind him, the square ahead. And to the right, the wide stone steps of the administration offices—ones he'd passed many times but never entered.

This time, he was gestured toward them.

The guards at the door stepped aside without a word.

Haldan led the way up the short stairway and through the tall arched entry. The heavy wooden doors shut behind them with a quiet finality, muffling the sound of the crowd like a curtain falling on a stage.

Inside, the air was cool. Still.

Stone floors stretched under thick rugs and tall windows filtered soft daylight through heavy velvet drapes. The scent of oil, ink, and old paper lingered—authority preserved.

Haldan moved though it like a man crossing his parlor.

He glanced back once, offering a smile.

"This way."

Calen followed him down a short corridor, past framed maps and burnished sconces until the mayor reached a carved double door and pushed it open without ceremony.

The mayor's office was exactly what Calen imagined it would be—large, lavish, and impossibly tidy. Thick rugs muffled every step, and tall bookshelves lined the walls like sentinels. A massive desk sat in the middle, its surface polished to a shine, every paper perfectly placed. A high, narrow window let in a slant of light, but most of the room was lit by lanterns.

"This is us," Haldan said, stepping aside. "Make yourself comfortable."

Calen stepped inside, uncertain whether to sit or stand.

Behind him, Haldan leaned back out of the open door and spoke to the attendant in a low, pleasant tone.

"I'm not to be interrupted. But—perhaps something light? A tray. Fruit? Or—pastries, I heard he likes."

The attendant made some muffled acknowledgment, and Haldan closed the door gently, the latch clicking into place with soft finality. The noise of the city beyond faded entirely.

He turned back to Calen with a genial smile and gestured to one of the high-backed chairs near the table.

"Please. Sit, if you'd like. I find conversation is easier when one isn't hovering."

Calen sat, not because he wanted to, but because standing any longer felt like a performance he couldn't hold. The chair was stiff, upright, and strangely distant from the table—as though placed for observation more than comfort. He folded his hands in his lap and kept them still.

He didn't know what this was supposed to be. An apology? A reckoning? Something in between? The day had already rewritten itself so many times it barely made sense.

Across from him, the mayor eased into his own seat with a careful grace, as though Calen was something volatile that might shatter or detonate if startled.

"I hope the accommodations are acceptable," Haldan said. "I understand this visit was...not planned."

He paused, letting the words sit.

"If there is anything Hearthmere can provide during your stay—housing, supplies, a dedicated liaison—we're prepared to be flexible."

"I'm not sure what I'm doing yet," Calen said.

There was a pause. Just long enough for it to register that this wasn't the reply Haldan expected—or perhaps hoped for—him to say.

"Of course," the mayor replied, adjusting seamlessly. "Forgive me if I speak too freely. I only mean to be courteous, not presumptuous. You've already shown a great deal of patience by agreeing to speak with me at all."

Calen didn't answer.

Haldan folded his hands on the desk. "I understand you've been staying with Dean and Ronan, yes? A fine household. Honest. A bit noisy, I imagine."

Calen's breath caught.

"No," Calen said quickly, his voice raw. "They—they had nothing to do with this. They don't know anything. Please, they have no idea about me."

He couldn't stop the words from spilling out. His mind raced with implications.

Haldan held up a hand, his tone softening, almost paternal. "I see. And of course, your...*disguise*, your cover, was impeccable. No one suspected a thing." His gaze seemed to hold a weight that Calen couldn't quite interpret, but the reverence in it was unmistakable. "Your presence here—a being of your power, your experience..."

"Consequently," he asked, an intrusive thought taking over, "How old are you exactly? It's always fascinated me..."

Calen blinked. "Oh, um—seventeen..."

Haldan's eyes widened, a grin on his face "Seventeen hundred years! Imagine..." His voice trailed off as though the idea itself had grown too grand to finish. But he quickly collected himself, then leaned forward slightly, watching Calen carefully before continuing with the gravitas of someone who had long thought on this very moment.

"I need not tell you that our city is under threat, not from petty concerns, but from forces far more dangerous than anything we've faced in years. The Empire is stirring, and they won't be pleased to know of your presence here." He leaned forward slightly, the movement slow, deliberate. "And that's why we must speak of this properly. I trust you understand the delicacy of the matter."

Before either of them spoke again, there was a sharp knock at the door—loud, urgent.

Haldan's posture shifted in an instant. There was a slight tenseness in his expression, a controlled irritation at the interruption.

"Pardon me," Haldan said, standing with deliberate care. "Please, make yourself comfortable."

The mayor crossed the room as the door opened with a low creak. Calen heard murmured voices from the hallway.

Just then, in his mind, a voice stirred—low, familiar, and steady.

*You're doing great, lad,* the stone said.

Calen jumped, worrying they'd be overheard.

*Don't worry. Only magical creatures and those who understand magic can hear me. Remember when I spoke with Mira? You didn't hear me then either.*

Calen took a slow breath. He wasn't sure whether he was happy to hear from the stone or deeply annoyed.

*If it gets to be too much, just charm the mayor and excuse yourself.*

Calen decided he was annoyed, although grateful for the reminder.

In the hallway, voices began to rise, muffled but unmistakably tense.

Then a sharper voice—closer now.

"—Dravess...on her way here to see *the wizard*. She insisted."

Calen felt the stone pulse.

He froze.

A beat later, Haldan's voice came through clearly—sharp but tightly controlled. "Dravess Merasha is on her way here? Now?"

There was a muffled reply from the attendant—apologetic, defensive.

*A Dravess,* the stone said, its voice concerned for the first time. *The Dravesses are sorceresses of the Emperor's inner circle—high advisors, powerful in their own right. They see him often, sometimes daily. They don't travel. Ever. They're not meant to leave the castle.*

There was a pause, like the stone was searching its memory.

*I know I've been away several hundred years, but I've never heard of one stepping outside the Imperial court. Something's wrong. She shouldn't be here.*

The stone's voice dropped lower, more serious than Calen had ever heard it. *This woman isn't to be trifled with, lad. If she notices you—and she might not, but if she does—you'll need to act fast. Hit her with your influence, hard. As hard as you can. Knock her teeth out with it and run!*

Before Calen could gather his thoughts, a woman's voice cut sharply through the door—smooth, crisp, with authority that needed no introduction.

"I heard there's a wizard in here."

Calen went still, every breath locked in his chest.

Outside, Haldan's voice rose in polite alarm. "Dravess Merasha, I had no idea you were in town. If I'd known, I would have arranged something more fitting. Perhaps we might speak over dinner this evening? A quieter setting—"

"Oh, I'm sure you would have," she interrupted lightly, as though the suggestion amused her. "But really, Mayor, let's not pretend Hearthmere is so bustling with statecraft."

"I've already heard the town talking—something about Imperial troops, a confrontation, a wizard appearing out of nowhere..." A pause, like she was letting the words settle into the air, "And now I hear he's walked into your office."

The door creaked open. She hadn't asked permission.

"I intend to speak with him."

The door swung open fully, and Merasha stepped into the room like she owned not just the building but the city around it. She wasn't tall, but her presence filled the space with an effortless command that made Haldan seem like a servant in his own office. A deep violet hood framed her face, the fabric heavy and lined with silver, shadowing everything but her pale, perfect features. Her beauty was too precise to be natural—like something designed, not born. Her lips were dark red, her eyes a piercing gray-violet that seemed to glow faintly when they caught the light.

Beneath the cloak, she wore fitted traveling leathers, black with fine silver filigree stitched along the seams. The bodice was drawn so tight it looked punishing, yet she moved with unbothered grace. A golden clasp fastened the cloak at her throat, set with a ruby so flawless it seemed to hold liquid blood under glass. Dust from the road clung to the hem, but somehow even that looked deliberate.

She scanned the space with cool precision, already preparing her greeting.

She was clearly expecting someone she recognized.

Her eyes passed over the desk, the shelves, the chair—then she stopped, mid-glide, and flicked them downward.

Calen.

She blinked once. Then turned sharply on Haldan, her voice laced with offence. "Well? Where is he?" she snapped. "I can't believe you'd stoop to hiding him from me."

Haldan, caught entirely off guard, made a confused little noise—half chuckle, half cough—and raised both hands to his chest, elbows bent awkwardly like he wasn't sure if he was surrendering or praying. With a small, hesitant gesture, he motioned toward Calen in the chair.

The Dravess turned slowly back.

She looked at Calen. Then looked again.

Her brows arched. Her head tilted ever so slightly.

She turned back to Haldan with a disdain so refined it bordered on art.

"That's not a wizard, Haldan. That's a twelve-year-old boy."

Calen cringed, and Haldan flinched, giving a sort of soft, startled half shriek—his arms still held at chest level as if he were protecting himself from being stabbed.

Judging from the sorceress's expression, Calen half expected her to pull out a dagger and do it.

"Oh no! No, I—I assure you," he stammered. "We have many witnesses to his power. The entire plaza, from what I hear, saw him do it. My own daughter was present during the incident."

He gestured weakly toward Calen, still clearly rattled by the morning's events.

Merasha gave Calen a sideways glance—detached assessment. The kind of look one might give something unexpected on a menu: not what she came for, but perhaps worth considering.

She took a slow step closer to him, her beautiful and terrible gaze never leaving his face. Then, head tilted, she looked him up and down with clinical precision.

"Well, he's not a wizard..." she said, not looking away.

A moment passed—long enough to be uncomfortable—and then her eyes narrowed slightly, curiosity blooming behind them.

"...but he is...something."

She took another small step, eyes drifting over him again, this time with the speculative air of someone trying to decide which colors might suit him best.

"Well," she said lightly, turning back toward Haldan, "either way, I'm sure I can figure it out for you."

She offered a thin smile. "I'll just take this boy off your hands. He can come with me. We'll poke and prod, see what shakes loose. In the meantime, you won't have to worry about him at all."

"No," Calen said, his voice small at first.

The Dravess had already begun turning back to the door, as if the matter were settled.

"No, you've got it all wrong," he said again, louder this time. "I'm just a normal lad."

He stood—awkwardly, stiffly—but when he spoke the words again, they carried a different weight.

"I'm just a normal lad."

There was a gentle push beneath the words, like silk sliding off a ream. The familiar warmth radiating forward enveloping the room.

Merasha paused mid-step.

She turned to look at him again. A curious smile on her face.

"Oh! He is!" she said, pleasantly. "This is wonderful."

Her eyes glittered as she took a slow step back to him, her gaze soft now, like a cat circling something warm.

"He must be a—siren of some sort—an incubus?"

She looked him over again, like he was a rare instrument she'd just discovered in a dusty shop.

Calen's breath caught. She wasn't backing off; she was *studying* him, amused, intrigued.

Panic surged in his chest. He pictured himself in a purple outfit, a slave entertaining guests at her parties.

He remembered that time in the smithy—when he took it too far, turned a man into a mindless thing, unable to speak or think.

He hadn't meant to do that. He barely knew how he'd done that.

But the stone had said to hit her hard.

Everything he had.

So he let go.

The charm poured out of him like a river, his eyes glowing yellow gold. Flooding the room before him.

"I. Am. Just. A. Normal. Lad," he said, staring into her powerful eyes, his voice cracking with the effort.

Her eyes, locked to his, glazed over, something inside going away. All the sharpness drained from her face in an instant. Her spine slackened just slightly. Her expression went soft, almost dreamy.

She blinked slowly, lips parted in sudden, confused contentment.

There was no need to talk to her now. She wasn't there.

# 14

Now was the time to depart.

He stepped around the sorceress without a word.

To the right of the door, the mayor stood in a mild stupor, hand still awkwardly raised, his mouth slightly open as if halfway through a thought he'd already forgotten. On the left, two attendants were similarly dazed—one of them still holding the fruit tray the mayor had ordered.

Calen glanced down and spotted a particularly nice pastry. He picked it up, looking at the entranced attendant.

"Thanks," he said, then he walked out the door.

He moved quickly through the outer hall and down the wide steps, out into the open space just inside the city's main gate. A few people milled about—traders, messengers, a pair of guards near the archway—but no one gave him a passing glance.

No one paid him any attention.

A few hours ago, he'd caused a citywide panic. Now, he was just another kid walking out of a government building.

Sure. Why not?

He took a bite of the pastry and began to walk home.

"Well," he said, directing his—magic? Warmth? Back at the stone. He didn't even know the proper name for it. "Now what?"

*You did it, lad!* the stone replied, excited. *She doesn't know what hit her!*

"Oh, really?" Calen remarked. "That makes two of us…"

He thought for a moment. "How long are they just going to stay standing like that? Forever?"

*Only a few minutes or so,* the stone replied, *or if someone interrupts them sooner.*

"And when they wake up. Then what?"

*They'll remember you as being just a normal lad—exactly as you told them.*

A pause.

*But, the Dravess…* The stone's tone cooled, and grew thoughtful. *She'll piece it together. Eventually. She won't know what happened, at first. But she'll come looking.*

"So…I can't stay."

*Not for long. A week, maybe two, if you're lucky. Longer if she leaves town before the charm starts to fade. But once it does—she'll remember just enough to want answers.*

***

The blacksmith's shop was closed.

Someone had stretched a line of rope across the open work-space with a hand-painted sign swinging gently from the middle: *Closed.* A set of burlap curtains had been drawn across the entrance, pinned at the top with iron nails and weighed down with bricks at the corners. A cart had been pulled partway across the front as a barrier, and an old barrel sat tipped on its side nearby, like a last-minute afterthought.

Calen stopped at the edge of the street, blinking at it.

This was his fault.

He didn't try to push past the front. Instead, he made his way around the side of the building to the gate, slipped through, crossing the narrow courtyard, and climbed the steps to the front door.

It wasn't locked.

He stepped inside.

Dean was on the left, arms crossed, leaning against the hearth like he hadn't moved in an hour. Ronan stood opposite him, hands stuffed in his pockets, his brow drawn. And Reeve—Reeve was sitting on the couch opposite the fire, but the moment Calen entered, he stood.

They all looked at him.

And then they moved.

Dean got to him first, crossing the room in three strides and pulling him into a hug that felt more like a tackle. Ronan was right behind, clapping a hand on his back and holding it there like he couldn't quite let go. Reeve hovered for a second, like he didn't know where to put himself, then stepped forward and pulled them all in, arms wrapping around the group like a seal.

Calen stood stiffly for a moment. And then—for the second time today, he broke.

The sobs hit fast, shuddering out of him before he could stop them. He'd expected fear, maybe blame. Another door slammed shut. Instead, he was held. Wrapped in arms that didn't flinch. Holding tight. Steady.

They didn't know what had happened.

They just knew he was home.

Ronan and Reeve backed off first, their hands lingering for a beat or two before slipping away. Dean stayed where he was, powerful arms still around him. Supporting him. And Calen leaned in—let himself collapse into the embrace like a branch giving way to the wind.

Dean held him.

Tight.

Like he'd been waiting for someone to hold.

For a long moment, he didn't move. His hand found the back of Calen's head, and he just stood there, jaw tight, staring at nothing.

Then, quietly, he guided Calen across the room. Half-carrying, half steering, Dean eased him down onto the couch next to Reeve.

Calen sat dazed, palms open on his knees.

Ronan stepped away and returned with a glass of water. He held it out without a word. Calen took it with a trembling hand.

Dean stayed kneeling in front of Calen, one hand remaining on his shoulder.

The room was still.

Dean shifted and pulled up a thin chair and sat.

Reeve leaned forward. "Are you okay?"

Calen looked up. His eyes were red, his face blotchy, but he met Reeve's gaze.

Calen opened his mouth.

Nothing came out.

He looked at Reeve. Then Dean. Then Ronan.

All waiting.

"It was..." Calen dragged a hand through the air, as if the space itself could explain. "I don't even know where to begin..."

He took a deep breath.

"I was walking with Lyra—on the road—and we got milk," he said, slapping the container down on the floor between them. "Then there were Imperial troops, and Lyra went up to them and started arguing, and then they were going to kidnap her, and then they attacked.

"And then—"

He swallowed. "Apparently there was a mage, and he used some kind of spell. And apparently—I'm some sort of magical being, and I deflected it.

"And then Lyra freaked out—like, really freaked out—and then the city locked me out and called all the guards on me, and—" His voice caught. "I ran into the forest. I was going to leave. I was.

"But the mayor came and found me. And he...he thought I was a wizard. Like, an old one. Like a thousand-years-old old.

"And then this scary lady came in, and she said I'm not a wizard, I'm a sigh-ren, or an inkybus, or something—I don't even know! And I got away, and they're not looking for me now. But they might. In, like, a week.

"And I don't even know what I'm supposed to do."

No one spoke.

Reeve glanced at Dean, then Ronan, then back to Calen. The three exchanged uncertain looks, as if trying to decide whether anyone else understood—or believed—this better than they did.

Calen stared into his glass of water, then took several loud gulps.

Dean's brow furrowed. He opened his mouth. "You—" He stopped, let out a soft hmm, and turned slowly to Ronan with a look that clearly meant, *Your turn.*

Ronan cleared his throat, shifted his weight, and ran a hand through his hair. "All that, huh?" He gave his thighs an awkward slap—more gesture than sound. "Well."

That was it.

Silence fell again. Then, slowly, all three turned to Reeve.

He opened his mouth. Closed it. Then blurted, all in one breath,

"Calen'smagicalI'veknownformonths!"

It tumbled out like a confession he'd been holding too long. He blinked, realizing what he'd said. "Sorry." A vague hand wave. "That's just been in there a while."

Dean and Ronan turned to look at each other. No words.

They exchanged a long, wide-eyed look—equal parts alarm, calculation, and something that looked suspiciously like resignation.

Dean cleared his throat first, his voice quiet and measured. "Did you hurt anyone?"

Calen shook his head. "No."

Ronan's arms crossed, brow low. "Is anyone else in trouble? Lyra? Anyone in town?"

"I don't think so," Calen said. "People were scared, but—more from the soldiers than from me, I think."

Dean and Ronan shared a glance. "Has this happened before?" Dean asked, as if he was piecing things together. "Before today?"

Calen hesitated. "Not like that. Not—not that big."

Dean's gaze shifted to Reeve. "How involved were you?"

Reeve blinked. "What? I—no, this wasn't my idea."

"What wasn't your idea?" Dean pressed.

Reeve shrugged.

"So, it was his idea?" Dean tilted his head toward Calen.

Reeve sat up, hands raised. "No! It wasn't anyone's idea—it's just…Calen has magic. He couldn't control it at first, and then he could."

Ronan rubbed his beard. "So, what exactly can he do?"

Reeve started to answer, stopped, and looked at Calen. Calen met his eyes. They froze for half a second—do not say it—and each shifted slightly where they sat.

"He can," Reeve began again, his voice a touch too high, "make people like him. A lot. And, um…do things. He can kind of…tell people what to do, and they just…do it."

Dean blinked. "Wait—what?" He let out a sharp laugh and clapped his hands once. "All right. Fine. You boys are being ridiculous." He spread his arms. "If you can actually do that, then go on. Make me do something!"

Calen's eyes widened. "Dean, I—"

"No, no, boy. Come on." Dean stood, relaxing now, clearly deciding it was a trick. "Impress me." He spread his arms wide, like a man daring someone to take a swing.

Calen cringed, then blurted. "Pour this water on your head."

Dean didn't even blink. He stepped forward, took the glass from Calen's hand, and tipped it over his head. Water ran down his face and into his collar. He froze, blinked again, and set the glass gently on the side table.

Reeve let out a low whistle.

Dean looked at Calen, his voice almost a murmur. "Fuck."

He stood slowly, wiping his hands on his pants, then wandered toward the window. He stopped there, staring out at nothing in particular—not angry, not afraid. Something heavier. Quiet. Contained. He was thinking.

Calen cleared his throat. "Can I take a shower?" he asked quietly, not looking at anyone.

Dean didn't answer—still fixed on the window—but Ronan gave a slight, unreadable nod.

"I'll go with him," Reeve said.

Calen wanted to be alone, but he didn't object. He didn't have it in him. Then he remembered how alone he'd felt in the forest and nodded. He rose, and together they stepped outside, leaving the two older men behind, still trying to piece together what had just happened.

***

Reeve stepped out and closed the door behind him. Calen was already a few paces ahead, walking with a tired, heavy gait. He followed in silence. He didn't know how to help, didn't have the right words or even the right instincts. But if Calen needed someone beside him, Reeve would be that someone. He didn't need to fix anything—he just wanted to be there.

The walk was quiet, but not uncomfortable. Just a few yards, barely enough time for the words in Reeve's head to catch up with his feet.

He followed Calen into the shower house, letting the door swing shut behind them. The tiled walls echoed slightly as they stepped inside. Reeve began to undress, folding his clothes and setting them aside, his thoughts still trailing behind.

The horns earlier, the panic. People yelling through the streets. He'd never seen the city like that before—so on edge, so afraid. And then the rumors started. A wizard was attacking the city, someone said. Another claimed Calen was involved—either helping the wizard, or he had been killed by the wizard. Lyra was involved somehow as well. Reeve knew that Calen was with Lyra, going to the dairy...and then nothing. Hours passed. No sign of either of them. Every possibility ran through his mind—none of them good.

Then the all-clear was sounded, and things started to settle, at least on the surface. But the rumors didn't stop. Whispers spread that the wizard wasn't all bad. That the mayor was handling things personally. The guards had been told to stand down. But no more mention of Calen. Not once.

Reeve had already been withdrawn before the tragedy. He wasn't one for crowds or noise, preferring quiet corners and familiar routines. But after the accident—after the bandits—killed Dean's wife and son—and his own mother—something inside him closed off entirely. The world lost its color. He stopped visiting the market. Stopped walking the city streets at dusk, or climbing the steps to look over the wall. Stopped laughing. It was easier to stay home, to fade into the edges of the household, where no one asked too many questions.

And then, Calen arrived. Bright, impulsive, endlessly curious Calen. Somehow, without even trying, he pulled Reeve back into the world. Not all at once, but slowly—like sunlight returning after a long storm. With Calen, he felt safe. Seen. Like maybe life still had pieces worth holding onto.

Now, he watched Calen pull off his shirt, unfasten his belt, and move to start the showers. Steam rose almost immediately, curling upward in soft tendrils. Calen didn't step in right away; he dragged a small wooden stool into the stream and sat down slowly, letting the water fall over him like rain.

His head dropped forward.

The water hit his shoulders, coursed over his chest, ran in smooth ribbons down his skin.

Calen was tall for his age, lean but strong, his muscles defined more by work than intention. There was a quiet strength in him, like a bow drawn and not yet loosened. His body was still that of a teenager, but it was leaning toward something more. He had dark hair, darker than Reeve had ever seen, almost black, even wet. It clung to his temples and neck now, and Reeve found himself watching the way it soaked and shifted with the water.

There was a dusting of hair under his arms. The same was true lower down, though Reeve tried to not let his eyes linger.

His skin was fair—too fair for someone who spent all his time outdoors—but it only made his dark eyes more striking. Dark, not in a cold way, but in the way velvet or still water is dark—deep and quiet.

Calen hadn't spoken. He hadn't really moved. He just sat there, letting the water run over him like he might like to dissolve into it.

Reeve let the water run hot over his shoulders. He didn't scrub. Just stood there, glancing sideways, watching Calen in the mist.

Without looking up, Calen asked, "Do you hate me?"

Reeve blinked. The question hit like a slap.

"Hate you?" he repeated, almost disbelieving. "Calen..."

Reeve pulled over a bench and sat. The water warm trickled down his skin, pooling at their feet.

"No," Reeve said, firmer this time. "I don't hate you. You're—you're basically my brother now."

Calen finally looked up, eyes glistening under strands of wet hair. Reeve saw the doubt in them, the weariness.

"Today was a lot," Reeve went on, his voice softening. "But I know you. I know who you are."

Calen shifted slightly on the stool, water splashing off his back into mist. He looked up and then away again, hesitant.

"There's something I haven't told you," he said quietly.

Reeve tensed, but didn't speak. It could be anything at this point. Perhaps Calen had a pet dragon.

Calen stood up and walked across the shower room to his belt and pulled something out. He walked back, an item in hand.

Then he offered it to Reeve.

Reeve started to stand, but sat down again, taking the stone. He looked at it curiously.

He looked back at Calen. Why would Calen hand him a rock?

"Okay," Reeve said, "a rock." This definitely wasn't a dragon.

Calen nodded. "It talks. It's magic. It's what sent me here."

Reeve frowned, glancing from the stone to Calen and back.

Calen offered a small, tired smile. "I know how that sounds."

Reeve pressed his lips together, unsurprised.

"At this point, Calen," he said soberly, "I'd believe anything you said."

"Actually..." Calen said quietly, "it's speaking right now."

Reeve couldn't hear anything.

Sitting back down, Calen reached out and gently took the stone back from Reeve's hand. Their knees touched.

He looked at it for a moment, then said, "He says...I mean, *it* says...I'm safe for now, but...the Dravess—the scary lady I mentioned before?—I actually had to charm her—she was going to take me away and study me—or worse."

He paused, then said, "I made her forget me, but the stone says the charm will wear off, and then she's sure to come for me soon after."

He looked at Reeve, his voice quieter still. "I can't stay here much longer. I think...I think I'm going to have to leave."

Reeve's heart sank. After everything that had happened today, the thought of losing Calen again was unbearable. There had already been too much loss, too much sadness. The idea of returning to the life he'd been living before Calen—gray, quiet, empty—felt like stepping back into a cave.

Calen was daylight.

Calen was a whole world full of magic and impossible things waiting to unfold.

Reeve wasn't going back.

"I'm coming with you," he said.

Calen looked up, surprised. "I'm... just going home," he said, uncertain. "Back to my house. My parents. I don't really know what else to do."

Reeve blinked. "Wait—you know how to get home?" He felt a flicker of betrayal and slid his stool back. "You said you didn't before. You didn't even know where you were..."

Calen hesitated, then he gave a small nod. "I met someone. In the forest. After the guards locked me out of the city. A fairy, actually. She said she could take me home." He obviously saw the change in Reeve's face. "It's a long story."

Reeve stared. "You met a... fairy?"

This story just kept getting stranger. Was Calen being truthful? He said Lyra was furious with him. Reeve had known Lyra for years. She was honest, loyal, responsible—there wasn't a more stand-up person in the whole city.

"Calen," he said, standing. "This is getting crazy. Wizards, a talking stone, fairies...?"

"I know how it sounds," Calen said.

His knees shifted apart, his head falling forward, fingers gesturing vaguely at the air like he could shape the words he couldn't find.

Reeve raised his hand. "Okay. Let's say I actually believe you. How can you just trust some random fairy? Don't they play tricks on people? Isn't that their whole thing?" He walked over and shut off the water, grabbing a towel and throwing another one at Calen.

Calen looked up and then away. "I actually know her. I trust her. She's...friends with my grandmother."

Reeve blinked, jaw slack. He let his arm drop and turned, pacing a few steps, snapping his towel once as he walked. This was so outrageous, it actually felt too crazy to be a lie.

He turned sharply and stared at Calen. "And you couldn't tell me because..."

Calen looked up, eyes heavy with regret. "Reeve, look at how you're reacting now—after knowing me for months. How would you have taken all of this the day we met?"

Reeve paused. Calen was right. But could he be trusted? A moment ago, he was willing to—Reeve wasn't even sure. But now?

"Tell me what happened. How did you get here?"

Calen shifted, throwing his towel over his shoulder, and moved to sit on a bench along the wall. "I found this stone in a river. It's dangerous. Powerful. It needs to go back to the castle it came from. It was supposed to send me there, but instead...it sent me here." He exhaled. "Lyra found me and brought me to the city. The stone only started talking today. The fairy only found me today."

Calen slumped forward, elbows on knees. "I have nothing left."

Reeve believed him.

He didn't know how or why—it didn't make sense, none of it did—but something in Calen's voice, the sag of his shoulders, the raw honesty in his eyes...it felt true. Besides, Calen, at any time, could skip all this uncomfortableness and just charm the situation away. But he wasn't.

Reeve walked over and sat next to him on the bench, their shoulders nearly touching. He didn't say anything. He wasn't sure what words could even begin to help.

So he just sat there.

Calen looked down at the stone in his hand. His expression shifted—disgusted, or maybe just exhausted. Without a word, he stood, crossed the room, and set it on the bench farthest away. The sound of it clinking gently on the wood echoed through the shower room. Then he walked back, dropped down beside

Reeve, put his arm around Reeve's shoulder as if to hold himself back, and glared at the stone like it had just insulted his mother.

Calen stared at the stone in silence. The tension in his jaw shifted slightly, then his brows lifted, faintly surprised. He didn't say anything at first—just nodded once, very slowly.

Reeve stayed quiet, watching.

Calen tilted his head, listening, then his expression grew more serious. Whatever the stone was saying, it wasn't casual. He responded with a quiet, "I see." He then blinked, his eyes darting back and forth as if tracing some unseen map in his head.

Still, Reeve said nothing.

Then Calen spoke aloud, not to Reeve, but to the stone. "So, the Valley of the Golems..."

Reeve shifted slightly. He didn't know what it was the stone had said, but the shift in Calen's voice—something between fury and exhaustion—told him the path ahead had just changed.

Reeve's curiosity finally got the best of him. "What was that about?"

Calen glanced at him, then back at the stone. He tilted his head, lips pressing into a flat line.

"Well, first of all, I'm thinking about tossing the stone into the nearest river."

Reeve blinked. "What? Why?"

Calen sighed, toweling off his wet hair. "Apparently, it doesn't want to go back to the castle like we thought. No, it wants to be taken to a place called the Valley of the Golems. Says there's a body waiting for it there. A body. So it can…take shape again. Be whole. Become a person, or something close to it."

Reeve sat in silence for a moment, towel in his lap. Then, slowly, he asked, "So…what's in it for us?"

Calen blinked. "What?"

"I mean…why do this?" Reeve said, thinking. "Why not just chuck the thing into the river like you said? Why go chasing after some golem valley?"

"*That's a good question!*" Calen said, eyeing the stone like he was moments away from walking straight through the city, bare-ass naked and dripping wet, just to toss it into the river himself.

Calen listened for a moment, then looked back at Reeve.

"He says he's lost, like I am. He doesn't know how he got in the stone—doesn't know what he is either, but he feels like there's answers in the forge, in the valley."

Reeve frowned. "Okay, but why us? What's in it for us? I've never heard of this valley. For all we know, it's across the continent. This could be really dangerous. Why should we be the ones who take him?"

Calen stared at the stone for a long moment. Then he sighed.

"He says…because we're already carrying him.

"Because we're the only ones who can. No one else can hear him. No one else would believe he's anything more than a lump of rock."

He paused, listening again.

"He says the magic in me—whatever it is—is tied to him now. That we're...connected. That maybe the answers we're both looking for are in that valley. This isn't just about him."

Calen dragged the towel over his head again. "He says I was never meant to go home."

Reeve let out a long breath.

"This is... a lot," he admitted finally.

"Yeah," Calen muttered. "It really is."

A beat passed.

"I'm going to bed," Calen said, standing.

Reeve blinked. "It's only, what, five?"

"Then I'm going to bed at five."

He picked up the stone and turned it once in his hand, as if still debating if it was worth holding onto. He walked across the shower room and tossed his towel onto the nearest hook. With no further ceremony, he grabbed his belt, tunic, and pants in a bunch and headed for the door, bare skin streaked with water.

Reeve stayed where he was, silent, watching Calen disappear.

He didn't say a word.

# 15

Calen didn't get out of bed the entire next day.

He didn't speak. Didn't eat. The room was hot and dim, silence heavy in the air. At one point, Dean knocked softly on the door. Calen didn't answer. Later, Ronan opened it just a crack and left a bowl of something on the dresser, but the spoon stayed untouched. He lay on his side with the covers shoved off, staring at the wall until the shadows shifted and deepened and the sky outside the window turned dark.

The stone stirred.

It had been silent since the night before, letting the boy rest. But now, it shimmered faintly from the satchel on the floor, and a whisper curled up from its surface.

"We should talk—"

Calen's eyes flashed gold in the dark. "Shut up."

A pause.

"That doesn't work on me," the stone replied, apologetically. Then, quieter. "But...point taken."

The glow dimmed. Calen rolled over and went back to staring at the wall.

***

A few nights later, the air was still too hot to sleep. Reeve lay on his own narrow bed across the room, stripped down and restless, staring at the ceiling. A breeze stirred the edge of the curtain, but it didn't help much. He turned onto his side to glance at Calen—still awake, still motionless.

He sat up. "You want to get out of here?"

Calen didn't move. For a moment, Reeve thought he might not answer. Then finally, a small shift.

"...out of here?"

"Yeah, outside," Reeve said. "Just for a minute. Get some air. We can climb out the window. Roof's right there."

Calen sighed. "Dean and Ronan's windows are open. I don't want them to hear anything."

"They're on the other side of the house. We'll be fine."

Calen sat up slowly, dragging a hand through his hair. He looked down at himself, then over at Reeve. They were both naked, which had become normal enough over the summer, but...

"Shirts," Calen muttered.

"Definitely."

They pulled on the long linen nightshirts folded at the ends of their beds—loose, wrinkled, and just long enough to pass for decent if anyone saw them from a window.

Reeve went to the window and climbed out first, crouching on the slanted rooftop just beyond. He turned and offered a hand. Calen followed, bare feet silent on the warm metal rooftop. The city was surprisingly silent. Dull voices in the air, footsteps distant, just an occasional snap of laughter or the bark of a dog echoing off stone.

"Too visible," Calen murmured, looking around.

"There's a ledge," Reeve said. "Here—boost me."

Calen gave him a lift, and Reeve hauled himself up to the peak of the house. A moment later, he reached down and helped Calen join him.

They sat together on the top ridge, feet braced on the slope, knees drawn up, shirts tucked under bare bottoms.

From here, the rooftops of the city stretched out in haphazard rows, clustered chimneys and crooked gutters catching moonlight. Reeve saw Calen looking across the city, toward the three-story houses of the town's wealthy citizens.

Lyra was over there. He had never been to her house.

A breeze finally reached them, soft and cool against their skin, blowing up their shirts and out their collars.

For a long while, neither of them said anything.

"I hate it," Calen said at last, voice low. "The stone. I wish I'd never found it."

Reeve didn't respond right away. He watched the glow of a lantern three streets over flicker and go out.

"You didn't find it," he said eventually. "It found you."

Calen huffed softly. "Even worse."

Another long silence.

"Have you told me everything now?" Reeve asked, not accusing—just tired, perhaps afraid. "Because every time I think I know everything, you say something new."

Calen rubbed his face. "I don't know. I think so. I want to say yes, but...what if I'm wrong?"

Reeve nodded slowly. "Then tell me when you remember. Just don't keep it to yourself."

Calen gave a small weary laugh. "You should just walk away, you know. You still can."

"I'm not going anywhere," Reeve said. "Just...don't keep pushing me out."

They sat a while longer in silence, listening to the wind.

Then there was a flicker of movement, a soft shimmer just beyond the chimney. A flutter of wings, like a giant barn fly, or a man-eater wasp.

The boys recoiled reflexively.

It landed at their feet.

Both jumped back, pushing their shirts down so the invasive insect wouldn't fly up.

"Ugh!" a voice sounded. "I've been looking for you!"

A glow appeared around the insect, faint and purple.

"I didn't know if I should come…"

Both boys blinked, looking closer.

In the faint glow, like a fading ember, a shape resolved—slim limbs, large, translucent wings that folded away into nothing, bare feet touching the metal roof.

Liri stood there, wringing her hands.

Reeve blinked at her, mouth slightly open. "…that's a fairy?"

Liri narrowed her eyes. "*Obviously.*"

She put her hands on her hips, looked up at them, and tilted her head. "Seriously? I leave the safety of my *sacred* forest once. Dodging hawks and blood-thirsty owls. And I'm here *two* seconds—and I've already got your *man bits* up my nose."

Both boys yanked their shirts again and sat down abruptly, legs crossed.

"Liri…" Calen said, leaning in. "What are you doing here?"

"I've been circling that forest since you left like a nervous bat," she said, flicking a bit of chimney dust off her shoulder.

Reeve squinted. "Wait, I thought you were, like, made of mist or something?"

"I am. Or *I was.*" She plopped down on the roof between them with a dramatic exhale, then immediately pulled her legs up and looked around nervously. "But when I leave the forest, I have to take form. And when I take form, I'm basically a very sparkly snack for *literally everything that flies.*"

She pointed upward suspiciously. "Birds are *everywhere,* you know. You look up, and they're just waiting."

Calen raised a brow. "At night?"

"Oh, *especially* at night," Liri said, dead serious. "Owls are murder goblins with wings—and necks that turn *all the way around*. It's not natural."

Reeve pressed a fist to his mouth, trying not to laugh.

Liri glared. She sniffed, then glanced back toward the forest, twitchy. "I shouldn't even be here. If someone swoops down and eats me, it's your fault."

"Can fairies die?" Reeve asked, leaning in to see her better.

"Well—yes!" Liri replied, offended. "I mean—I would wake up again in the forest in a few decades, but I'd rather that be avoided…"

"Why did you come then?" Calen asked, gentler now.

Liri hesitated, then shrugged, voice smaller. "Because I didn't know if you were okay. I wanted to go back to Mira. I *should* have gone back. But I couldn't. I kept thinking…what if you needed me?"

Calen looked at her—really looked at her—and something in his face finally eased.

"I did," he said. "I do."

Liri blinked hard, then quickly waved it away as if he'd sneezed on her. "Ugh. Gross. Don't get sentimental. You're sweaty, and I'm emotionally brittle."

The laughter faded, and for a moment, the rooftop was quiet again. The stars shimmered overhead, and the breeze stirred the edge of Calen's shirt.

Reeve shifted where he sat. "So...are we gonna talk about it?"

Calen blinked. "Talk about what?"

Reeve gave him a look. "The stone. What it is. What it wants."

Liri perked up instantly, narrowing her eyes. "Oh, *please* tell me you're not still listening to that thing."

Calen exhaled. "I don't know if I'm listening. I'm just...not ignoring it."

Reeve raised a brow. "Which means you're listening."

Calen hesitated, then looked between them. "It told me something the other night. It said it wants...a body."

She winced. Liri froze.

"Now it wants a body?" she said, voice pitching up. "Oh, no. No, no, no."

She threw her hands in the air. "*Never* trust anything that wants a body. That's like...rule one!"

She held up a finger, looking at Reeve. "Rule two is don't flash fairies."

Reeve coughed, half-laughing, and put a hand between his legs.

Calen gave her a look. "Liri..."

She dropped her hand, suddenly more serious. "That thing you've been carrying? It's not just some enchanted trinket. It was embedded in the Wizards' Council's castle. Deep magic. Old magic. It's layered and complicated and probably way too smart."

Reeve frowned. "So, it's...enchanted."

Liri nodded. "Probably a lot more than enchanted. I mean—*it's speaking.*"

Calen stared at her. "Why didn't anyone tell me that? And what's a Wizards' Council?"

Liri shrugged. "Well, I mean...you didn't *really* need to know. The original plan was you'd just pop up next to the castle, stick the stone into the wall, walk down the hill, meet me, and go home. As far as the council goes, it's a meeting place for about a hundred fifty brilliant but conflicted wizards who could burn this city down with a snap of their fingers, and the only reason the Empire rules over the entire continent. You don't mess with them."

She waved a hand as if they should disregard that. "Anyway, this could've taken ten minutes. Maybe fifteen, if you'd stopped to pee. There was no reason to dump a bunch of details on you."

Calen began to think about when he'd found the stone, and he wondered if Liri had—

But before he could finish his thought, Reeve cut in. "You were 'just' gonna send *him into a castle full of ancient magic* without telling him what he was carrying?"

Liri replied, clinically, "Technically, yes. But it was a *very solid* plan."

Calen paused, feeling a bit used.

"So...what if we don't?" Reeve asked, glancing between them. "What if we don't go to the castle? What if we do what it wants?"

Liri squinted at him. "You *want* to listen to a rock?"

Reeve shrugged. "I don't know. What else are we doing?"

Calen's voice was quiet. "It did choose me..."

Liri turned slowly. "I don't think that's—"

"No, I mean it," Calen said, more serious. "What if this isn't just some accident? What if it picked me because I'm supposed to do something more?"

Liri stared. "Or, maybe you were just the first person to pee near it."

Calen gave her a sharp look, finally finishing the thought he started earlier.

He looked away, but didn't let it go. "Still. It's trying to go somewhere. It wants to be more than it is. Just like me. And even if it is lying to me, it isn't lying about that."

Reeve leaned in. "Where is it trying to go again—the Valley of the Golems?"

Liri exhaled slowly. "I think it's talking about Lord Daetari's Valley."

Calen blinked. "Who?"

Liri shrugged. "He's one of the Lord Wizards—old wizards, more like gods. They talk with the gods..."

Reeve's eyes widened. "Is that even possible?"

"Yes," Liri replied solemnly. "The gods are real."

Calen sat up, suddenly excited. "And we can go talk to one... to see one... about getting the stone a body?"

Liri's mouth twisted. "Well, *technically* Lord Daetari isn't a god—but yes?"

Reeve raised an eyebrow. "Wait, you said he's more like... How old is he?"

Liri tilted her head. "As old as I can remember. I think he was one of the first wizards."

Calen leaned back slightly. "But, if he's there...and we brought him the stone...he would know what to do."

Liri didn't answer right away. Then, finally, she said, "Maybe. The stone wouldn't be anything compared to him, that's for sure. He would be able to handle it safely."

Calen thought for a moment. "Can we use your fast-travel spell to get there?"

"No." Liri looked down, suddenly sorry to disappoint him. "That only works in Gregor's Forest."

Reeve looked up. "Wait—fast-travel? What's that?"

Liri tilted her head. "Hmm, it's hard to explain. The magic in the forest is thick. Uh, ancient. I can shape a path through it—something that feels like walking down a deer trail, but it skips miles at a time. You can't even tell it's magic except for the beginning and the end."

Reeve thought for a moment. "That's...actually kind of amazing."

She shrugged. "It's nothing special. To me, it's just faster than having to flutter at someone's side while they walk and walk. But, outside the forest, the magic's broken."

Calen processed that for a moment. "How long would it take, then...to get to the valley?"

Liri grimaced. "I'm not sure... It's really far, and I don't travel like you do."

Reeve grinned faintly. "So, we'd be doing this the hard way."

Calen nodded at Liri. "But we'd be doing *something*."

They sat in silence for another few breaths, the city's lights flickering beneath them like fireflies.

Eventually, Reeve stood and stretched. "Well, guess we should sleep while we still can."

Calen nodded, then carefully climbed back down and through the window. Reeve followed, both of them landing with soft thumps on the wooden floor.

As they peeled off their nightshirts and tossed them aside, Liri flitted in through the window behind them, perching on the dresser like she'd been invited.

She blinked once. "Seriously? You're naked again?"

Calen didn't even look at her. "You sound just like my mother."

Reeve snorted, already climbing into bed.

Calen flopped onto his mattress with a sigh. "She never stopped complaining about it."

Liri crossed her legs and folded her arms. "If you both die on this trip, it's not going to be because of monsters, it's going to be because you're *very stab-able*."

Reeve yawned. "I sleep better without pants. Let fate deal with it."

Liri muttered something in a language neither of them understood, then fluttered down the edge of the washbasin, where she curled up beside an old hairbrush like it was the comfiest bed in the world.

Calen was already asleep.

# 16

Over the next few days, the boys gathered what they needed. Calen picked through the market for supplies—bedrolls, flint kits, a whetstone that smelled like sulfur. Reeve talked a reluctant merchant into parting with a series of travel maps and even found a battered field guide on edible plants that he claimed to remember from his school days. They each brought packs large enough for the road ahead and stuffed them with food, tent supplies, soap, thread, and everything they could think of.

For Liri, they found a tiny cricket cage tucked behind a row of dusty charms in a curiosity shop near the back of the market. It was brass, slightly dented, and lined with a scrap of purple velvet. She rolled her eyes, but approved of it in her own way—declaring it "tolerable." It was at least somewhere she could hide if she sensed any overt bird danger. They were ready to go by mid-September.

Back at the shop, Dean had barely spoken to them since they gave notice. He grunted once—maybe in approval, maybe in irritation—but didn't say goodbye. Ronan had already replaced them with two other boys. They weren't as fast, but they worked without complaint.

Many in the city had asked about the events from the previous month. Calen had lightly charmed them all, and now no one did. The day slipped quietly from public memory.

When it was time, they left in the morning, without fanfare.

The sky was overcast that morning, the kind of dull gray that made the world feel muffled. The air was cooler than it had been in weeks, soft on the skin but still damp from the rain during the night before.

They walked without speaking, their packs slung over their shoulders, boots striking the packed dirt on the main road. The North Gate loomed ahead of them—a pair of guards stood at the base, silent and disinterested, while a few more watched from above.

Calen slowed as they approached. He was walking forward, but part of him felt like he'd left something behind with every step. The shop. The rhythm of the work. Dean's gruff voice echoing through the rafters. He'd done half his mourning for the loss of his life in the city that day in the forest, already broken about what could have been. But now, walking here, the city soon to be at his back and the world ahead, it ached in a quieter way.

A part of him thought of home—how easy it would be to just go and forget all of this like a dream. Instead, his grip on his pack tightened, and his eyes scanned the trees beyond the gate. The world was wide, and the stone was in its place at his waist.

Reeve walked behind him, quieter than usual. His jaw was tense, his eyes fixed ahead. Calen knew he'd never left the city before. Everything beyond the gate felt too big, too open, too unknowable for them both. But Calen was walking forward, and so Reeve was walking forward as well.

They passed through the gate. No one stopped them.

Behind them, the city breathed without them.

Calen caught the scent of bread baking on the wind and thought of Lyra.

He remembered the way she wrinkled her nose when she was trying not to laugh, how she always braided her hair before going to the market. The lunch breaks in the alley behind the workshop, sharing bread and dried fruit. The time she brought him a scarf she made herself—lopsided and too long—but she'd been proud of it. The way she'd reached for his arm that morning at the dairy, the warmth in her eyes. He missed that warmth.

He thought of how they'd walked together, how light the day had felt. How, for a few hours, it had felt like there was a long, happy future in store, and how everything would be okay.

And then the fire in her voice. The betrayal in her eyes. The way she'd turned from him like she never wanted to look back.

He'd hoped that someday he'd find her again, that he'd tell her the truth and fully explain what happened. Then she'd understand. Then they could go back to the way things were.

***

They cleared the outer city and continued until midday. The road narrowed as the city fell farther and farther behind. From there, they followed a narrow road north until it bent sharply right—into the forest.

As soon as they cleared the tree line, Liri burst from her refuge—which she insisted on calling her *refuge* and not a cage, as she was not a circus animal. She rose in a flash of violet light, wings unfurling as her form shifted. The hard, delicate body she wore in the outside-world—thin, like a carved insect—softened and bloomed. Her skin deepened into a glowing amethyst hue, her limbs stretched, and the edges of her figure blurred with the light. Her wings, no longer needing to flap to hold her aloft, became an extension of her movement, guiding her along like currents of winds she didn't need to catch.

"Ooh," she sighed, drifting just ahead of them. "That feels better. I don't know why I ever leave the forest."

Calen and Reeve both paused to watch her settle into the air like she belonged there—because she did.

"Liri!" Reeve gasped. "You're beautiful!"

She spun lazily in the air, the light around her catching like dust in a sunbeam. "Well, *thank you*," she said with a wink. "Nice to finally be appreciated in my proper form and not mistaken for a lightning bug, or a wasp, or something a bird might like to *enjoy for lunch*!”

She flitted sideways, wings flickering with sunlight. “Now then. Are we ready to skip a few miles?”

“Yes,” Reeve said. “My legs are already a bit tired.”

Calen looked at him. That wasn’t a good sign.

Liri flew lower, a trail of dust and sparks behind her. She flew north and then cut a precise line west to east. She began spinning, her wings catching and refracting the light. The air around her began to bend. Leaves stirred on the ground as a warm breeze seemed to come out of nothing. The edge of something unseen pressed against the air, and an arch formed before them—outlined in shimmering green.

The air in the arch gave way, and what was behind no longer matched its surroundings. A pale, sandy looking trail lay before them, cut through the woods, dodging between massive trees that seemed to go all the way up into the sky. The air had an emerald tint, and golden light cut through the trees. A rushing sound filled the air, loud but soothing, like distant waterfalls or wind moving through endless leaves.

The forest air smelled like a thousand woods all at once—mulch, bark, blossoms, wild fruit, Liri. The fairy had changed as she passed inside. She was larger now, and instead of her usual pinkish skin and lavender glow, she was pure white and glowed like starlight.

As the boys stepped inside, the arch vanished behind them.

"Now, boys," Liri said, in the tone of someone tending small children, "there are a few rules here—"

"Where is this place?" exclaimed Reeve, looking around in wide-eyed wonder.

Liri, clearly annoyed at being interrupted, pressed her fingers into her temple and began again.

"First of all..." A pause. Then her brow furrowed. "I don't know where this place is. It only exists while we're in it, but it's always here, except the part you can see isn't really the part that's here."

She blinked hard, like someone trying to unfog a dream. She looked seconds away from overloading herself.

Calen cut in gently, "Okay, Liri, what were you saying about rules?"

She straightened, collecting herself. "Yes, the rules." Then she lost it again. "Though—they aren't *all* the rules, and these are the just important ones."

Calen gave Reeve a pointed look and gestured toward Liri. "See what you did?"

Reeve shrugged. "I'm sorry. I'm not used to..." He trailed off, still looking around in awe.

Calen narrowed his eyes. "Oh, not you too."

He turned back to the still rambling fairy. "Liri. The rules."

"Ah, yes." Liri nodded. "Rule one: stay on the path. You can wander a little to the left or right, but don't step in the bushes."

"You'll fall off," she added casually.

Reeve startled. "Fall off?"

But Calen put a hand on his arm, calming him.

"Rule two," she said, "we need to keep moving. Lingering in this place gets weird."

Reeve opened his mouth, then closed it again. He obviously decided not to ask what *weird* meant, considering their location. Calen was feeling confused himself since he stepped in. Maybe they should have had this conversation prior to entering.

"So," Liri continued, "if we need to camp and stuff, we'll just exit like we came in."

Then the voice of the stone drifted in—calm, patient, and grand.

"I can explain," it began. "Around five hundred years ago—give or take a decade—the aggressive and unwarranted expansion of the Empire threatened the sanctity and security of the Great Forest, which led Lord Gregor—or just Gregor at the time—to begin laying the elementary foundations for the protective—"

"Enough," Calen snapped, catching Reeve by surprise.

"Wait!" Reeve exclaimed. "I could hear that! The old man—was that the stone?"

Calen and Liri exchanged a quick look.

"Yes!" Calen said, visibly excited. "You can hear it here! It must be because...everything's magic in here.

"That's amazing!" he added, his voice lifting with fresh energy.

He paused, then said, "Did you *want* to hear that?"

Reeve considered it. "Not really."

They both laughed—and with that, they began to walk.

***

They walked for what felt like hours—or maybe not long at all.

Time was slippery here, refusing to move right. The light shifted softly overhead, never dimming, never quite still. It reminded Reeve of trying to wake from a dream—but the dream wouldn't let him.

The trail curved through the forest, winding left, then right, with a faint spill of pale sand marking the center. It looked like whoever walked before them had a hole in their pack. Reeve kept glancing back, trying to fix landmarks in his mind, but there was no real *back* anymore. The trail behind them just melted into the trees.

"I think I hear water," he said, squinting into the haze.

Calen nodded. "Me too."

Liri floated beside them, slowly "It's not water," she said. "It's the trees."

Reeve frowned. "The trees make that sound?"

She tilted her head. "Or maybe the space between them. The magic here is so thick, it almost feels like we're underwater."

They walked in uneasy quiet after that.

Eventually, Reeve stopped, leaning forward with his hands on his knees, lungs tight.

"You okay?" Calen asked.

"Yeah. Just trying to pretend I didn't grow up shoeing horses. I can stand all day, but I'm just not used to walking like this."

Calen chuckled, slinging his pack off his shoulder. "You're doing fine."

Reeve dropped onto a low root, stretching out his legs until his knees popped. He took a long drink from his flask, wiped his mouth with the back of his hand, and exhaled. "I don't know how you're not winded."

Calen sat beside him. "I think it's the stone."

Reeve glanced at him. "The stone?"

"I've been sort of noticing it," Calen said, resting a hand at his waist, "but now that I've been walking with it...I don't feel heavy. My legs aren't sore. I'm not even really tired."

Reeve raised an eyebrow. "Must be nice. You want to carry my pack too?"

Calen hesitated, then unbuckled the belt. "You want to try?"

Reeve blinked. "Seriously?"

"Why not? I'm curious what happens."

Reeve took the belt carefully, half-expecting it to buzz or spark, and fastened it around his waist.

The change came fast.

He straightened without thinking, the dull ache in his calves gone. His shoulders lightened, like he'd just shrugged off a coat he didn't know he was wearing. Even the air felt thinner, easier.

"Whoa," he breathed.

Calen smiled faintly. "Feel it?"

Reeve nodded, testing his balance, one leg, then the other. "Yeah. It's like—I don't know. I feel amazing."

Calen laughed.

"You okay?" Reeve asked.

Calen glanced down at his empty belt. "Yeah." He nodded once, though his tone said otherwise.

Reeve grinned, already walking backward down the trail. "Then let's go."

They moved on in silence.

They'd gone about the same stretch they'd done earlier, but now Calen was lagging.

He rolled his shoulders and muttered, "Okay, now I feel it."

Reeve slowed, glancing back. "You want to switch again?"

"No," Calen said. "I'm glad you're feeling better."

They kept walking.

Then Calen said, "I wonder if there's a way to share it."

Reeve looked at him. "The stone?"

"Yeah," Calen said, thinking. "Like...split the effect some-how. Maybe there's a way it could help both of us at once?"

Reeve smiled. "Like we hold hands around it?"

Calen laughed. "Well...? Maybe. What if we attach each end of that belt to our normal belts...like a tether between us?"

Reeve looked down at the belt. "That's...weird enough that it might work."

They stopped. Calen unhooked the ends of the stone's strap from Reeve's waist, then handed one strap back to him. They clipped the ends onto the side of their regular belts, forming a bridge—just a few feet—between them.

"All right," Calen said. "Let's see what happens."

They started walking again, side by side.

Calen felt the usual cloak settle over him.

"Mine's working. How does yours feel?"

Reeve smiled. "I feel the same!"

It worked!

***

They walked for hours, almost in a trance.

The forest never dimmed. The light continued to glow around them—soft, diffuse, directionless. No shadows moved. No color changed. It felt like walking through a painting.

After a long while, Reeve glanced sideways. "How long have we been walking?"

Calen shrugged dreamily. "No idea."

Reeve slowed a little, looking around. "Shouldn't it be... like, later?"

Calen frowned, then turned to Liri. "Do we know what time it is?"

Liri had been drifting behind silently. "Time?"

Reeve raised his brows. "Yes, you know. The thing that makes the sun move?"

She squinted into the branches overhead, then nodded as if just remembering. "Oh. Right. It's um...almost sunset."

Both boys stopped walking.

"Sunset?" Calen repeated. "It was morning when we started."

Reeve thought for a moment. "That means we've been walking nine or ten hours!"

Calen turned to Reeve, wide-eyed. "We didn't even stop for lunch!"

Reeve looked down at his stomach, mildly betrayed. "That explains a lot."

They looked around. Everything was the same as when they'd entered. Calen sighed.

"Let's stop for the night."

Liri slowly floated ahead of them. "We'll have to step out."

Reeve blinked, "Out of the trail?"

She nodded. "Just like before. We can't linger in one spot. If we have to stop, we have to leave."

She slipped her hands through her hair, slowly floating to the ground. She fluttered her wings once and floated over to the left side of the path. She slowly ascended again, forming an arch, which shimmered green.

The air rippled, and the regular forest appeared before them—hot air rushing in around them, the smell of mud and birdsong in the air.

They stepped through, and the enchanted path faded behind them.

The clearing wasn't large, but it was flat enough for a tent, and the undergrowth had been pushed back from years of deer traffic or luck.

For a moment, neither of them spoke.

Reeve turned in a circle. "Is it just me, or...does this look like exactly where we started?"

Calen glanced around. Same trees. Same forest smell. The sun had moved. "Yeah, it really does."

He looked at Liri. "Did we even go anywhere?"

"Oh yes," she said brightly, back in her pink and purple form. "You've moved."

Calen narrowed his eyes. "Where *to*?"

She tilted her head. "The forest."

"That's not helpful," Reeve muttered.

Calen rubbed the back of his neck. "We were heading north the whole time, right?"

Liri nodded. "Of course."

"Are we still near the forest edge?"

"Yes."

Calen pointed off to the left. "I think the road we were on before cuts up through this stretch. If I pop out real quick maybe I can get a look, see how far we've come."

Reeve looked up at the sky. "We're losing light. You go—I'll start setting up camp. Here, you take the belt." He started unclipping himself.

Calen nodded and slipped through the trees, picking his way back toward the road.

It wasn't far. The underbrush thinned after a few minutes, and soon he stepped out onto packed dirt—ruts from wagon wheels, and the remains of an old signpost.

A man walked in the distance, leading a donkey with baskets tied to his sides.

Calen jogged over. "Excuse me. Can you tell me where we are?"

The man blinked at him. "Near Redstone. Town's just three miles west."

"Redstone," Calen repeated. "Thanks!"

The man gave him a funny look and kept walking.

Calen turned and bolted back to the trees.

When he stepped back out into the clearing again, Reeve was crouched beside the half-assembled tent, trying to figure out how the poles locked in place.

Calen was breathless. "I found a guy. He said we're three miles from Redstone."

Reeve stood up. "*Redstone?*"

Calen nodded.

Reeve started pacing, taking in the news. "That's over five-hundred miles from where we started."

They stared at each other.

Then Reeve broke into a stunned laugh. "We've been walking for nine hours."

Calen grinned. "Nine hours."

They both looked down at the crooked tent.

Reeve nudged it with his foot.

"Maybe we should have practiced putting it together before we needed to put it together."

They went back to work—one holding poles steady while the other adjusted straps and canvas. It wasn't exactly graceful, but it was faster on their second try. The stakes gave them trouble, and at one point, Reeve tripped over the corner and swore loudly, but eventually things stayed up.

They stepped back to look at it.

"Not bad," Calen said.

Reeve gave it a final tug. "Honestly? Proud of us."

Next came the fire.

Lucky for them, Calen had tons of experience making fires.

He didn't say much—just knelt by the edge of the clearing and started cleaning out a small space, brushing away leaves and scraping down to bare earth. He built the fire base, then opened the flint kit and set it beside him.

He pulled out a pouch with shavings and sprinkled them over the nest. Then he topped them with thin sticks.

Reeve watched closely, crouched nearby. "You've done this before."

"A few dozen times," Calen said, striking the flint.

Sparks leapt, catching the shavings. The moss crackled, then lit, and in seconds the fire was alive.

He added thinner sticks, slowly building it up.

Reeve grinned. "Impressive."

"Thanks," Calen said with a nod. "What's next?"

Dinner was more improvisation than recipe.

A few hunks of dried meat, some trail cheese wrapped in cloth, two flat loaves. They placed a flat rock near the fire to warm things—mostly symbolic, but it made them feel like they were doing something.

One of the cheeses rolled off and landed in the dirt.

Reeve groaned. "That was the one I liked."

Calen picked it up and tilted his head, "It's just a little dirt." He dusted it off and took a bite, handing Reeve his clean piece.

They ate cross-legged on their blankets, food in laps. They didn't talk much. Just the sound of chewing, the flicker of fire, and the first chirps of nighttime insects beginning to stir.

The fire popped softly. The clearing was quiet, except for the soft whir of insects and the occasional rustle of leaves.

Calen leaned back on his hands, looking up. The sky above the treetops was already dark.

Reeve stretched out his legs with a groan. "So...now what?"

Calen looked at him. "What do you mean?"

"I mean...do we just go to bed?"

Calen blinked. "I guess."

Reeve glanced around. "It's not even that late. Just sunset."

They sat there in silence for a beat, both of them slowly realizing the same thing.

"We didn't bring anything to do," Calen said.

"Nope."

"No books, no cards, no dice..."

"No weird travel games."

They looked at the tent, then at the fire, then at each other.

Calen shrugged. "I guess we just...try to sleep?"

Reeve raised an eyebrow. "You think we'll actually *fall asleep*?"

"Probably not."

Reeve sighed and flopped backward onto his blanket, staring at the darkening sky.

"You know," he said, "Redstone is just three miles from here... We're not short on money. We could have gone to town, had a nice dinner, and got an inn room."

Calen blinked, then groaned, tipping his head back. "Gods, why didn't we do that!"

Reeve smirked. "Because we're rugged adventurers."

Calen rolled his eyes. "Right. Rugged, who won't eat dropped cheese..."

They both laughed softly.

The fire crackled. The forest breathed all around them, growing slightly cooler now. Above, the stars were starting to appear.

Calen glanced around. "Where's Liri?"

Reeve sat up a little, looking into the trees. "Huh, I hadn't noticed she was gone."

They both looked up.

Liri was perched high on a branch, legs dangling, wings tucked behind her like folded silk. She fluttered down slowly, landing on a low rock near the fire.

"I've been here the whole time," she said. "I just didn't want to interrupt your very serious dinner and tent building ritual."

Calen blinked. "Right. Sorry. We sort of forgot about you in the chaos."

Liri gave a dismissive wave. "It's not like I can hammer stakes or build fires. You two had it covered."

Reeve smirked. "That's generous."

She looked at the tent. "It's standing, isn't it?"

"Barely." Calen laughed.

Liri sat with her knees drawn up, wings folding tighter, as she looked into the firelight. "Still counts."

For a while, no one spoke.

Then Reeve stirred. "How old is this forest, anyway?"

Liri didn't answer right away.

Calen looked over at her. "You grew up here, right? Do you know how the path works?"

She tilted her head slightly, listening—but still didn't speak.

Calen leaned back on his hands. "I mean...you don't have to tell us everything. But you've seen things. We barely even understand how magic works."

Reeve nodded. "Yeah, I mean, is it something anyone can use, or... is it just built into people like you?"

Liri blinked, then raised her hands in mock surrender. "Woah, guys. What's with all the questions?"

Calen shrugged. "We're just curious."

Reeve added, "You're kind of the first magical person we've really talked to."

Liri sighed dramatically, then rested her chin on her hand. "Fine, but short answers."

Calen leaned in. "How old is the forest?"

Liri rolled her eyes. "Really old."

Reeve scoffed. "What kind of an answer is that?"

"Fine," Liri answered, dusting off her skirt. "It's not as old as the moon, and it wasn't the first forest, but it was one of the first."

Calen and Reeve exchanged a look.

Reeve raised an eyebrow. Calen gave the smallest shrug.

It was the kind of look that said, *What sort of answers do you expect from a fairy?*

Reeve started next. "Okay. How does the path work?"

Liri shifted toward Reeve. "Well, the stone started to say, in a really *boring* way, that the fast-travel magic spell was embedded in the forest so that friendly people could quickly flee from invading Imperial troops. It originally worked with lamps and green flames, but then the fairies figured it out too."

Calen asked, "Is this the same Empire that's threatening Hearthmere?"

Liri suddenly became very serious. "Not just the same Empire, the same *emperor*."

Reeve sat up more now. "I didn't know that. But, the stone said the conflict was five hundred years ago—surely it can't be the same person. Unless—he's a wizard?"

Liri sat up more and leaned in, her voice low. "That's just the thing. He's *not*. Somehow—and no one knows how—he figured out how to stay alive all this time."

"So," Calen joined in, "the troops I ran into. The Dravess... They work for *that* emperor?"

Liri nodded slowly. "There's a reason the Empire controls half the continent."

"Whoa," Calen replied, shaking his head.

"And... magic?" asked Reeve, a bit of hope in his voice, "What is it? Can anyone use it?"

Liri relaxed and shook her shoulders. "Magic? Yes! It's everywhere! It's like air or sunlight—it's all around us." She thought for a moment, then added, "I mean, sometimes it's thicker or thinner in places..."

Reeve nodded. "And anyone can use it?"

"Oh yes," replied Liri, causing Reeve to smile. "Everyone can use it. It's kind of like being able to sing, or dance, or whatever. Some people are just naturally better at it."

Reeve asked. "But, you're made of magic, aren't you?"

Liri nodded, flapping her wings. "And some people are partly made of magic, like Cal—" Her eyes got wide. She'd said too much. "But anyway! Wow, it's so late! You guys should get to bed! I'll see you in the morning!"

And with that, she fluttered away into the forest.

They both sat in silence, staring at the spot where Liri had vanished into the trees.

The fire crackled.

Reeve furrowed his brow "Wait...did she just say...?"

"I think she did," Calen whispered.

Reeve turned to him. "What does that mean?"

Calen shook his head. "I don't know."

"But it would explain a lot of things..." Reeve said, leaning in again.

Calen nodded silently.

They didn't say anything after that.

Just sat there a moment longer, letting the silence stretch between them—neither willing to break it, neither knowing what to say.

Eventually, they began packing things up. Folding blankets. Scooping up loose bits of food. Knocking dirt off utensils and tossing them back in the bag. It was quiet work, half-distracted.

When they had reached the tent, Reeve pulled open the flap and peered inside.

"Whoa," he said softly. "It's darker in here than I expected."

Calen leaned in behind him. "Yeah, I thought we'd get some firelight in, but…"

Reeve stepped inside and held his hands out slightly. "Can we even see anything?"

They both crouched low, trying to feel their way around the limited space—just enough room for two, maybe three bedrolls and their packs. The tent smelled faintly of pine and canvas, and their movements made the fabric rustle softly in the otherwise still clearing.

They fumbled with blankets and bags in the dark, bumping elbows and whispering short directions. It wasn't graceful, but eventually the bedrolls were laid out, packs shoved toward the back corners.

After a while, they were able to lay out and finally get some rest.

Calen farted.

"Calen!" cried Reeve, coughing.

"It doesn't smell," Calen replied quickly.

Reeve sniffed a couple times. "*Thank you!*"

# 17

The forest was already loud when Reeve woke.

Birds were calling from every direction—some voices sharp and familiar, others strange and layered. Insects clicked through the brush, and something far off gave a hollow hoot that rolled under the canopy like a drumbeat. The whole place had been awake long before they were.

He groaned first, dragging an arm over his eyes. "What time is it?"

Calen blinked at the tent wall, where light spilled through the canvas in soft gold. "Morning."

"No kidding," Reeve muttered. "It sounds like a parade out there."

A bird shrieked right outside the tent, and Reeve flinched hard enough to make the bedroll creak. "Ugh—stupid bird. Now I feel like Liri."

He shoved his way out, hauling his bedroll after him. The air was cool and green, smelling of damp leaves and sun-warmed bark—the kind of scent that meant the night had been peaceful enough for the forest to forget them.

They moved quietly through the routine: folding blankets, packing, eating. No talk, just the small sounds of morning.

Liri didn't show up until they were almost done. She drifted down from a high branch, wings beating lazily, brushing her hair with a twig like it was the most natural thing in the world.

"Ready to go?" she asked, yawning. "The path's waiting."

Calen slung his pack over one shoulder. "Yeah. Let's get back to it."

He tightened the last strap and glanced west, toward the road he'd run from the night before—just a dark line behind the trees.

"So much for visiting Redstone," he said under his breath.

Reeve followed his gaze. "We'll come back through someday."

Calen nodded but didn't look convinced.

Liri tilted her head, and the familiar shimmer opened ahead of them. The enchanted path unfolded like a memory—soft light, endless green.

"Door's open," she said.

They stepped through. The forest changed instantly—sound deeper, air heavier. No matter how many times they saw it, Reeve's brain couldn't seem to hold on to what this place really looked like.

They followed the curve of the trail down a hill that hadn't existed a heartbeat ago.

After a while, Reeve slowed. "Hey...we should probably hook the stone up like we did yesterday."

"Oh. Right." Calen unclipped the pouch from his belt and handed it over.

"Still one of my better ideas," Reeve said with a grin, tightening the strap.

They walked in comfortable silence until Reeve spoke again. "You ever think about how weird this is?"

Calen raised an eyebrow. "Only with every step."

"I mean really weird," Reeve said. "We're just walking, but out there—" He gestured vaguely at the forest, at the world beyond it. "People are working, living, doing normal things, and they have no idea this place even exists. A magic road through a magic forest." He shook his head, half-laughing. "It's wild."

Calen smiled faintly. "Sure beats firing up the forge."

They fell quiet again. The sound of their boots and the low rustle of trees filled the space.

After a while, Calen shifted his pack strap and unclipped the belt. "I'm gonna step off for a second," he said, nodding toward the trees, tugging at the front of his pants. "Back in a minute."

Reeve nodded automatically—then something stirred in the back of his mind. Liri's warning. About *falling off*.

Before he could say anything, Liri, who'd been floating nearby, straightened in midair.

"Wait—hold on, let me open a—"

But Calen was already stepping through the brush when a flash of green swallowed him whole.

Reeve froze, heart hammering. "Calen?"

Liri spun toward him, eyes wide. "It's okay! He's fine, really—it's just—" She darted to the spot where Calen had vanished. "I just need to go get him."

Then she turned sharply, pointing at Reeve so hard her tiny hand trembled.

"Listen to me—it's *really, really important* that you don't move. At all. Where you're standing right now? That's where you stay. Don't take one step. Don't even lean."

Reeve nodded fast. "Got it."

"I'll be right back," she said. "Right back."

And with that, she vanished into the brush.

***

Calen stumbled forward, expecting mossy underbrush and dappled light—only to find mud underfoot and the taste of rain in the air.

He stopped abruptly.

Everything was different. He looked up.

The forest no longer glowed. The light was flat, gray. The air hung damp and heavy around him, cool against his skin. Wind shifted through the branches above, making them groan and sway with the low rustle of an approaching storm. Leaves shuddered. Insects fell still.

The soothing, lulling drone of the enchanted forest trail had vanished.

Calen looked down as he felt the cold sprinkle of rain on his skin. The ground was muddy.

He didn't even see the ravine.

He took a step to his right, and the ground gave way beneath him.

He tumbled down the slope with a startled yell.

He hit the incline hard, rolled sideways, caught a root—lost it—bounced off the thick bark of a tree.

He slammed shoulder-first into a fallen log, then slid again, twisting to brace himself.

His knee clipped a rock.

His back scraped rough bark.

A jolt of pain lanced through his side.

He reached out blindly for something—anything—but the world tilted again, and he went down one last time.

His head smacked against a stone.

Then stillness.

He lay there for a moment, breath knocked out of him, body sprawled awkwardly at the bottom of the ravine.

Then, slowly, he sat up.

No pain.

He looked down. No blood. No bruises. His clothes weren't even dirty.

His fingers went instinctively to the stone in his belt.

"Okay," he whispered. "Thank you."

He stood, testing his legs. Everything worked.

He looked around, trying to get his bearings.

"Well," he asked himself, "what now?"

Then he remembered what he'd come here to do.

Right.

He relieved himself against a tree, shaking his head at what had just occurred.

When he turned back, Liri was there.

"Okay," she said, voice calm but firm. "So. Let's not do that in the future."

Calen blinked. "I—yeah. Noted."

"If you need to use the bathroom," she continued, "you tell me. I open a door. You do your business. Easy."

She lifted a hand and made a small circular motion in the air. A person-sized portal shimmered into existence behind her—tighter, more precise than the usual grand arches.

Calen gave a small nod and followed her through.

They emerged back onto the enchanted trail.

Reeve was standing frozen like a statue in an awkward pose—arm up, mouth open, eyes fixed. He looked like he was holding his breath.

Calen stepped forward.

The portal vanished behind him.

Reeve took a deep breath, relaxing. "You good?"

"Yep."

"Did you 'fall off?'" Reeve asked, breathless.

Calen blinked. "Nope," he said, walking past him.

Liri just grinned.

Reeve tossed up his hands. "Fine. Whatever."

They barely took a step forward before Reeve stopped again. "Now I have to go," he admitted.

"Great!" chirped Liri. "That is how you do it!"

She gave Calen a long stare as she slid over and opened a portal for Reeve.

"Just pop back in when you're done."

"Will do," Reeve said, stepping out.

***

They continued the day without incident, taking proper breaks when needed, their rhythm falling into something steady and familiar.

The trail wandered onward under the canopy of green, quiet and unchanging.

At the end of the day, Liri flitted forward, drawing the line of the large entry arch.

The air shimmered.

Beyond it stood the outworld forest—and everything had changed.

There was a clearing outlined with dark trees under a churning sky. Wind rushed past the portal, whistling and cracking. Rain swept sideways, and somewhere in the distance, a rumble of thunder rolled like a warning.

A gust of wind blew in, sharp and cold, while lightning forked through the sky above. The sound came late, booming hard enough to vibrate in their ribs.

Calen stared through the arch, frozen.

Reeve shifted beside him. "Do we...do we close it? Just keep walking?"

They hesitated.

Another gust of wind tore through the gap, scattering outworld leaves down the enchanted path behind them.

"I mean, we're tired," Reeve said. "We've probably walked as far or farther than we did yesterday."

Calen nodded slowly. "I don't know how long we can keep going."

"We could test it," Reeve offered. "See how far we get before we're too worn out."

Calen's voice was low. "And then what? We reach the point where we're too drained to even set up the tent?"

Reeve didn't answer.

The rain picked up.

Liri hovered at the edge of the arch, her expression unreadable. She looked at them both at once, then said lightly, "I'll see you boys tomorrow." With a flick of her hand, she drew the arch forward. It swept over them in a blink and sealed before they could protest.

Rain hit hard—cold and fast, like needles against their skin. The wind shoved them from the side, nearly knocking Calen off balance. He gritted his teeth and pulled his cloak tighter. It was already soaked.

"Go!" he shouted over the noise.

They ran forward into the clearing, boots slipping on wet grass. Calen dropped his pack with a heavy thud and tore at the tent straps.

The sky opened up.

Sheets of water fell in thick curtains, flattening the grass around them. The wind howled through the trees, bending and breaking branches, tearing leaves loose and whipping them into the clearing.

Thunder cracked overhead—loud enough to make Reeve flinch. "This is so bad!" he yelled. "I don't think this is going to hold!"

"Just keep going!"

They wrestled with the canvas, trying to force the poles into place as the tent flapped violently between them. Rain soaked everything—bags, clothes, hands. Calen could barely feel his fingers. He was breathing fast, blinking water from his eyes, struggling to keep the panic from breaking through.

The fabric snapped like a sail. One of the poles clattered to the ground.

Reeve cursed. "We need to call Liri! We need to get out of here!"

"She's gone!" Calen snapped. "She already left!"

Another burst of wind rocked the clearing. The tent nearly tore loose from Calen's grip.

He couldn't catch his breath.

Not just from the cold, or the fight with the tent—but from something deeper. A memory.

The same wind. The same sky.

A tornado had taken nearly half his town only months before.

He dropped to one knee and shoved the final stake into the ground.

"Get inside!"

They forced themselves through the flap and yanked it shut behind them.

Inside, it was pitch black.

The tent shook violently around them, the fabric snapping and groaning like it might tear apart. Rain pelted the outside in steady waves, and the roar of the wind made it feel like they were inside a drum. Water pooled near the edges, seeping under the floor tarp. Every gust sent a jolt through the walls.

Reeve scrambled to one corner, soaked and shivering. "I don't think this is going to hold!" he shouted, but the sound barely carried.

Calen ducked low, trying to breathe. His heart was pounding. His cloak clung to him, heavy and cold, and his hair was plastered to his forehead. He couldn't see anything—just blackness and noise and the violent push of air around fabric.

"What do we do?" Reeve asked.

Calen didn't answer.

He remembered the trail, the feeling of protection. He remembered how his house hadn't been touched by the storm.

His hand found the belt between them, still clipped in place. He searched hand over hand for the pouch, the stone.

The tent buckled again.

Calen felt along the side of the tent, an inside seam, where there was a pocket. He quickly shoved the stone inside.

At first, nothing.

Then, slowly, the wind began to dull. The fabric began to settle. The roar outside continued, but inside, the air began to still. The floor stopped quivering. Even the cold began to lift, little by little.

Reeve looked around. "Wait!" he yelled, then must have realized he could hear his own voice clearly now. Then, in a normal volume, he said, "Wait...is it over?"

Calen was still catching his breath.

Reeve crawled forward and cracked the flap just enough to peek outside. Rain blasted in sideways, trees bent under the wind.

"It's worse," he said. "It's way worse than before."

He turned. "Why isn't the tent moving?"

Calen stared at the inner pocket. "It's the stone."

They didn't speak for a while.

The storm raged just beyond the thin canvas, but inside, the silence was strange—like being back on the enchanted trail.

Reeve sat back, breathing slowly. Calen stayed where he was, shoulders rising and falling, his damp hair still clinging to his face.

Then Reeve frowned slightly. "It's warmer in here."

Calen blinked. He hadn't noticed it at first, but he could feel it now too. The biting chill was gone. The air felt comfortable—mild, almost cozy.

Reeve reached up and touched his shirt. "My clothes are almost dry."

Calen glanced at his own. The edges of his sleeves, once dripping, were only just damp. The floor beneath them, where water had been pooled seconds before, was no longer wet. The fabric was dry to the touch.

He looked at the pocket again.

Reeve let out a breath. "That thing is invincible."

Calen didn't answer right away. He just sat still, listening to the muffled storm and feeling the warmth slowly spreading through the fabric around him.

They sat in the dark for a while, listening to the wind buffet the tent walls, though none of it touched them now.

Reeve shifted, his voice low and tired. "You hungry?"

"Yeah," Calen said quietly. "But I don't know how to find anything the way we tossed everything in here."

They dug through their pockets by touch, hands fumbling over damp fabric and loose straps. Somewhere, Calen found a wrapped heal of bread. Reeve found a large lump of cheese. It was awkward trying to sort supplies without being able to see.

Reeve gave a frustrated sigh. "If only we had some light..."

A golden glow filled the tent.

The pouch where Calen had stored the stone was lit from within, casting a hazy illumination through the walls of the tent.

Reeve sat up. "Okay, that's new."

Calen stared at the glow.

Then he heard it.

"Since I saved you today—twice," came the warm, old voice of the stone, "perhaps you might reciprocate some kindness and allow me to speak for once."

Calen didn't answer right away.

He just looked at the glowing pocket.

He looked over to Reeve. "It's talking again."

Reeve leaned in. "What's it saying? I can't hear it anymore."

"Nothing yet," Calen said, moving closer. He asked the stone, "What is it?"

"Just some conversation. Is that too much to ask?" the stone replied kindly.

Calen shifted even closer to the glow. "Okay, but some questions first."

"As you wish," the stone replied.

Calen hesitated. "Are you alive?"

The answer came without pause. "I think so."

Calen looked at Reeve. "It said he thinks so."

Reeve pressed his lips together. "That's not comforting."

Calen ignored him and turned back to the stone, "Have you always been in the stone?"

"I can't remember."

"Were you once...someone?"

"I don't know that either. I woke up in the riverbed when I met you."

Calen tilted his head slightly. "Do you remember anything before being in the stone?"

"I remember facts, knowledge. But not experiences. Not of my own, anyway. I know things—but I don't remember living them or seeing them."

Calen relayed it almost word for word to Reeve.

The other boy frowned. "So, it's like a library—that thinks?"

Calen leaned back a little. "Do you know who created you?"

There was a pause. "No."

Calen's eyes narrowed slightly. "Hmm," he said aloud, then added to himself, "That's interesting because Liri said that you were part of the castle of the Wizards Council. You should know that. And I believe her."

He didn't press further.

"Do you sleep?" he asked instead. "When you're not talking?"

"Yes, sometimes I lose awareness entirely. Especially when the stone is tired, like when you first got to Hearthmere."

Calen nodded slowly and relayed the information to Reeve.

Reeve scratched the back of his head. "Weird. But you said—uh he said, when the stone is tired, but isn't *he*—the stone?"

Calen understood the distinction and asked the stone.

"I am not the stone; I just inhabit the stone. Although I am within, I don't control or have knowledge of its workings."

Calen thought about this. How was he able to activate the spell that transported him, and how was he able to choose the location?

"But what about when you transported me?" he asked.

"For that one time, yes. And perhaps I could muster some other small doings, but in general, no. I have no control. The stone's powers are reflexive. There's a system inside—spells arranged, sorted, embedded. I don't select them. They respond as needed. There are likely thousands."

After relaying this news to Reeve, Calen turned to the stone.

"How come Reeve could hear you on the fast-travel trail, but not now?"

"Your guess is as good as mine. Perhaps it's the saturation of magic on the path—some kind of auditory enhancement?"

"Do you recognize Liri? Or other fae?"

"I know none of them specifically," the stone said. "But I am aware of many fae. And other beings like her. Mystical, old, frequently dangerous to men."

After Calen passed that along, Reeve gave a snort. "Sounds like her. She almost got us killed kicking us out into this storm."

Calen asked, "Have you spoken to anyone before now? Before me?"

"No."

"Are you bound to me now?" Calen asked next.

"No. Whoever carries the stone receives its protection, but there is no binding. Binding spells are for the most advanced wizards. Very tricky. Often dangerous."

"Can you feel what I feel?"

"No, but I observe you. I can guess, most of the time."

"What happens if I lose you?"

"Then I am lost."

That answer hit Calen heavier than the others.

Calen didn't speak for a moment after relaying it to Reeve.

The other boy thought for a moment. "So, if we were to set him down...he could be lost forever?"

Calen nodded, thinking. "Can you teach me magic?" he asked the stone.

"A little. If there's something you want to learn, I can help where I can."

Calen smiled faintly. "That's a yes."

Reeve perked up. "Wait, really?"

"That's what he said..." Calen's face suddenly changed. He asked the stone, "Wait, are you an 'it' or a 'he'"?"

"'He' is fine."

Then to Reeve. "He says he's a he."

Reeve exhaled. "Finally. That one was hurting my brain."

Calen thought for a moment, then said, "Wait, is there a limit to your protection?"

"I can protect something roughly the size of a house—maybe less, depending on the strain. If I'm overwhelmed, the magic depletes. It refills from ambient magic, but that takes time."

Calen looked over to Reeve. "The shield runs out if you use it too long."

Reeve ran his hand against the enchanted tent wall. "Good to know."

"He can hear me, right?" Reeve asked.

Calen nodded.

"If you're not the stone...could you leave it?"

"That is what I'm hoping to learn in the valley. If I could gain a body there, then I could be as free as either one of you."

Silence settled again.

Then Calen shifted slightly, his voice quiet but deliberate. "Do you know what I am?"

Reeve's eyes widened, and he shifted forward slowly as if to hear better.

The stone's tone changed—lower, heavier. "I want you to think carefully before you ask me that again."

Calen squinted and tilted his head, confused.

The stone continued, "You may still be under a protective spell—something woven to shield your true nature from harm. If you force the truth to the surface, that shield might fall."

"Imagine you were a vampire," he continued, "and you didn't know. So long as you were nameless, you walked freely in the daylight. But the moment you knew—truly knew—the sun would burn you, and you'd be bound to the night forever."

The stone paused. "You could be confined to the forest, like Liri..."

Calen sat very still.

Reeve's patience ran dry. "Well? What did he say?"

Calen looked over to Reeve, unable to keep the sadness from his face.

"He said I need to think before I ask that again. That the answers might have consequences."

"Consequences?" asked Reeve.

"Yeah, like, I could be trapped in the forest, kind of like Liri."

He thought for a moment. "Yes, she can leave, but she hates it, and it makes her weaker..."

"And that could happen if you know what you are?" Reeve asked quietly.

"Yeah, I guess it could."

"Anything else, young man?" the stone asked.

"No, I guess that's it.." He looked at Reeve.

Reeve shook his head. "That's it."

The stone shimmered in his pocket.

"It seems that's all I have too. Talking like this is actually very tiring for me, but I do enjoy it. If you want the light out, just touch the stone again."

After that, there wasn't much to say, so they made their beds, now dry and warm, and fell asleep to the sound of rain they couldn't feel and wind that couldn't reach them.

***

Calen woke first.

The air was still. Too still. No birdsong, no rustle of branches overhead—just the soft snoring of Reeve beside him and the faint scent of damp soil.

For a long moment, he lay motionless, watching the golden light filter through the canvas walls of the tent. For a few more minutes, they were tucked safely in their little cocoon of warmth, the chaos of the night held at bay by canvas and sleep.

He undid the flap and stepped outside into silence.

And destruction.

The clearing was a mess of broken branches and scattered leaves, and about thirty feet away, a massive tree had fallen, its trunk split lengthwise. One branch—big enough to crush a wagon—was lodged just shy of their tent's edge. A few more feet, and they would have been flattened in their sleep.

He heard Reeve stir behind him. "Shit."

Reeve stumbled out like a baby deer, rubbing his eyes. He followed Calen's gaze and went still. "That wasn't there yesterday."

"No," Calen said. "It wasn't."

Reeve looked over the destruction. "I thought this forest was enchanted," he said. "Protected."

A voice spoke from the tree line. "Storms are part of nature."

They both turned.

Liri flitted over and perched on a nearby branch. Her wings shimmered faintly where the light caught them. She looked completely unaffected, as if she'd spent the night somewhere warm and dry.

"You look well-rested," she added.

Reeve crossed his arms. "No thanks to you."

"What do you mean?" she asked, pouting like her feelings were hurt.

"You dumped us in the rain!" Reeve began removing their gear from the tent. There wasn't much camp to pack.

Liri followed him with her eyes. "I don't do wet. My hair poofs."

"Oh, no," Reeve said dryly. "Not the poof."

"It's tragic." She sighed. "And you're welcome, by the way."

"For what?"

"For not staying and screaming the whole night. I'm adorable, but I'm not exactly calming in a crisis."

Reeve tossed her a look. "You think abandoning us makes you less annoying?"

She shrugged. "Less noisy, at least."

Calen stepped out of the tent and glanced between them.

"She's explaining how leaving us to die was actually charity," Reeve said, tearing down the tent.

"Oh, good," Calen said. "That clears it up."

Liri smiled sweetly. "See? He gets it."

Reeve shook his head and folded the tent. "Next time there's a storm, I vote we tie her to a tree."

"You'd miss me," she said, walking along the branch like a tightrope walker.

"Not if the tree's far enough away." Reeve said, tying the last flap of his pack. "We're moving faster than I expected, and we—"

"You're welcome," Liri chimed in, arms wide and smiling.

"As I was saying," Reeve said. "We have some extra time. We could take a look around. Try to figure out where we are."

Calen glanced up at the tree line. The destruction seemed to stitch in every direction, the storm having carved through everything without much care.

"I don't think there'll be much sightseeing to do around here today," he said, eyeing the fallen tree again. "We should just keep going." He handed Reeve a sandwich he'd just made.

"Very well!" Liri sang. She floated over before them. "Make sure you're hooked up to your tether-buddy!"

Calen clicked the spare belt onto Reeve's and then his own as Liri opened the portal to the enchanted path.

He looked around one last time and stepped through.

***

Reeve adjusted his pack over his shoulder. "So, how far are we, really? From Ultara Orralis?"

Calen shook his head. "No idea."

"Come on. We did, what, five hundred miles the first day?"

"Roughly. But yesterday...?" he said, thinking. "That storm could have slowed us down. Or sped us up. There's no way to tell."

"So, we're guessing."

Calen shrugged.

Reeve sighed and looked up at Liri, drifting slightly ahead of them. "Hey. Fairy girl. Any idea of how far we've got left?"

There was a pause.

Then her voice came drifting back, dripping with offence. "Fairy girl? Okay, Boy-who-smells-like-horses, *now* you want my help?"

Reeve blinked.

Calen laughed.

They both glared at him.

She continued, "Now you're all *'please, Liri, use your magical insights, you glittering beacon of wisdom.'* Funny how that works."

Reeve retorted, "The glittering beacon of wisdom would be the stone."

Calen closed his eyes briefly, trying not to smile. He reached over and slipped his fingers in the stone's pouch. "How far now to Ultara Orralis?"

"You'll arrive on the third day, if you keep this pace," he replied wisely.

Reeve smiled. He could hear the stone again.

He turned to Liri, repeating. "Three days, if we keep this pace."

She turned up her nose and slowly floated ahead without a word, her glow flickering in silent protest.

Calen watched her drift forward, then adjusted the strap on his right shoulder.

"Well," he said, "looks like we've got three days ahead of us."

# 18

Suldric woke with a jolt, sweat on his chest and forehead. He half-sat up before collapsing back onto the pillow, breath shallow, ribs tight.

The room was dark, but he saw everything with perfect clarity—the chipped edge of the washbasin, the hairline cracks in the ceiling, the unlit candle on the far table that he never touched.

Fragments of the dream clung to him like cobwebs.

Blood on the ceiling. Screams.

Wet footprints smearing the stone floor.

A knife sliding between his ribs—slow, deliberate, almost reverent.

He reached down and touched one of the many scars across his chest, thumb tracing the raised seam of memory. Then he turned his head to the window. No light through the blinds. Still night. Still raining.

Suldric sat on the edge of the bed, shirtless, sweat clinging to his skin in a slow crawl.

The air in the room was heavy—thick with heat, and thick with silence.

He could see perfectly, thanks to his new talents. The dark had stopped being a barrier. Now, it was something like home.

He could fade into it now—vanish into shadow until no one could see him. Not even the magic-sensing guards that patrolled the city.

A basin sat on the table across from him, a faint sheen on the water clinging to its rim. Coins rested beside a folded note, the parchment beginning to curl from the humidity.

He reached for the note.

The parchment was softened from being folded and unfolded too many times. He smoothed it flat against his knee.

The handwriting was precise, almost mechanical. No greeting. No signature.

*The price remains the same.*

*One week left. Then it's gone.*

Below that, a number. It hadn't changed.

He stared at it for a long time.

His jaw ached from clenching. He hadn't noticed until just now. He dragged a magic laced finger across his jaw. The pain faded.

He let the note slip from his fingers and watched it float to the floor.

His mind drifted back to the basement.

It had smelled like candle wax and old paper. It had taken weeks to find. Threats had been made, bribes had been paid. Now, it was his turn.

Books were stacked in uneven towers, crammed onto narrow shelves, or left open on the floor in strange arrangements. Not all of them were written in ink.

The goblin hadn't greeted him. Just raised a lantern, blinked once, and blew it out. Neither of them needed it to see.

Suldric followed the goblin deeper down. Wooden stairs gave way to stone. The air cooled, thick with dust and silence.

The book wasn't on display. It wasn't even shelved. It had been hidden under a stone in the floor, wrapped in oilcloth and animal skins.

When the goblin unwrapped it, the room shifted, and the unmistakable pull of black magic rippled through the air. Ancient. Hungry.

Suldric knew it instantly. This was what he'd been searching for. Anything to advance his knowledge.

All black magic materials were considered highly criminal and carried the punishment of death. News of a tomb like this could start an inquisition.

And it was almost in his possession.

He'd thought about stealing it, of course.

But this goblin wasn't some back-alley charlatan hawking hexes and love dust. This one was old. Quiet. Patient.

There were wards to the walls that Suldric didn't recognize—magic older than anything the Empire taught. Maybe older than the Empire itself.

And the goblin watched him like he already knew what Suldric would decide. Like he'd seen a hundred other desperate mages make the same calculations and leave with lighter pockets or heavier guilt.

Suldric hadn't even reached for it. He knew better.

A loud noise from the city behind him brought him back to the room and the note on the floor.

Suldric stood and began to pace.

The sweat hadn't cooled. It was still clinging to him, soaking the waistband of his shorts, running down the curve of his spine.

He ran a hand over his face and played with the hoop in his left ear. He walked across the room to the chest of drawers and picked up the original letter.

Two payment options.

The first: a sum so high, he was sure it had been a mistake.

The second: six names in red ink. No explanation. Just the names.

He'd already been working for weeks, quietly selling his talents and his love to people who didn't ask questions. Exploiting their desires. Manipulating their fears. Smiling when he had to. Staying silent when it mattered.

Healing wounds that were unhealable.

Fixing things only he could.

A whispered word here, a well-timed glance there.

He left with gold, jewels, secrets—sometimes more.

Every job brought him closer to exposure. And still, the total barely scratched the surface of what the goblin had asked.

He hadn't resorted to murder. Not yet.

But that list was starting to look like the only way.

He told himself—more often lately—that he didn't need the book.

He'd made it this far. Learned more than most mages ever would. He could keep going without it.

Find another path. A safer one.

Find a different book. Buy a home—or a castle with the riches he'd amassed.

He could pay for protection, discretion, servants, silence.

He could start a cult if he wanted to.

But the lie never held for long.

Because he knew—deep in the quiet core of him—that this wasn't about survival anymore. It was about *becoming something more*. And that book was the next step.

He picked up the dagger from the table, placed his hand flat beside the coins, and in one swift motion, brought the blade down.

All four fingers came off cleanly.

They hit the wood with a soft, wet sound. Blood poured freely across the table's edge.

He watched them bleed for a while, as if the answers to his questions would appear there.

Then, slowly—methodically—he picked up each severed finger and pressed it back into place.

The wounds healed instantly. The blood evaporated into smoke.

He exhaled once through his nose.

Then he reached for the original note again.

Six names.

None of them familiar.

Well, maybe one.

He squinted, just slightly. A memory tugged, just out of reach.

He stared harder. Slowed his breathing.

If he was going to do what he was thinking about doing, he had to be sure.

And for that, he'd have to go to the GutterGlass Sideshow Underground.

Back to Zesty Matilda.

The madam always insisted on seeing the goods before she'd connect you with a client. And Suldric had shown her—just once—back when he'd needed access to a noblewoman's jewel collection and didn't feel like starting a war to get it.

The entire ordeal had been humiliating. Loud. Perfumed. Moist.

He'd promised himself he'd never go back.

And yet here he was, and it would have closed nearly two hours ago.

It wouldn't open again until the following night.

Suldric sat back in the chair, listening to the rain.

Sixteen hours.

Give or take.

He would have to wait.

***

That evening, the air in the room was thick—warm like breath on skin. The rain had slowed to a lazy patter against the high window, but the heat hadn't broken. Suldric stood shirtless in front of the previously warped mirror. He had fixed it, of course. His power over aesthetics was near unlimited.

His hair was still wet from the shower. He'd been waiting all day, and now it was time to perform.

He ran long fingers through his hair. Magic shimmered along the strands, sliding them into place like water over stone. The spell made everything just a little too perfect—enough to catch the eye and make someone forget what they were about to say.

Suldric stared at his reflection for a long time. He removed the shirt from the chair near him and pulled it on. He ran his hand along the fabric, and it flicked from black to crimson to deep, sharp sapphire. He studied each color critically, let the blue settle in, then whispered to himself. Leaning in, he ran a finger across his lips; they darkened, flushed with enough color to suggest that something obscene had just ended—or was just about to begin.

His pants were already tight, but he dragged his fingers slowly, deliberately along the seams. The fabric shifted under his touch—adjusting, tightening, climbing. The waistband lowered, hugging his hips, and the back seam pulled snug within the cleft of his ass. Just enough stretch, just enough definition. It was uncomfortable, but the front of his pants left no doubt in any onlooker: he was a big boy.

Not subtle. Not tasteful. Intentional.

He stepped into his boots and reached for the dagger on the dresser—slim and dark enough to vanish in shadow. He slipped it in its usual place up his left sleeve. The other, smaller one, he secured in a sheath at his right ankle. He never left without both.

Then came the finishing touch.

He picked up a pin from the dresser and stabbed his finger. He rubbed the blood into his palms, then raised his hands and ran them slightly along the curve of his neck, behind his ears, and across his bare chest. The magic spread with every movement—warm, invisible, intoxicating. A slow-blooming spell. It compelled a deep desire, but the target's face needed to be within inches of his skin.

Black magic was a close-quarters art—intimate, invasive. It didn't reach. It took.

He gave himself one last look in the mirror, further buttoning his shirt.

Then he left.

The stairs would have creaked under his boots as he descended to street level, but they didn't. The door closed behind him without the usual thud.

The street outside was cobbled and wet, slick with oil and old rain. Lamplight flickered—some gas fed, others glowing with faint magical runes etched into iron castings. A carriage clattered past, wheels loud against stone, the driver shouting at someone in the road. On one side of the street, a man sat huddled under a canvas awning, coughing into his coat. On the other, a woman in fox fur and satin gloves was laughing too loudly at a joke no one else heard.

Suldric moved through it all like a mist—between classes, between glances.

He passed three districts, two guard stations, and one drunk noble being sick behind a fountain. The buildings changed—stone giving way to brick, then to plaster, then brick again.

Eventually, the street narrowed. The lights dimmed. The night thickened with the scent of perfume, sweat, and street smoke.

Here, the lamps burned lower and redder—intentional, suggestive. Music spilled from open doorways—strings, drums, distant singing. Somewhere, a woman screamed in delight or pain. A shirtless man stumbled past him, laughing with his arms around two companions.

The order of the city was lost. Here, there was only heat and appetite.

He passed bars, bordellos, and the many lines at food carts.

Then he saw it half hidden by a leaning alley wall: the cracked red door. Brass gargoyle knocker with its tongue out.

As he approached the door, a narrow slit scraped open.

"Who is it?"

Suldric beamed. His entire face softened, brightened, lit up like someone had just offered him dessert.

"Oh, come on, you know me!"

A pause. Then a grin behind the slit.

"Pony?"

"Evening, Bucket."

The door flew open so fast it rattled in its frame.

"Ha! Would you look at this! Ladies are done for tonight!"

Bucket beamed—all muscle and joy, towering at least two heads over Suldric. He was built like a siege engine wrapped in skin, with a thick, barrel chest and little pointed ears that hinted that he wasn't all human and twitched when he got excited—which was apparently *right now.*

He didn't hesitate, just swept Suldric into a full-body bear hug that cracked something in Suldric's spine and lifted his boots three inches off the floor.

"You look gorgeous, you wicked little bastard."

"*I always do*," Suldric purred into his chest.

Bucket laughed, loud and stupid-happy, and set him down with a thump.

"Zesty's going to lose her *mind*. She misses you!" he gushed.

"Yes, but I missed *you*!" Suldric flirted.

"Oh, you charmer! I could just eat you up!" Bucket held a hand over his face.

"Promise?" Suldric replied, rubbing his hand over Bucket's giant pectoral.

Bucket giggled like a schoolgirl.

"Well, get in there, Pony. The nights've been boring without you!"

Suldric gave him a wide smile and sauntered into the brothel.

The velvet curtain inside muffled the noise from the street like a secret. The moment it fell back into place behind him, the world changed.

This wasn't a tavern with a back room. It wasn't some pleasure house for soldiers on leave. The GutterGlass, or "GG," catered to the wealthy, the powerful, the discreet. It was invitation-only. You didn't walk in off the street. You were brought. Vouched for. Or someone owed someone enough to get them past Bucket.

It had been a pain to infiltrate, but money flowed here like cheap wine.

A wave of warm-air rolled over him—scented with jasmine, smoke, and something sugary and low-burning. The music inside was slow, dreamlike. Laughter echoed from behind curtains. He heard a man moaning from a back room.

Suldric stepped into it like he owned it.

Because tonight, he did.

Suldric had barely taken three steps into the lounge when the girls saw him.

A cluster of them peeled away from a velvet dais, all sheer fabrics and bare legs, bangles clinking like soft wind chimes. They moved as one—fluid, delighted, dangerous in their affection.

"Pony!" one of them squealed.

"You didn't tell us you were coming," another pouted.

He gave them a glowing, performative smile just before they reached him—and then they were on him.

Soft hands slid along his shoulders, his chest, his waist, the front of his pants. One nuzzled into his neck, exhaling with a sigh as if he were made of cinnamon. Another cupped his ass with both hands and squeezed.

"You always smell so good," one whispered, licking just below his ear.

"You taste even better," another mused, kissing his collarbone.

Suldric laughed—low and playful—tilting his head to let them press closer. His hands moved among them with practiced ease, stroking hair, waist, and cheek.

"Ladies, you're spoiling me."

"That's the point," someone whispered and kissed his lips.

One of the girls had already undone all the buttons on his shirt when a sharp voice cut through the room like a whip crack.

"Pony, *darling*. If the upholstery stains, I'm sending you the bill!"

The girls scattered with practiced grace—laughing, sighing, a few casting looks over their shoulders like they'd only *just* gotten started.

Zesty stood at the top of the stairs, framed by dark velvet and low golden light. She was tall, draped in something black and glossy with a neckline that defied physics and sleeves like knives. Her eyes were lined in black, her mouth painted like sin. She looked like she hadn't slept in two decades and would never apologize for it.

"Pony," she repeated, "you better be here to make money or spend it, but I won't have you stirring up drama *again*."

"Zesty!" Suldric beamed, buttoning his shirt and pants. "Just the lady I've come to see!"

"Which means you're about to make my life hell."

She didn't sound mad. She sounded *resigned*. And maybe just a little bit entertained.

Zesty descended halfway down the staircase, heels tapping like punctuation.

"Upstairs, Pony. To my office. Before you start humping the furniture."

She turned and disappeared behind the curtain before he could reply.

Suldric gave all who were watching a cheeky wink, adjusted his collar like it was armor, and followed.

The hallway above was quieter—thick carpets, closed doors, the faint rustle of silk and muffled gasps behind them. Her office door was already open. He stepped in.

The room smelled like cloves, old perfume, and ink. Books stacked in messy piles, scrolls spilling out of drawers, candles leaning in drunken angles across a desk cluttered with vials and ledgers.

Zesty was pouring herself a drink.

"You caused me quite a bit of trouble," she said, not looking at him. "When the heiress's jewels went missing the night after your visit—a lot of fingers were pointed."

She sipped, then turned to face him. "You sure you don't know what happened to them?"

Suldric smiled sweetly. "Absolutely not."

Zesty snorted, "Uh-huh..."

She leaned across her desk. "You know she cried for hours. Said you made her feel 'seen.' That she must see you again. But, of course, I have no idea how to reach you once you...depart."

"I have that effect on women," Suldric said, as if he was sure he was having that effect right now.

"You also have a tendency to make them lose things...like jewelry worth more than this entire building. And not for the first time."

He stood slightly and tossed a round pouch. It slid across the wood and came to rest near her fingertips.

Zesty didn't move for a beat. Then she set down her glass, untied the pouch, and poured the contents out on the desk. Gold coins—heavy, old.

She counted slowly, which took some time, with long fingers and long silences.

"Well," she said at last, sweeping the coins into an open drawer and tossing back the pouch. "I consider that matter to be closed."

She looked up. Her eyes were sharp again, but not angry. Just *interested*.

"What can I help you with tonight, Pony?"

Suldric's smiled faded—not abruptly, but in pieces. Like a candle burning out slowly. His shoulders shifted. The glimmer in his eyes dulled—not gone, just...replaced. And what replaced it was something far colder. *Still beautiful*, but not meant to be looked at for long.

Zesty noticed immediately. Her expression didn't change, but the air between them tightened.

"Discretion," he said, "and information."

Zesty leaned back slightly, one brow rising. Her tone stayed light, but it had lost all its playfulness.

"That's awfully vague. I'll need to know what kind of arrangement you're after. My clients know I'm a beacon of discretion."

He didn't blink. "The scope is...considerable."

Zesty tapped the desk with her fingernail. "Oh."

A silence stretched between them, then she nodded—slowly, once. "I see."

He reached into his pocket and pulled out a list he'd written based on the names the goblin had given him. He slid it across the table with two fingers.

"I need to know who these people are," he said, "and where I can find them."

Zesty reached for the paper. No dramatic pause, no hesitation—just a fluid, practiced motion. She picked it up like it was laced with something unclean and unfolded it.

Her eyes scanned the list once. Then again.

She didn't speak.

She folded the paper neatly, placed it in her bra, and looked him square in the eyes.

"How soon?"

"As soon as possible."

She nodded once—no sarcasm, no smirk, no sass. Just a calculation clicking into place behind her eyes.

She tapped the desk a few times with her fingernail.

"Pony...some of these people... They don't just kill you. They peel you apart slow and mail the pieces to your friends."

He lowered his eyes—not in shame, but with the kind of heaviness that settles in the spine when you've already decided something you can't take back.

"I know."

She looked at him. "This is gonna cost you." She nodded toward her desk drawer. "And a lot more than *this*."

He nodded.

She knew he was good for it.

"I'll have the information, day after tomorrow."

He nodded again, standing. And just for a heartbeat—his mask slipped.

Zesty saw it.

The fear.

Buried, brief, but real.

"You don't have to do this—whatever this is, kid," she said quietly.

He met her eyes. No smile. No act.

"Actually, I do."

He turned and left.

***

The rain had picked back up sometime after midnight. Now, it pattered softly against the window, distant and lazy, as if the city were settling in for something it didn't want to name.

Suldric sat cross-legged on the bed, shirtless, a half-finished glass of dark liquor on the table beside him. The parchment note lay open in his lap. Creased once, then twice. The six names written now had details under them—Zesty's hand, neat and efficient. Occupations. Habits. Schedules. Weaknesses.

He read them again, slowly this time, tasting the shape of each life.

"Six people in three and a half days," he mused, almost admiring the ridiculousness of it. He set the letter aside and fell back, letting the pillow catch him.

She'd only asked for a fourth of what he'd been ready to pay.

Zesty, ever the queen of underworld flair, had played her part like she always did upon delivery—arched eyebrows, dramatic pauses, that little speech about "the risks, Pony." And he'd let her say it. Let her think it was high-stakes. Let her count coins slowly, pretending not to be impressed.

He chuckled to himself now, a little dry sound in the quiet.

"She thought she took me for a ride."

He'd been ready to give her four times that amount.

He could easily make it up again in a few months if needed.

No amount of money mattered now. Only the book. Only the list. Only the ticking clock.

Three and a half days.

He'd have to start tonight.

He sat up again and dragged the note back into his lap. No hesitation this time, just calculation. This sixth name was totally out—he had no idea where to begin. He didn't know these people even existed before now.

He skimmed the others. The archivist was too well-shielded, and the merchant was never alone. The bureaucrat, though…

Halvar Dren. Minister of Trade Regulation.

Suldric tapped the name with the pad of his finger. Normal hours. Same route. Predictable. A man who felt safe wrapped in his routine.

That made him first.

***

The streets were quiet in Feather Falls—a quiet slope on the eastern side of Ultara—the kind of quiet that came with deep confidence, the belief that money alone could ward off danger. The houses weren't houses, but estates, with whitewashed stone, arched windows, and glowing oil lanterns that never flickered.

No guards. No wards that mattered.

Suldric stood at the edge of the street, head tilted back, letting the rain fall against his face. For a moment, he simply breathed—then he let the magic slip in.

The shadows didn't just wrap around him. They *sank into him*. Into his skin, his bones, his breath. His outline blurred. His heartbeat softened. His presence vanished.

He crossed the street without hurry. Lifted a hand. Touched the front door.

The lock opened to him with a sound like a polite sigh.

He opened the door without making noise and stepped into silence. Somewhere below, soft music. A servant, maybe two. But they wouldn't see him. Wouldn't feel him. He moved like air, like fog, like something already forgotten. Up the staircase.

He found the door.

Inside, the room was warm and gilded—paneled in dark wood, embroidered drapes half-drawn. The man inside lay sprawled across a velvet coverlet, bare chested, silk nightclothes tangled around his legs, his mouth slightly open.

Halvar Dren.

Minister of Trade Regulation—and probably not friendly to goblin trade.

Dreaming of coin, probably. Or power.

Suldric stepped forward and let the invisibility melt away. It was unnecessary now.

He climbed into bed. Slowly, deliberately. No sound.

The man stirred just slightly—turned his head—and Suldric was on him.

A hand to his chest. A leg across his hips.

He curled around him like a lover, a serpent, a spell made flesh.

Halvar gasped, but no sound came out.

The life didn't leave him in a scream. It left him in waves.

Suldric pressed his body flush against him, every inch connecting, consuming, drawing in. Heat rushed up through his spine—power, rich and terrible, flooding every cell, sharpening every nerve.

His lips brushed the man's ear as the last breath left him.

Not a kiss. Just closeness. Intimacy.

And then...stillness.

What remained of the minister was shriveled—collapsed in on itself, blackened and lifeless, like a rose left in smoke.

Suldric stood. Adjusted his shirt. Slipped through a side hallway, past the empty kitchen, out the servant's door and into the night.

He didn't look back.

Didn't slow down.

Didn't stop until he was back in his room.

Then he sat, cross-legged again, as before.

"That was too easy."

He picked up the goblin's first letter, as if to brag to it.

The minister's name—Halvar Dren—no longer shimmered in red. Now it was ink. Black, neat, and struck through with a single line.

Final. Clean.

One down.

Suldric let the paper fall back to the bed and sat with it, breathing in the aftershock of the spell. His heart had slowed, but everything else buzzed—vision clear, skin sharp, thoughts slicing through fog like polished steel.

No tremble. No guilt. Not even a flicker of hesitation. Just...clarity.

He closed his eyes and replayed the kill—not the death, but the *method*. The way his skin had pressed into the target, the way the magic had responded. It had moved faster than expected. More eagerly.

The spell in the book—rudimentary, now that he thought of it—called for *full body contact.*

As if the closeness itself was the trigger.

But that wasn't quite right.

*It was connection.*

The skin didn't need to cover every inch. The current had run through his hands first; maybe that would be enough next time.

*Arms? Chest to back? Maybe even just one hand on the back, the chest alone?*

He opened his eyes again, already cataloging changes. His breathing was deeper. His senses sharper. Even his skin felt tighter, more reactive.

So much power.

He looked down at his hands, flexed them slowly.

"I can do it cleaner next time."

***

The café wasn't far from the central plaza, tucked beneath an overhang of flowering stonework and wrought iron railings that still glistened with fresh dew. The storm had broken right after dawn, and the sky now was a flawless blue, the last of the clouds fading from view in the east. It seemed a joke almost, considering the night's work.

Suldric sat beneath a striped awning, one leg crossed over the other, a porcelain cup in his hand, a half-eaten croissant on his plate. Sleep hadn't come, but it wasn't missed. He'd taken out half the list in one night.

Suldric leaned back in his chair, letting the late morning sun warm his face.

The third soul had faded sometime around dawn along with the rain, but the magic lingered like steam in his blood.

He wasn't just killing. Each life he drained left traces behind: vitality, energy, strength—enough for weeks, maybe months. It sank into his bones, sharpened his focus, clarified his thoughts. So much power. So much potential.

Three days remained. Three more names. Two of them, at least, were familiar now—accessible. But the last...that one was different. Zesty's notes had been vague, almost reluctant, offering no address, no pattern, no real identity. Just the implication of power, of secrecy, and a location wrapped in whispers. Some kind of spy, hidden deep within the city's spine, protected by something that made even her tread carefully.

He would need time for that one. Maybe two full days if it came to it.

Better to move quickly now and handle the fourth and fifth tonight. The sooner they were dealt with, the sooner he could shift his focus to the real challenge.

And maybe tonight, he thought, he'd try it one-handed.

***

The evening after, the sun was low—air thick with leftover heat and the scent of flowering vines. A horse clattered past, pulling an empty cart.

Suldric sat on a bench beneath a leaning gas light with one leg stretched, the other bent. He looked casual, like a man waiting for someone who was already late.

He held a copy of the day's paper. Cheap ink smudged faintly across his fingertips.

*"Third Prominent Death Baffles City Officials—No Evidence Left Behind."*

*"Shriveled Bodies Discovered in Three Districts—Are We Safe?"*

*"Sources Say Magic May Be Involved."*

Suldric smiled without meaning to and thought, Two more on the way, boys.

The fourth and fifth had been quick, clean and easy. One had slumped in a basin while shaving—and not his face. The other never made it past their front gate.

Mustn't go out after dark...

There were no patterns, no signs, no spells that could be traced.

Only emptied corpses and a city's growing sense of unease.

And across the street?

There was a building no one could name at all.

It had taken him all day to find it.

Even with all his senses, all his tricks, even with the energy of five souls still running within him—the building refused to be real.

From the corner of the eye, it was nothing, perhaps a shadow between shops or the side of a warehouse. But when he looked straight at it, it half materialized, as if made of fog or in the process of fading away.

A low, square structure of old red stone, fronted by four pale columns and a pair of white doors with no handles. It looked like a bank or courthouse: regal and cold.

Above the doors rose a modest dome, and at its heart, a boulder of etched stone with gold lettering that seemed to fade as he looked at it. Runic lettering was carved so tightly it looked like chains. He couldn't read them.

He couldn't even try. It seemed to hurt his eyes when he looked directly at it.

And from there, light. Not torchlight, nor gas or flame, but something colder, older. A soft wash spilled down over the front steps and sidewalk, pale and deliberate, like a watchful eye. It marked the boundary like a warning no one had written, but everyone understood.

Layered spells, stacked one over another, woven so tightly they looked like a single pulse.

To step into that light would be to step into someone's awareness.

Even now, it made the hair on the back of his neck stand.

Black magic didn't belong here, and neither did he.

So, he waited.

Outside the light.

Watching and listening.

Something in his gut twisted at the thought of stepping into that light. Not death—at least, not immediately—but something just as final.

He didn't know exactly what the runes would do, and he didn't care to find out.

He'd seen wards before.

Broken them. Evaded them. Turned their purpose to his own advantage.

But this? This was *not* that.

And there was no way in.

Not with disguise or stealth—not even an army, probably.

He was *sure* of that.

He wasn't even certain what kind of being could create something like this.

The magic was wrong. Off the scale. Dense and complex in ways that hurt to look at.

And then, as he stared at this fortress in wonder—this impossible thing, baffled by its very existence—a slow, suffocating dread began to rise in his chest.

There was no way to complete the list.

Not unless something shifted. Not unless the final target walked out into his waiting hands. And what were the odds of that?

He looked at the soft pool of inspecting light.

It had been a long time since he'd felt this helpless.

And longer still since he'd admitted it.

He couldn't just sit here all night.

Not across from *that*.

If the people—or things—tied to that building were even half as dangerous as the protective spells suggested, it wouldn't take long before someone noticed the man that didn't belong.

He glanced up and down the street. He watched a boy deliver bread to the shop on the corner. He watched a man in gold-trimmed robes nod at a passing guard. He watched as the shadows crept longer across the walls as the sun dipped lower.

And then he noticed a narrow, slate-colored inn tucked against the alley behind him.

It had a small sign and very few windows, but one of them—a second floor room—looked directly at the front of the building.

He stood, folding his paper and slipped it in his coat.

*It's worth a try.*

The room was small but clean—but neither of those things mattered. The window across the room had all of his attention and a thin curtain he didn't plan to close.

Suldric sat in the dark, one leg folded beneath him on the bed, the other drawn to his chest. He hadn't lit a lamp. He didn't need to.

The building across the street was still there—barely. Still flickering at the edge of perception like a mirage in torchlight.

The pool of spell-light on the sidewalk had grown stronger as night fell. It wasn't brighter, not exactly. Just...sharper. Like it was waiting.

He'd been watching for five hours.

No movement. No visitors. No sign of anyone going in or coming out.

And yet, somehow, it didn't feel empty.

It felt like it was buzzing with activity, like a hive.

He reached for a glass of water on the table, then stopped, realizing he'd barely moved since he sat down.

His eyes hadn't left the building.

"Come on," he whispered. "Someone walk out."

But no one did.

The sun rose without ceremony, flooding the city in soft gold and cutting sharp lines across the windowsill.

Suldric hadn't moved.

He sat exactly as he had all night—one leg folded, one leg drawn up, eyes fixed on the building that refused to exist.

He felt no fatigue.

The power he'd stolen from the others still thrummed quietly in his veins. Apparently that meant he didn't need to sleep. Not for a while.

*Wonderful.*

And yet, he was irritated.

Worse—he was anxious.

His fingers drummed against the mattress as he stared.

Still no movement. Still no opening. Still that same unnatural spell-light, now dulled by daylight but no less real.

He picked up the folded parchment Zesty had given him. He skimmed it again.

"An inconspicuous building in the south ward. Hard to find, but you'll know it when you see it. Might want to reconsider this one. You'll know the man when you see him as well—always flipping a coin in his hand."

He scowled.

How the fuck did she even know this name in the first place?

He'd bribed, manipulated, seduced, and terrified half the city's underworld over the past three months, and *this* was the first time he was completely blank.

There was no one he could ask—no one he could trust.

He looked back out the window.

And then a thought hit him—hard.

The goblin.

He'd put this name last.

And now—now Suldric was staring down the one name he couldn't touch—the one target protected by the gods themselves.

Maybe it wasn't just coincidence.

Maybe the goblin had sent him to knock out five people who had inconvenienced him, slighted him, or obscured his path in life.

Maybe this last name was an impossible task.

A trap.

Maybe he'd been played from the start.

A pawn? A weapon? A fool!

Worse than Zesty.

His fingers curled into the parchment in his hand.

***

It was just past midday. The street below shimmered with heat, the kind that made shadows ripple like water. Suldric hadn't moved from the window.

He was starting to think he'd wasted the morning. Wasted the night. Wasted his shot at power. Wasted everything.

Had he left the Empire for this?

He had been somebody there. A rising star. A tactical mage with clearance, purpose, control. Brutal training from a young age, yes, but structure. Rank. Fear. Respect.

Now he was sitting in a dingy inn, alone, watching a building that didn't exist, waiting on a man that probably didn't exist, chasing a book that was never available to begin with.

What am I doing? he asked himself.

Maybe...revenge? Maybe I could go back and find—

And then the door opened.

Suldric's head tilted.

He didn't breathe.

Didn't blink.

From the haze of the spell-light stepped a man.

Not a soldier or a priest—something with wings that could come from such a building.

Just a man.

Ordinary clothes. A narrow hat. An unassuming gait.

And in one hand—casual, practiced, thoughtless—he flipped a coin.

Suldric was standing before he realized.

Shit.

He hadn't thought of what he would do past seeing *him*. He hadn't accounted for the door, the stairs, the delay.

He had to get down there.

He slipped out the door, into the hall, down the steps.

The midday light caught him off guard—white and blinding on eyes that had spent the night in shadow.

He bit back a scream, panic rising in his chest.

*Where is he?*

He scanned the crowds—vendors shouting, carts creaking, pedestrians drifting in waves. A dozen hats. A hundred shirts. All wrong.

He took a step forward, breath caught halfway.

And then—

There!

Mid-block. Turning left.

Calm. Unhurried. Still walking.

Got you.

Suldric moved.

Not rushed.

Not reckless.

Just...fluid.

He slipped into the current of the crowd like a shadow falling into place. No bumps into bystanders, no stares. He was nothing to anyone here. No one to be noticed.

A predator again.

This—he knew how to do.

It was strange, doing it in the daylight. His craft belonged to the night. Shadows and moonlight. But he adapted.

He shrouded himself lightly—just enough to dull attention, blur the edge of his outline, make the eye slip past him.

Within seconds, he was only a few paces behind the man.

Close enough to see the relaxed set to his shoulders.

Close enough to hear the soft clink of that coin still dancing in his palm.

And that's when it hit him.

What if he isn't like the other targets?

The building, the runes, the light.

What kind of person walks out of that fortress like it's home?

He studied the man's movements, looking for a limp, a weakness, a crack...and found none.

Is he magical? Trained? Cloaked in wards? What if my spell doesn't work on him?

Suldric's fingers brushed the end of his sleeve, comforted by the familiar weight of the dagger hidden there. It was enchanted—heavily. He could cut through leather, armor, and even basic shield spells like butter. It cleaned itself. It never dulled. It was hard for others to see once drawn.

Always have a backup.

Still, it was mostly early in the day. Too many people. And this wasn't just any target.

He had time to wait, watch...learn.

Suldric eased back half a step and kept following.

Not yet ready to strike.

Not yet.

He followed for several blocks, keeping a steady distance.

The man didn't hurry. He didn't glance back.

Didn't seem to notice the way the crowds made space for him without him realizing it.

Then he veered—right, through a tall stone arch—into a market.

Suldric slowed.

The scent of fruit and spice rolled past him. Fresh bread and grilled meat. Voices: laughter and bartering.

And there, at the far end of the square, the man stopped. He turned, scanning the crowd.

Looking for someone.

He didn't seem concerned. If anything, he looked polite. Civil. He stood like a man accustomed to power, but not obsessed with showing it.

Then his gaze settled—on a young man. Maybe seventeen, standing alone, looking at necklaces. He walked over to the young man, and they began talking.

Suldric drifted closer, weaving through the stalls and people, never breaking stride.

He drifted to a stop, three steps behind, letting the crowd move around them. Timing was everything.

I get in. I get out. Lost in seconds. His body won't even fall before I'm gone.

Suldric noticed the men seemed to be arguing now. There was a scuffle between them.

This was the moment.

He stepped forward, one arm rising as if to embrace a friend, wrapping it around him, palm open. He pressed his hand into the man's chest—right over the heart.

The spell worked instantly with no resistance. Five seconds was all it took.

It was over. He turned and left.

Time to get my book.

<h1 style="text-align:center">19</h1>

The balcony curved gently with the shape of the room, lined in smooth black iron that curled at the edges like climbing vines. Beyond it, the city stretched out in layers—spires and domes, glowing sigils in shop windows, the shimmer of the sky—bound lanterns still drifting from the night before.

Calen leaned forward on the railing, arms crossed, letting the breeze lift his hair. The sun hadn't quite cleared the rooftops, but the light already had that clean golden tone, as if the rain had scoured everything for their arrival.

Behind him, Reeve stepped out barefoot, holding two mugs. He handed one over without speaking, and Calen accepted it without looking.

"I still can't believe this place exists," Reeve said after a moment.

Calen took a sip, letting the warmth of the drink settle in his chest. He didn't know what he'd expected when he arrived at the emerald gates, but it wasn't this.

"It feels too clean," Reeve said, looking around. "Too shiny."

Liri laughed, but it was soft, almost sad. "Give it time."

***

The hotel restaurant sat on the edge of a curved walkway draped in flowering vines, half-suspended over a stream that gurgled beneath the planks. Somewhere nearby, wind chimes rang in the breeze.

Calen and Reeve sat under a woven canopy of silver branches, still dewy and glowing with the morning light. Liri sat beside them on the table in a special chair for the hotel's smaller guests.

Plates were arranged with near ceremonial care. Goldenfruit had been peeled into soft spirals, laid beside pastries still warm from the oven. The server poured a clear, shimmering nectar into stone cups, bowed, and floated away without a word.

Calen blinked. "Is it...safe to eat glowing fruit?"

Liri didn't look up. "Only the ripe ones glow."

Reeve leaned in and sniffed his tea. "This smells like cinnamon and roses had a fight and both won."

The pastries were impossibly soft, brushed with jam and dusted with powdered bark-sugar that melted instantly on the tongue. The eggs had been piped into curling ribbons and dotted with a purple spice that none of them could name but all found completely enchanting.

"I think I love this city," Reeve mused, licking his finger.

Calen didn't respond at first. He was too busy chewing and eyeing the silver-tipped leaves on the vine above. They were slowly shifting color with the light.

"You know," he said eventually, "if the Empire ever finds this place..."

"They won't," Liri said, wiping her mouth with a petal-shaped napkin. "They can't. The entire forest from here to beyond your house is protected by the Green."

"The Green?" Calen asked, glancing over at her.

"Yes," Liri said, reaching for another slice of goldenfruit. "The Green is the spell that protects the entire forest. It's the same one Lord Gregor cast centuries ago—the one that makes fast-travel paths possible. But it does more than that." She gestured vaguely to the horizon. "It shields the forest. The trees. The cities. All of it."

Calen raised his brows. "All from *one spell*?"

"It's the most powerful spell that's ever been cast." she said. "In the history of all spells."

Reeve let out a low whistle.

Liri continued. "The emperor could send every soldier in the Empire and their mothers and still never make a dent."

Calen looked down at his tea, the glow of it soft against the stone cup. "So, we're safe here?"

"It's the safest city in the world," Liri said matter-of-factly. "At least, from being attacked."

She picked up a piece of pastry, then added with a flick of her wings, "There can still be dangerous people. It *is* the second biggest city on the continent."

Reeve shook his head, staring across the courtyard. "And all this was from a spell cast hundreds of years ago?"

Liri nodded and sipped from her cup.

"That's...I can't even imagine meeting someone powerful enough to do something like that."

"You might—if you're lucky," she said, glancing toward the skyline.

Reeve blinked. "Wait—he's still alive?"

"This is his city," Liri replied. "He's not as easy to get a hold of these days, but yes. Lord Gregor lives here."

Calen sat back slowly, the cup forgotten in his hands. "He's really here? Somewhere in this city?"

Liri nodded. "He's got a temple in the center of the city. There's a huge forest there. And a shrine to Aelira, the Goddess of Nature. He's...a really kind man. Soft-spoken."

Reeve dropped his spoon. "You've *met* him?"

"Of course," Liri replied, as if it were obvious. "I live just east of the city, in the forest. I've been through here thousands of times!"

Reeve stared. "You live...here?"

Liri scoffed, "Um, yeah. What do you think I do when I'm not traveling with you guys? Dance around trees all day?"

Reeve opened his mouth, then closed it again.

Calen, feeling just as sheepish, cleared his throat. "So...what are we doing today? Did you want to see the shrine?" He turned to Liri. "Can people just go?"

She nodded.

"Great," Reeve said. "Let's go."

***

The walk to the city's center was anything but quiet.

Liri flitted between stalls, pointing at fruits she liked or laughing at signs written in the wrong dialect. Reeve kept pace with Calen, holding a folded map he didn't need and mispronouncing half the street names just to make him laugh. Even the buildings around them seemed to join in on the chatter—tall and regal, carved stone and iron balconies, all packed tightly like gossiping nobles pressed into a ballroom.

This was the city's heart. Expensive, elegant, impossibly dense. But at its center, the forest still breathed.

They'd seen the canopy rising in the distance, but now the forest stood directly before them, a wall of green.

The surrounding promenade looked like any other city park—stone benches, tidy hedges, a few flowering trees—but just beyond the low wall, the forest loomed, thick and overreaching.

A four-foot stone barrier marked its edge with a curling vine motif. Trees rose just beyond, ancient and thick, their roots spilling into the walkway and their branches reaching out to brush the windows of nearby buildings. Some vines had even claimed ironwork above shopfronts.

As they stepped toward the entrance, a tall stone archway framed the threshold, carved with winding roots and ancient symbols worn soft with time. No gate barred their path—just the quiet invitation of something vast and alive beyond.

Calen crossed first, and the moment his foot touched the mossy path beyond—silence.

The sounds of the city vanished—no voices, echoes, or clatter of hooves. Just stillness.

Reeve froze mid-sentence. Liri, who was now flying ahead, didn't even glance back.

Birdsong rang from all around them, accompanied by the sound of water trickling through stone. A warm, fragrant breeze stirred the ferns by the path.

Calen tuned slowly. Behind him, the street and its towers were still visible—right there, as if through glass. But the sound was gone.

The path wound gently through the trees, the air thick with moisture and floral spice. Leaves the size of cloaks swayed overhead, and soft green light filtered through layers of vines and blossoms. It felt warmer here—more humid, lush, and alive.

Fae drifted lazily through the air, glowing with soft colors. Some paused to blink at them. A few trailed after Liri, chirping in high, chime-like voices. She responded similarly, grinning as they pulled her into a hovering, spiraling dance.

Calen ran his fingers along a thick branch wrapped in flowering moss. "It's like another world," he whispered.

Reeve didn't reply. He was too busy edging around a brightly colored toad that seemed to be glaring at him.

Liri floated back down to them, looking distraught.

"What is it?" Calen asked. He'd never seen her look this way before.

"Well," Liri said, laughing, "I haven't been back here in quite some time, and..." She looked over her shoulder as if she was being watched. "Well, I used to be somewhat popular."

She looked down one arm shyly.

"And?" Reeve asked, stepping closer.

"Well..." she started, shaking her head. "Well—anyway. I didn't think anyone would recognize me for sure—not after all this time had passed."

"So, what does that mean? Why are you acting like this?" Calen pressed.

"Well! It just means that I didn't want to draw any attention to you, and I thought we would sort of be lost in the crowds—and it doesn't mean anything. I just think we shouldn't be hanging around here exactly." She straightened her dress. "The shrine is boring anyway. It's just a statue and people walking around quietly. And Lord Gregor isn't seeing people today, so there's no reason to stay here is all..."

Calen considered this for a moment, then smiled. "Anyone up for lunch?"

They agreed, following the path back away from the temple.

Afterward, they wandered the merchant district, admiring the displays. Looking around, Calen laughed quietly. "We look like we just walked in from a pig farm."

Reeve smirked. "That's because we basically did."

It wasn't hard for them to find a clothing shop that catered to visitors. The clothes were simpler than the noble fashion they'd seen at dinner the night before, but still elegant. Liri declined a new outfit but tried on every tiny hat in the shop.

They spent the next hour or two simply walking. The city was full of strange and lovely things—a street of wind catchers that made music as they passed, a vendor with glass birds that chirped when held, a square where various magical-looking creatures danced slowly. Sculptures and fountains seemed to be at almost every corner.

The tone was light, the air was warm, the day passed easily, and they made their way back to their hotel for dinner.

The dining room of the hotel was nothing like the sun-drenched breakfast terrace. Here, everything gleamed in candlelight and shadow—deep maroon walls, heavy velvet drapes, gold trim catching every flicker of flame. Crystal chandeliers floated like low stars above polished tables dressed in cream linen and delicate glassware. The air smelled faintly of roasted citrus, fresh bread, and something richer, like cardamom or cloves. People crowded the dining room. They all seemed to be having whispered conversations.

Calen and Reeve were seated near a tall, arched window, though the glass reflected only the room's glow now, the city swallowed in night. Liri perched in a velvet nook beside them, wings folded and silver eyes quietly scanning the room.

Calen shifted in his seat, stretching one leg under the table. "Ouch. My legs are sore from all the walking the last few days."

Reeve chuckled and leaned away, rubbing his lower back. "You're not kidding. My legs, my feet—my ass hurts. We've been walking nonstop for three days, Cal."

Calen smiled at the new nickname. "We didn't feel it before, back on the road, because we had the stone on us."

Reeve glanced toward the ceiling like he'd just realized something. "I'm glad, though, that we left it in the hotel room. With all the magic people and creatures—and even a wizard walking around this city. It might have drawn attention to itself."

Liri snorted. "You two are soft."

Calen grinned. "Oh, and how many steps did you take today?"

Reeve laughed.

Just then, a server approached with a small bowl, placing menus in front of them and pouring crystal-clear water into tall, stemmed glasses. Reeve caught him before he left.

"Sorry," Reeve said. "Is something going on? People seem...tense."

The server hesitated, then offered a processional smile. "There's been news, sir. The evening papers released an early edition. Several prominent citizens were found dead in their homes overnight. No one heard anything. Their bodies were just found randomly."

Reeve looked to Calen and Liri, concerned.

The waiter continued, leaning in. "I guess the bodies were all shriveled. Like they'd been eaten from the inside out. Magic investigators have been dispatched from the university—it's all anyone can talk about."

Reeve turned back to the table, then looked at Liri. "Are magic murders common here too?"

Liri looked shocked. "No. Not at all..."

The server shifted slightly, possibly remembering his manager. "Of course!" he cut in confidently. "None of these were in this part of the city. The hotel is perfectly safe."

Reeve offered a tight smile. "We'll take your word for it. And maybe a bottle of whatever people drink when they're only pretending not to be on edge."

"I'll bring the drink menu at once!" the server said with a small bow and slipped away, leaving them with their thoughts.

"I haven't had anything but cider before," Calen mentioned.

"Me either," Reeve replied, smiling. "But now seems like a good time to try new things."

***

Dinner passed in a slow, velvet haze. They tried a few drinks from the menu—clear, fruity liqueurs, spiced spirits that went down like fire. More than they needed, maybe. Enough that they started to laugh louder, talk a little easier, the tension from the waiter's story dissolving under warmth and candlelight.

Eventually, they made their way upstairs, a little flushed, a little unsteady, leaning into each other as they crossed the hall. The city outside kept glowing, but the night belonged to them now.

Back in their room, they peeled off their new clothes carefully, smoothing and hanging them on the stand by the wardrobe. Their feet ached. Their legs ached. Even their backs had begun to complain.

"I need a bath," Reeve groaned, rolling his shoulders. "A hot one. My whole body's sore."

Calen, sitting on the end of the bed and tugging off his boots, looked up. "That sounds really good, actually."

They padded into the large bathroom.

The tub wasn't a tub. It was a basin fit for royalty—deep, oval, wide enough to lay down facing each other. The walls were tiled in cream stone, the edges lined with small, glowing orbs that pulsed with warm light.

Next to the faucet sat a heavy glass bottle filled with pale, iridescent liquid. Liri, now perched on the sink, gestured to it with a wingtip.

"If you want bubbles, pour that in."

"Seriously?" Reeve asked.

She gave him a look. "I would never lie about soap—and you need some!"

Reeve laughed and started to lower his trousers, threatening nudity.

"Well!" Liri said, fluttering to the balcony. "You two enjoy. I'm going to visit an old friend. I'll be back in the morning."

"Bye, Liri!" Calen called after her.

He was trying to figure out the faucet system.

Reeve laughed and tipped in half the bubble bath bottle. The water foamed instantly, filling the basin with thick, perfumed bubbles that smelled like grapefruit and fresh air. Calen ran his hand through it, nodding in approval.

Reeve slid into the bath first with a deep sigh. Calen followed, stretching out across from him. They sat in silence, the bubbles hiding all but their shoulders. Their feet were at each other's knees.

Outside, the city glowed. Inside, the night folded in gently around them.

***

The next morning, they dressed in their new clothes—simple, stylish, and far less "villager." Calen laced his boots while Reeve leaned over the small hotel desk, studying a city map.

"The Southern Market looks promising," Reeve said, tapping the parchment. "Bigger than the others we've seen. And if we're looking for anything interesting—or a gift to send back home—that's where it'll be."

Calen nodded, fastening the last button of his shirt. "Sounds good to me. Let's make a morning of it."

The sun was already bright outside, spilling through the open balcony doors in golden shafts. Liri fluttered in.

They gathered up their things. As they were about to leave, Calen thought of his still sore legs.

"Maybe I'll just take the stone with me today," he thought. He grabbed his usual pouch belt, snapped it on—stone in place—and left the room.

They spent the morning wandering side streets and tucked away courtyards, sipping chilled drinks from clay cups and stopping to watch a troop of fox-masked dancers near a fountain. By the time the noon bells rang out from the southern clock tower, they had arrived at the Southern Market.

The square buzzed with noise and motion. Stalls lined the brickwork paths in lazy arches, bursting with woven fabrics, dried and fresh flowers, charms that swayed in threads in the wind, and various food stalls. Reeve slowed near a stand selling enchanted hammers—some no longer than his palm, others etched with foreign runes and bound in leather cord.

"Hey," he said, nudging Calen. "You think these are just for show?"

Calen glanced at one, unimpressed. "Maybe. I've seen enough hammers to last a lifetime."

Liri hovered nearby, head cocked. "If you're looking for something nicer, there's a smith across the square. He does wood and rune-inlaid grips. They do shipping as well."

Reeve's eyes brightened. "That might be worth sending home. My dad would love an enchanted hammer!"

Calen nodded, stepping back. "You two go on. I'll catch up."

He wandered away, past a table of dyed scarves and another of glass marbles. At a quieter corner, a narrow jewelry stand stood tucked between two linen carts. Strings of pendants dangled lazily—crescent moons, suns, spirals, and one small necklace that had a charm pendant in the shape of a cow.

He froze.

He reached out and lifted it gently. It was made from metal—something mixed with gold, from the looks of it—and when he turned it over, he discovered it was attached to a tiny chain for a tail that wagged as he held it.

It was cute. Silly. Charming.

It made him think of Lyra.

She would have laughed at it, he was sure. Called it ridiculous, probably. Maybe he would've moo-ed at her, and she would've laughed.

He rolled it between his fingers. Maybe he could bring it back with him and give it to her. Tell her he'd been thinking about her, and how he was sorry about everything. He imagined her glaring at him, but taking it, seeing the little tail and then smiling...

"Excuse me, son."

The voice wasn't loud, but it cut clean through Calen's thoughts. Authoritative. Calm. A tone that made you listen before you even knew why.

He turned.

The man who'd spoken stood just a few feet away. Tall, trim, maybe forty—or maybe far older. There was something timeless about him. Crisp clothes. His posture was relaxed, but he had a sense of authority.

"I'd like you to come with me."

Not a question.

Calen blinked. "I don't understand."

The man stepped forward—not aggressive, but practiced.

"You have something of ours. And I think we need to have a quick conversation about how we're going to go about returning it."

Calen's mouth opened, then closed again. "I...I don't know what you mean."

The man smiled—polite. Empty.

With a smooth, practiced motion, his hand dipped into Calen's pouch. He held it up between them. The stone.

"This, perhaps?"

Calen's heart dropped. He reached instinctively, but the man pulled it back, firm but not hostile. On his hand, a ring caught the light. Black, too perfect. The surface seemed to swirl faintly, like smoke sealed under glass. The man in the market—

"Easy. You're not in any trouble," he said smoothly. "We just need to talk. After that, we'll take this, let you and your friends go on your way, and you can come back and buy that necklace for the pretty girl. Sound fair?"

Calen hesitated, his fingers curled.

"I'd rather not," he said, more force in his voice than intended.

The man's eyes sharpened. "Son—"

"Give it back," Calen said. Not a request.

The charm behind his voice hit like a note beneath the surface—low and warm. The man flinched, just slightly. His hand twitched. For a moment, it looked like he might obey.

Calen stepped forward, reaching.

The man blinked, snapped out of it, and pulled the stone back again. "That's enough. Come with me." His hand started to close around it.

"Give it back," Calen said again, stronger now—something golden rising in him, touching his eyes.

The man stumbled for a moment. Calen grabbed the stone, and they struggled, twisting for control. Calen won.

Just then, a shadowy hand reached around the man and grabbed his heart.

He turned blue for a moment, then gray, then black. His body shriveled in on itself like a dying plant, crackling, collapsing.

The body fell, crumpling at Calen's feet.

Something was moving away. He could barely see it. Its form shifted like it was underwater, features swimming in and out of focus. Like smoke caught in sunlight.

"Stop!" Calen cried after it.

The shape faltered.

For a breath, it froze—like a puppet with cut strings—then it kept moving.

Calen's grip tightened on the stone. It felt hot again. His power was already rising, drawn from the fight, the fear. Now, it poured into the stone, amplified, focused.

"I said *stop!*" he shouted, his voice crackling across the square like thunder. A flash erupted, bright as the sun, blinding everyone, including Calen.

Calen staggered back a step, vision spotted, ears ringing. The stone burned in his hand, pulsing like a second heart.

Gasps rose around him. Then screams.

"He killed him!"

"Gods, look at the body!"

"Call the guards—get the inquisitors!"

Shapes moved in the periphery—people backing away, pointing, shouting.

Calen blinked hard, trying to clear his vision. The world was too loud, too bright. Too fast.

Then—

A figure stepped through the light like it wasn't there at all.

Tall. Striking. Calm in the chaos. His eyes were impossibly blue.

"Come with me," the man said, gently, urgently. "You don't have time. They think you did this."

Calen froze. "Who—?"

"I can explain later." He reached out. "Please, I can get you out of here."

Calen's grip clenched the stone.

"Go with him, boy," the stone said. "You can trust him."

Calen didn't think. He took the man's hand and ran.

# 20

The world had changed. Or maybe it was just him.

Calen followed without question, his feet moving in the rhythm of the man's.

He didn't speak. Neither of them did. It was as if the city had slipped sideways, quieted like it had been lowered into water. The crowds blurred at the edges. Noises dulled, colors softened. People turned to look at them and then didn't. Faces passed without focus. He might have been dreaming, except for the heat of the man's hand in his.

That part was real.

The fingers wrapped around his were large, soft, and firm, but not tight. A guiding grip. Calen stared at their hands, legs still moving automatically. It had been years since someone had led him like this. He remembered it suddenly—another hand, calloused, his father's tugging him along at the edge of the orchard fence after he'd wandered too close to the thorns. The same firm pull. The same unbroken promise: *I've got you.*

But this wasn't his father. This was a stranger whose hand he had taken without a second thought.

And still they walked. The stone was back in its pouch now, at his waist.

He hated it.

This was the second time it had ruined him. The first with the villagers. Loving faces that became terrified—hateful. Now, this city of marvels, magic, pastries, warm baths—peace—saw him as a killer.

For once, he thought bitterly, I had something good. I was happy here. I was safe.

And again, it was over.

The part that made his throat close was that he felt like *this was it.* The end of him. Worse.

Just let this man take me into oblivion, he thought.

They moved through alleys, across bridges, up crooked stairwells of iron and narrow brick. No one stopped them. No one *could.* The world slid past like oil on glass.

Finally, the man stopped in front of a door. Third floor, plain wood, brass knob. He let go of Calen's hand and opened it.

Inside, the space was dim, quiet. The man stepped inside, held the door, and looked back at him.

Calen stepped through. The door shut with a finality that felt like the end of something.

It was pitch black.

Calen stood motionless in the dark, heart loud in his chest. The air was still—no echo of steps, no street noise. The apartment swallowed sound like velvet. There was a faint smell, clean and sharp: stone, soap, old books, wood, leather, and the scent of the man—musty and sweet.

Calen's eyes strained, but there was no light to adjust to. He took a cautious step forward. The floor under his feet felt polished like stone or lacquered wood. The air was cooler here, still humid from the storms and thick with that strange scent.

A soft click—a lock, or latch—echoed behind him.

Calen flinched slightly, his shoulders rising.

There was a pause. Then the sound of a slow inhale.

"I'm sorry," came the man's voice—low, smooth, almost regretful. "That was...unkind."

Calen didn't turn. His breath was tight in his throat.

He heard the soft footsteps, barefoot against the polished floor. Without speaking, the man reached the far wall and drew back three sets of enormous curtains—floor to ceiling, thick as cloaks and the color of deep ink. They hissed against the track, then spilled open like something exhaled.

The city beyond them surged into view: rooftops drenched in sunlight, spires shining in the heat.

From here, they could see the arc of the river, the curve of the old district—even a bit of the central forest, where green shimmered like glass beneath the afternoon sun.

The man stood at the glass, backlit by daylight. "I never open these," he said softly. "There's no need. I see perfectly in the dark." A small pause. "But that doesn't mean you do."

He turned, his expression open, almost tentative—like someone trying to please. "Better?"

Calen nodded, his eyes still adjusting to the sudden flood of light. He didn't move far from the doorway.

The man turned away from the light and stepped gently back into the room. He gestured to a low sitting area—two chairs angled near a table carved from some dark stone and a long sofa.

"Come sit," he said quietly. "If you'd like. You must be hot."

Then, with a glance at a nearby sideboard, he said, "There's water. Or wine. If that's easier."

He didn't wait. He crossed to one of the chairs and sat cross-legged.

Calen hesitated, then stepped farther in. He moved slowly, watching the man the whole time.

Finally, he sat.

The man stared at him deeply. The silence stretched—not hostile.

It was unnerving, having someone that beautiful stare at him like he was the mystery in the room. It felt...awkward, almost romantic. Like he'd stepped into a moment meant for someone else.

Then the man leaned forward, elbows at his knees, eyes still locked on Calen.

"Now," he said softly, "what exactly did you do to me?"

Calen blinked at the question. "What do you mean? I didn't do anything."

The man tilted his head, brow drawing slightly. "You told me to stop. I did for a moment. I kept going. You shouted it. And then—" He paused, the memory threading its way through his expression. "You hit me with something—a spell. I don't know what it was."

Calen stared at him, lost.

The man sat back, eyes never leaving his. "What was *that*?"

Calen opened his mouth, then closed it again. He genuinely didn't know.

And then it hit him.

The stone. The fight. The man crumpling dead at his feet. The shadow.

The thing that had reached around the man and—killed him.

Calen's stomach dropped.

He stood, forcing the couch to scrape back behind him.

He was alone. With a man he didn't know—a killer.

And now, they were in a quiet apartment. Shut inside. Possibly with no one to hear him scream for help.

"You," Calen said, the word sharp. "You killed him."

The man didn't flinch. "*Yes,*" he said. "And then *you* spelled *me.*"

Calen stared. "I didn't—" He shook his head. "I didn't 'spell' you. I don't know what I did."

"But you did." The man leaned forward again, voice still calm—but eyes lit with accusation. "You changed something. Inside me. You reached out and put something in my head—I felt it."

"I didn't mean to," Calen said, pulse loud in his ears. "I was—I wanted to..."

Calen's breath came fast now. His hand went to his belt on instinct, fumbling for the pouch. He pulled the stone free, and it tumbled into his palm.

He looked at it like it might explain itself.

"I don't know," he choked. "I didn't mean to do anything. I was just trying to—to stop you from getting away. You—"

He held the stone up, as if it might answer.

The man across from him narrowed his eyes. "What is that?"

Calen didn't speak.

The man stood up slowly, gaze fixed on the object in Calen's hand. He took a cautious step forward, not threatening, just...drawn.

His brow furrowed.

"The runes," he said, voice lower now. "Those are the same runes that were on the boulder—at the building..."

Calen looked down at the stone.

The air shifted.

Then: "Yes," said the stone.

The man froze.

"To answer your question. The spell Calen performed was the Mojet'thar, or King's Oath."

The man stumbled back, falling into the chair behind him. A look of shock and dread on his face.

"Mojet'thar," the man repeated, almost inaudibly, nodding to himself.

He sat in silence, eyes distant, thinking.

Then, he slowly said, "But that can't be cast *on* someone."

He looked up at the stone, voice low, uncertain. "It's...given. Freely. It has to be. An oath between master and devoted servant—a pledge of eternal loyalty." He shifted his attention to Calen. "Unbreakable."

Calm, absolute, the stone replied, "You are bound to Calen until your death."

The words hung in the air like a divine decree. Cold and final.

The man put his hands on his face in horror.

Calen just stared, too stunned to speak.

The man stayed like that for several minutes, hands over face, elbows on his knees—like he was trying to press the words out of his head.

Then, slowly, he lowered his hands.

His expression was pale, his eyes haunted.

"That is not possible," he whispered.

He looked down at his own hands, like they no longer belonged to him.

"That spell is *not* something that can be cast. No one can force it. Not even the Lord Wizards."

He looked at Calen now—really looked at him. Not with suspicion. With fear.

"You're not supposed to be able to do that," he said. "Not unless..."

Something inside him recoiled from the thought.

"What *are* you?"

Calen didn't answer, but the stone did.

"He is the result of forbidden magic. The product of a wizard's bloodline—something that should not be possible."

The man listened, wide-eyed.

"A child born of magic itself," the stone continued. "A wizard's progeny. The union of power and life."

He let the words hang, then said, "That is why the spell worked: chaos magic."

The man looked at Calen like he was seeing him for the first time. Not a boy. Not a man. Something else.

"Wizards can't have children," he whispered. "It's—it's one of the oldest laws of magic. The power consumes the seed."

"And yet here he is," the stone replied solemnly. "He didn't know until just now. I'm sorry."

Then the stone asked, "What is your name, young man?"

The man blinked, surprised—like he'd forgotten he had one. "Oh. Um...it's Suldric."

"Suldric," the stone repeated. "This is Calen."

The man looked up. "Pleased to meet you…" he murmured, unsure if he meant it.

Calen hadn't moved.

He was still standing—rigid, uncertain, one hand clenched around the stone like it might shield him if things went wrong again.

Suldric hadn't so much as blinked.

Then the stone spoke again. "There is nothing to fear, Calen." His voice was gentle this time, almost kind.

"You've had a terrible shock. You weren't meant to find out in this way. Please, sit down. You are perfectly safe here. It is impossible for Suldric to hurt you. The spell has seen to that.

"In fact, he loves you now—more than you can possibly know."

Calen sighed and sat, pulling the couch back in place behind him.

Suldric leaned forward slightly, expression lost—vulnerable in a way that didn't suit someone so powerful.

"Do I…love him?" he said, almost to himself. Then louder: "I do…feel it."

He looked over at Calen with something like awe.

"Not romantic. Just—" He pressed a hand to his chest. "It's just there. Like he's…mine to protect. Mine to serve. My king. My…student… My son. My teacher. All at once."

He swallowed, tears forming in his eyes.

"I would...die for you...?" The words shocked even him. Then, more resolved: "Right now. Without hesitation."

Calen just stared at him.

The words *I'd die for you* echoed through his head like a threat—even though they weren't.

Even though he knew Suldric meant every word.

It didn't feel safe. It felt wrong.

"I didn't ask for this," Calen said, his voice tight. He swallowed. "I don't even know you."

He stood up again, too fast. "You can't love me. That's not real. That's just the spell."

Suldric didn't argue. He just nodded slowly and said, "I know."

And somehow, that made it worse.

Calen didn't move.

Neither did Suldric.

The room had gone still again—curtains drawn wide, sunlight pouring across the floor, catching the faint gold veins in the stone table between them. Outside, life continued. Somewhere, someone was laughing. A carriage clattered past. The world hadn't noticed.

But in this room, everything had changed.

Calen's chest felt tight. Not in pain, just full. Like there wasn't enough space in him for everything he was feeling.

The stone was warm in his hand.

He didn't speak. No one did.

For a long time, they just sat there. Not as master and servant. Not as strangers.

Just sat. Trying to understand what had been done to them.

The silence held.

Until—

A knock at the door.

Not loud, just *present*.

Three short raps, then nothing.

Calen flinched.

Suldric looked at the door like he'd forgotten it existed.

The knock echoed once more.

Suldric stood, suddenly alert. "Would you mind...just go in there for a moment?" He gestured to a narrow door down the hall.

Calen hesitated.

"Please," Suldric added. "Take the stone with you."

That got his attention. Calen stood up and slipped into the other room.

***

Suldric crossed to the front of the apartment and opened the door.

A small man stood there, holding a parcel.

Suldric's chest tightened.

The man handed him the package, muttered "Pleasure doing business," and wandered off.

Suldric closed the door, pulled his dagger from his sleeve, sliced the twine, unwrapped it.

And there it was.

The book.

Suldric exhaled through his nose. He couldn't have Calen disturbing this. It was too important. If Calen saw it and objected, he knew he would happily throw it away, and he couldn't allow that to happen. He opened the small cabinet by the door, slid the book in, and closed it tight.

He returned his dagger to its normal place and called out, "You can come out now!"

***

Calen stepped back into the room, the stone in hand.

Suldric was just returning from the door, expression unreadable but calm. "Just a book delivery. Something I ordered a while ago."

He walked past Calen and settled into the chair again like nothing had happened.

Calen stood there a moment longer, unsure of whether to sit, speak, or run.

They sat in silence for a moment, Calen still clutching the stone. Suldric watched him with quiet devotion.

Calen kept his eyes on the floor. He still didn't know if he was safe. He shifted in his seat, uneasy.

Finally, without looking up, he asked, "So...are you just coming with me now?"

Suldric didn't hesitate. "I think so."

Calen's brow furrowed. "Just like that?"

"I don't want to go back to what I was doing before," Suldric said.

Calen looked at him then.

There was a weight to Suldric. Not just magical—personal. Like someone who had been on the wrong side of the line too many times and crossed it repeatedly anyway.

Calen hesitated, then asked, "Did you kill those three people? The ones in the papers?"

Suldric didn't flinch. "Six, actually—including today's... Yes."

Calen's stomach twisted. He stared at the floor for a long moment, then asked, "Why?"

Suldric's tone stayed even. Not proud. Not ashamed. "For knowledge."

Calen looked up. "What kind of knowledge?"

Suldric met his gaze without hesitation. "Black magic."

Calen blinked. "Black magic? That's forbidden."

Suldric tilted his head slightly, almost amused. "Oh? Says the *being* that's forbidden."

Calen opened his mouth to argue—then closed it again. "Right," he muttered. "Fair."

They sat there a moment longer, the weight of black magic and quiet truths still hanging between them.

Then Calen glanced up, brows drawn, voice uncertain. "So... are we like...friends now?"

Suldric gave a small smile. Not mocking. Just sad.

He got up and sat down next to Calen on the couch. "More like family," he said.

Calen blinked. "Oh."

They lapsed into silence again, the weight of it all settling into the spaces between their words.

Then, quietly, Suldric said, "Can I see it?"

Calen blinked. "The stone?"

Suldric nodded.

"Why?"

Suldric's voice was calm. "Curiosity. Nothing more." He paused, then added, "If you don't want me to touch it, I won't. I can't, actually. Not if you don't want me to."

Calen hesitated. He looked down at the stone in his hand—still faintly warm.

"You can look," he said slowly. "But you can't keep it."

Suldric offered a small nod. "Fair enough."

Calen extended it to him.

Suldric took the stone, then stopped. His gaze landed on Calen's hand.

The skin across his palm and fingers was red and blistered, the edges shiny with moisture. Angry welts crisscrossed the skin, just beneath where the stone had been resting.

Suldric's expression shifted.

He gently set the stone on the low table.

He reached for Calen's wrist, turning it to examine the damage. He didn't say a word.

Suldric brought his other hand to Calen's, and with a magic-coated finger, traced a slow, deliberate line across the burns.

A faint trail of smoke followed the movement—wispy, gray, scentless. The blisters faded, the redness gone.

When he was done, Suldric cradled Calen's hand between both of his, massaging gently.

Only then, after Calen was whole, did he lift the stone.

Suldric held the stone in both hands now. It reminded Calen of his grandmother when she examined it.

Suldric's expression shifted—no longer gentle, but focused, his eyes closed.

"It's..." he began, brow furrowing. "It's enormous."

He opened his eyes and set the stone down on the table.

"In my mind, it's like...a room. No. A whole library. Volumes stacked to the ceiling. Thousands of spells. Thousands."

He glanced at the stone again, reverent now. "I don't even know where to begin."

Calen leaned forward slightly. "Can you read any of it?"

Suldric shook his head once, slow and deliberate. "No. Not yet. Most of it's...locked. Shielded. Protected in layers."

He looked at Calen then. "But the outermost layer? That's protective magic. Shielding, detection, warding. It's not offensive. Not on the surface, anyway. Was there something in particular you wanted me to look for?"

Calen shook his head.

"You should know," Suldric said quietly. "You're safe."

Calen blinked. "What?"

"No one saw your face. The ones who might have—blinded. Panicked. You're not in danger."

Calen leaned back, unsure. "You don't know that."

Suldric was quiet for a moment. He hadn't considered it before—but now that he did. That man...the one who he killed at the market...he hadn't been acting alone.

He was part of something. A network. An order.

That building with the dome—that hadn't been his personal fortress. It had been a hub.

And if one spy had fallen, the others wouldn't scatter. They'd close in.

They'd want answers.

Or revenge.

Calen noticed Suldric thinking. "What's wrong?"

"The man who died...he wasn't alone. Not in the way I'd assumed."

Calen tensed. "What do you mean?"

"I think he's part of a network."

Calen thought about it.

The rings.

His stomach turned.

"The man in the market," he said. "He was wearing a ring."

Suldric nodded. "So?"

Calen's voice dropped. "The same ring as someone else I met before. A vendor who I bumped into back in Hearthmere. Weeks ago."

Suldric's expression darkened.

"How many of them are there?" Calen asked.

"I don't know," Suldric said. "But a lot more than two." He leaned back, eyes narrowed. "And they've been watching you longer than either of us realized."

They compared what they knew—what each had seen, what each had missed.

It didn't take long to piece it together.

Calen had likely been under surveillance for weeks. Maybe longer. They probably knew where he'd been staying, who he'd been traveling with. And if they saw the stone on him this morning, that would explain why they struck when they did.

Calen went still. "Reeve," he whispered. "And Liri."

His stomach twisted.

He hadn't thought about them once—not since the market. And suddenly, his mind filled in the silence with something horrible.

He saw Reeve lying motionless on the hotel floor.

He saw Liri—a tiny crushed shape next to him, wings torn, curled like a broken leaf.

His stomach lurched.

"I need to check on them," he said, already rising from the couch. "I—what if they—?"

Suldric stood too, calm but serious. "Then we go. Now."

Calen was already moving to the door when Suldric asked, "Where are they?"

Calen paused. "We've been staying at the Broadleaf Hotel. Fourth floor. Room 416."

Suldric crossed to the wall beside his door and reached for a narrow brass handle, half hidden in a carved wooden panel.

He gave it a single pull. Somewhere below, a quiet bell rang.

He didn't wait too long. Barely two minutes later, there was a soft knock on the door.

He opened it just enough to reveal the face of a young man in a fitted gray coat. Polite. Neutral. Exactly the kind of person you sent for things you didn't want recorded.

Suldric handed over a small envelope sealed in black wax and slipped a silver coin into the runner's palm.

"Please take this to the concierge desk at the Broadleaf Hotel. Please stay, and then bring me their reply."

The runner nodded once and walked away without a word.

Suldric closed the door behind him and turned back to Calen. "Give him fifty minutes," he said. "We'll go in from the inside."

Suldric returned to the couch again, watching Calen absently run his fingers over the smooth surface of the stone.

"Why today?" Suldric asked, almost offhandedly. "If they've been watching you for weeks, why confront you now?"

Calen blinked. "What?"

Suldric met his eyes. "What changed?"

Calen looked down at the stone. "Oh," he said, a wave of guilt washing over him. "This is the first time I've carried it."

Suldric tilted his head. "Why today?"

Calen's cheeks flushed. "I was sore," he said despairingly. "We'd been walking around the city for days, sightseeing. My legs, my back, everything was sore..."

He turned the stone in his hand, "When you carry it, it...helps. You don't get tired, or hungry, or thirsty. You don't feel the sun as much. You can carry more. Move longer. And if you put it in a building or tent, it protects that too. Our tent in the woods, my house back home. Horrible storms passed over us like nothing."

Suldric's brows rose slightly. "That makes sense, based on what I could tell from examining it. Those aren't minor en-chantments. That kind of passive effect from something so small is..." He thought for a moment. "That's wizard magic. It must have been made by a group of wizards—or even a Lord Wizard."

"Like Lord Gregor?" Calen asked.

Suldric nodded.

"Do you think this is his magic?" Calen asked, shifting to face him.

Suldric thought for a moment. "No, he's a green wizard. This is mainly golden magic."

Calen looked down at the stone again, the surface catching the afternoon light in a way that seemed...warmer now. Familiar.

"My magic..." he said slowly.

Suldric studied him for a moment, then asked gently, "May I touch you?"

Calen sat up straighter. "What?" he asked, the edge of fear rising again in his throat.

Suldric looked away, tone soft. "I was just hoping to see if I could read you. Like I did with the stone."

Calen hesitated. His thoughts turned inward. This might give him answers. Real ones.

After a breath, he said, "Yes."

Suldric looked back at him. "Yes?"

Calen nodded, more certain now. "Yes."

Suldric slid a little closer, reaching to place his hand on Calen's chest.

Calen recoiled. That was how Suldric had killed the agent.

Suldric stopped instantly, his hand frozen midair. Then he stood, taking a step back with both arms lowered and palms facing out. "It's okay!" he said quickly. "Gods, I'm sorry. Calen, I would never hurt you. I'm so sorry that you saw that. I didn't mean to scare you."

Calen sat motionless, heart pounding. He couldn't reconcile the handsome, caring person in front of him with the shadow that had killed without hesitation. Who had killed people in their homes. Government ministers, wealthy merchants. Men with names and families and locked doors.

Calen's voice was low. "You killed them…"

It wasn't a question.

Suldric didn't look away. "Yes."

Calen stared at him. "Those people…the ones in the papers. The murderer everyone is afraid of. That's you."

A long silence.

Suldric sat back down facing forward, eyes on the wall. "That was before."

Calen blinked.

Suldric's voice was steady, but softer now. "Things have changed."

Calen tilted his head in frustration. "What, now you're some kind of good person?"

Suldric's head bowed. His eyes searched the floor as if the answers were written there. "I guess," he said simply.

Calen stared at him. "Why?"

Suldric turned his head, looking directly at him. He leaned in, staring into his eyes.

"Because *you* are," he said.

It wasn't said tenderly; it was just the truth, spoken plainly. Like it had been sitting there the whole time, waiting to be named.

Calen felt it now. There was a part of him in Suldric's eyes looking back at him. Like something passed between them the moment the spell was cast and never left.

It was true.

Calen didn't know how he knew—only that he did. Something deep and wordless bound them now. He felt it in Suldric's eyes. He felt it in his own chest.

He didn't think. He just leaned forward and wrapped his arms around him.

Suldric tensed—but only for a breath. Then he returned the gesture, careful and solid. Not pulling him in—just being there.

They just sat there, holding each other. Long enough for the world to feel quiet again.

They leaned back slowly, almost at the same time. The silence between them had changed—no longer tense, just still.

Suldric exhaled. "It is golden magic."

Calen blinked, eyes still a little dazed. "What?"

"I read you," Suldric said, "When you embraced me." He thought for a moment. "No one has done that—held me like that—since I can remember... Thank you."

Calen nodded.

"Golden magic. That kind of clarity, influence, vitality. It resonates the same way. That may be why you're so compatible with the stone."

Calen sat with that for a moment, turning the words over.

"That makes sense," he replied. "I have the ability to make people like me, to do what I say. I can...command them."

Suldric was quiet for a moment, then he said flatly, "Chaos magic."

Calen turned to him.

"Golden magic," Suldric clarified. "But much more powerful. Wild. Untamed. It doesn't follow the laws the others do."

He looked at Calen now, not with suspicion, but with reverence. "That's what you are."

A sharp knock broke the silence.

Both of them looked at the door.

Suldric rose with practiced calm and opened it.

The same gray-coated runner stood outside, now holding a slim envelope sealed with a wax imprint from the Broadleaf.

Without a word, Suldric accepted it, slipped another coin into the runner's hand, and gave a faint nod. The man tipped his head in return and walked off down the hall.

Suldric didn't close the door. He opened the envelope. Room keys.

He glanced over at Calen, then gestured with a small tilt of his head. "Let's go."

Calen stood.

As they slipped into the hallway, Suldric mumbled something under his breath. The air shimmered around them. "No one will see us now," he said. "No eyes. No ears. Not even magical ones."

And together, invisible to the watching world, they made their way to the hotel.

# 21

They remained veiled until they were inside the room. The curtains were already drawn. The air was still. When the door closed behind them, the magic dissolved with a hush—like a breath being let go.

The two stood in silence for a moment, the weight of everything still lingering between them.

Then Calen glanced at Suldric. He replied with a quiet nod.

Calen crossed the room to the adjoining door, opened it slightly, and knocked twice.

There was a pause.

Then a muffled voice—Reeve's. "Who is it?" Wary. Tight.

Before Calen could even reply, a much smaller voice shrieked from the other side, "Calen?! CALEN—if you're a ghost, I swear I'm going to salt this whole room!"

The door opened fast.

Reeve stood there. He looked like he hadn't slept in days. He blinked, stunned and froze when he saw Calen standing there—alive.

"You disappeared," he said, voice barely holding. "I thought..." He couldn't finish.

"I'm okay," Calen replied.

Reeve pulled him into a tight embrace, arms locking around his back like he was anchoring him to the world. He didn't let go and guided him into the suite, half-walking, half-carrying him to the couch like he was afraid he might vanish again.

"Oh my gods, you're not dead!" Liri shouted mid-flight. "Okay, now I can kill you myself!"

But the moment she caught sight of Suldric, she slammed to a stop in midair like she'd hit a pane of glass.

"What the hell—Calen!" she shouted, pointing with both hands and floating backward. "Why is he here? That's a black mage! That is a full-blown forbidden, first-degree, cloak-and-dagger murder mage!"

Calen didn't flinch, flopping down on the couch, exhausted.

Reeve froze where he was, looking over at Suldric, half sitting down.

Liri's wings buzzed hard. "You know? *Why* is he standing in our hotel room?"

Calen stayed calm. "This is Suldric. He saved me. He's good."

"*Saved* you?" She threw her hands up, flew over, and hovered in front of Calen's face. "From what, the consequences of trusting tall, dark, and soulless?"

"I'm telling you," Calen said again, steady, "he's safe."

Liri grabbed Calen's face and turned it to look at Suldric. "Look at him! He's got black magic dripping off him like cologne. I don't even know how he got past the city guards!"

She flew up and started to spin. The air in the room began to shimmer. "In the name of the forest and the protection of. I hereby invoke the Green to banish—"

Calen grabbed her out of the air. The spell halted.

"I'm telling you," he said again, even steadier, "he's safe."

Calen let her go and she flitted back, offended.

He pulled the stone from his pocket. "Tell her, stone."

The stone glowed to life, alive in a golden mist. "I assure you, young lady, Suldric is safe."

Calen forced the stone to go dim and put it back in its pouch.

Liri muttered something very un-fairy-like, swooped across the room, and landed on the dining table. She crossed her arms and legs and glared at Suldric like she was trying to set him on fire with her face.

"Fine," she muttered. "But the second he starts chanting or glowing weird, I'm flying straight into his eye."

Only now did Reeve think to sit down. "You brought him back?"

"Yeah," Calen said. "He saved me."

Reeve studied Suldric, then Calen again. He placed his hand on Calen's shoulder and nodded once. Processing. Accepting—for now.

Reeve looked between Calen and Suldric, noticing their black hair. "Hey, you two kind of look like brothers."

Calen and Suldric glanced at each other, both surprised...then smiled.

Reeve smiled too. Just a little. The tension in the room softened. He leaned back with a sigh. "Is anyone else starving, or is it just me?"

Calen smiled, surprised by the normalcy of the question. Then he realized he was hungry too.

Liri gave a nod, stretching her arms overhead. "I don't need to eat, but I enjoy it!"

Suldric took a step back. "If you don't mind, I'll have it sent next door. It's quieter. And safer." He looked to Calen. "No extra attention. I'll cover the bill."

Calen nodded gratefully. "Thanks."

They all gathered themselves and moved into the adjoining suite. The curtains were already drawn tight, blocking the city beyond. They moved to the dining room, identical but reversed from their own.

It wasn't long until dinner arrived. The covered trays held warm, fragrant food, and the soft clink of silverware filled the space.

No one spoke much at first. They were all too tired. Too full of unspoken things.

Finally, Reeve broke the silence. "We were about a hundred yards away when it happened," he said, staring at the edge of his plate. "I was looking at these enchanted hammers—really nice ones! One of them could triple your swing!" He got excited, but collected himself before continuing. "I was really debating which one to get. I found two I liked, but they were fairly expensive, so I couldn't just get both..."

Liri gave a tiny smile. "He was really taking forever."

Reeve nodded once. "Then it hit! The flash. I thought I'd gone blind!"

"It was like the whole market exploded," Liri said. "Like the sun had fallen from the sky."

"They still don't know what it was—some sort of killing magic, they supposed," Reeve continued. "I tried to get to you... I ran. But people were screaming, tables were all knocked over, everything was chaos. And then I saw the body. Crumpled. Over by where you had been standing."

Calen lowered his fork. "You thought it was me."

Reeve nodded.

Liri added, "They quarantined the whole area. They questioned everyone as they let people out. We waited at the exit, thought maybe you got caught inside or were hiding. But you never came out."

Reeve looked across the table. "We thought you were gone, Calen. Really gone."

A silence followed—not sharp, not bitter. Just deep.

Then Liri exhaled through her nose and shifted in her seat. "Hey, Calen?" she said softly. "Can we talk? Just us?"

Calen looked at Reeve, then Suldric. A subtle unease passed between them.

"Yeah," he said. "Sure."

He followed her out of the suite and into the other. He could hear Reeve asking Suldric about how he saved Calen.

"Want to step outside?" she asked.

Calen shook his head. "No. We can't open the curtains. I think we're being watched."

Liri nodded in understanding. Calen sat at the dining table.

"Hey, so...I wasn't sure when to say this," she began, hands clasped in front of her. She landed on the table. "But after what happened today...when we thought you were dead..." She hesitated, then pushed forward. "I went to see Mira last night."

Calen blinked. "You did?"

"She was frantic, Calen. Scared. Your parents are going crazy. She wanted to know if you were okay. When I told her you were alive, she started crying with relief."

Liri took a few steps toward him.

"But...Calen...she wants you to come home. Right now. And after today, I think it's best too.

"You can keep the stone. Take it with you. We can figure out what to do with it—how to get it a body later. But you need to go home. Maybe even tonight. Especially if you think we're being watched."

She paused.

"We can pack up. Reeve can come with us. Let's just...go."

Calen looked down at his hands. "I can't."

She stared at him. "Why not?"

Calen's voice was quiet. "Because I know what I am."

Liri tilted her head slightly. "What do you mean?"

"My grandfather was a wizard."

Her breath caught.

He looked up at her. "She lied to me. Mira. My parents. All of them. My whole life, I thought I was normal."

"Your parents don't know," Liri said softly.

"Well, then Mira lied to them too."

"She thought it was safer if—"

"She didn't even tell my dad?"

"No." Liri's voice was quieter now. "He doesn't know."

Calen was still for a moment. "Is he like me then?"

Liri thought, then said, "I think so..."

"And...my little brother?"

"He's just human. No magic in him at all."

Calen nodded slowly, taking it all in.

After a moment, Liri looked down, twisting her fingers. "I knew," she said quietly. "I've known this whole time. I was helping Mira keep it quiet."

She hesitated.

"But when I saw the seal on your magic, I just...unlocked it. I didn't ask. I didn't warn her. I just did it."

She looked him up and down, guilt clouding her expression. "I thought it would help. I didn't realize it would change everything."

He didn't speak.

"That's why Mira was so angry," she whispered. "She knew."

He exhaled. "There's more."

Liri gave him a tired look. "Of course there is."

"I performed the King's Oath..." He paused. "The Maja...Thara—something."

Her eyes widened in horror. "You what? Calen, that's ancient magic. It's permanent! Why would you pledge yourself to this black mage? Was that his price for saving you?"

"No!" Calen said, frustrated, a hand pulling his hair. "He pledged to—to me..." He exhaled hard.

She froze. "He... what?"

Calen looked away. "I didn't ask for any of this," he said. "I didn't want it. But—I'm still me. I'm still the same person—the same Calen—I always was."

Liri studied him like she was seeing him for the first time. Something shifted behind her eyes.

Then she said quietly: "That's the most dangerous lie of all."

***

Calen stepped back into the suite, his expression somber. Liri drifted behind him in silence, her wings barely whispering in the quiet.

Suldric looked up, lounging with a wine glass at the head of the table, one brow rising as they entered. Reeve sat near the far end, arms crossed, his eyes snapping to Calen's face with visible concern. No one spoke.

Calen just walked past them without a glance and began gathering the dishes from the table. The clink of ceramic on wood broke the hush. Reeve moved to help cautiously. Liri joined in too, stacking utensils with slow, precise movements. Suldric did not rise. He watched them like one might watch a fire—casually, with the knowledge that it might shift at any moment.

It was domestic, almost peaceful, but the silence was tight. Everyone could feel it. Something had changed.

Once the dishes were stacked and ready for retrieval by the hotel staff, Calen dried his hands on a cloth and turned back to face the others. His voice was steady.

"We need to talk."

He walked to the table and, without ceremony, set the stone down in the center. It landed with a soft weight—more than it should've had, somehow—and sat quietly, unmoving.

"You too," Calen said to it. "You're part of this."

The stone glowed from within, a slight golden mist forming. Suldric finally leaned forward, slightly amused.

Reeve took a seat across from Calen, lips tight, unsure of where this was going. Liri curled into a coffee cup she'd stuffed with a napkin.

Calen sat at last. He looked at everyone around the table once, then exhaled.

"There's something you don't know," he said, looking straight at Reeve. "The flash you saw in the market." He paused. "That was from me. I—accidentally cast a spell—on Suldric."

Liri's eyes narrowed. She hadn't heard this part.

"And it bound him to me... Permanently."

Reeve blinked. "I don't understand."

Calen looked down at the stone, as if maybe he would help explain, but he didn't.

"I, uh...I found out that my grandfather was a wizard, and that because of that, I have chaos magic. I—it's uh...forbidden." Calen shrugged, wringing his hands. "And because of that, and because I had the stone...Suldric is bound to me until one of us dies."

Reeve frowned. "You just...*did* this?"

Calen nodded. "I didn't know what I was doing. It just happened. After that, Suldric took me to his apartment to recover, and then we came back here."

The silence that followed was long and close.

Calen finally looked up. "I think I need to go home."

Reeve leaned forward slightly, his voice low. "What does that mean for us?" he said, looking at Suldric and Liri. Then, softer, "For me?"

Calen responded quickly. "It doesn't change anything." But even as the words left his mouth, they felt empty. In his mind, he heard Liri: *the most dangerous lie of all.*

"That's why I need to go home. I don't know what I'm doing. I don't know who I am. I don't want anyone else getting caught up in this until I figure things out."

Liri sat up in her cup. "I agree," she said, her voice unusually steady. "This is too big. Too fast. And it's not slowing down. Calen's grandmother knew about all this and was keeping it a secret. She will have a better grasp of our situation. She can help us sort it all out and regroup."

She looked at Suldric. "He's just a kid. He should go home. He shouldn't be here dodging spies, or whatever else there is."

Suldric nodded.

The stone pulsed, the mist expanding. "If you return home, you will not be returning alone. You are already being watched. Not by the city. Not by the council."

The light dimmed, then flared again. "You are under the watchful eye of the Aracel."

The name landed like a cold wind in the room.

Liri climbed out of her coffee cup and stood on the table. "What?" she said sharply. "When did they get involved?"

The stone answered without pause. "They have been following him since Hearthmere."

A hush followed. Suldric looked more serious now.

"Calen saw them when no one else did," the stone said. "He looked through their veil and saw what shouldn't have been seen.

"He saw the ring."

Calen's stomach turned. He remembered the strange vendor and then the man that was killed at the market. They both had worn strange, smoke-filled rings.

"They knew then," the stone continued. "They have known ever since. Calen is not normal."

The stone quieted, its voice fading into its core, leaving only its glow behind.

Reeve looked around, puzzled.

"Wait...is the stone talking again?"

Everyone nodded.

He exhaled sharply and rubbed his face. "Everyone can hear it but me," he muttered. "Of course."

He pointed a glance at Calen. "Well? What's it saying now?"

Suldric signed dramatically and slid his chair over to the left. He reached out and placed a single hand on the top of Reeve's head like he was blessing an altar boy.

"Okay," he said, deadpan. "Continue."

The stone pulsed. "Calen was seen in Hearthmere. He saw a ring that should not have been seen, and they've been following him since."

Reeve blinked hard, then looked over at Suldric. "Okay, yeah. Heard it that time." He then added, "That's a neat trick."

Liri exhaled slowly, her voice unusually quiet. "You boys do not get how bad this is. The Aracel don't chase you through alleys with knives. They don't send letters. They don't knock. They just appear. Right before things get really bad."

She looked at Suldric. "They work for Lord Daemion."

Suldric's eyes widened. He pulled his hand back from Reeve's head as if it had started burning.

He stood. Not dramatically—just with the quiet urgency of someone realizing they were suddenly standing on the wrong floor of a collapsing building. He began to pace, running a hand through his hair.

"Lord Daemion is the most powerful wizard in the world—the most dangerous," he said. "And not necessarily the nicest either."

He stopped suddenly looking at them. "Zesty warned me," he whispered sharply. He looked at the ceiling, his face pale. "She said the people you're messing with don't just kill you. They peel you apart and mail your pieces to your friends."

Liri tilted her head. "Sounds like what I've heard as well."

Suldric let out a long breath through his nose. "I thought she was being dramatic."

Calen started, "The man you kil—" but he caught himself, biting his tongue. "Um. He had a ring like that."

Everyone looked at him.

He didn't elaborate.

Suldric dragged a chair out from the table, turned it around with one hand, and dropped into it backward, arms resting across the top like he'd never been rattled in the first place.

"They don't know us, though," he said. He pointed to Calen. "They don't know me, and they don't know you."

Liri gave him a look. "Well, they're curious about Calen."

Suldric's face fell. "Yes."

The stone flared gold. Suldric reached over and placed a hand on Reeve's head again.

"You cannot go home."

The stone's glow deepened, not brighter—but denser, like honey thickening in the light. "Calen. You have power even elder wizards fear. Without training, without guidance, you are already stronger than most who walk the council halls. With me, you're more powerful still. You cannot afford to go back until you have mastered your powers enough to keep the ones you love safe. If you go back now, you'll be handing them to the Aracel.

"Suldric, you are bound to Calen. Even if he does nothing under their scrutiny, they will perceive your magic and come for you. Black magic is forbidden. There is no more hiding, not for either of you. Your only protection is each other. The strength

I lend to both of you will make you more than formidable. You may become unstoppable, or at least invulnerable—perhaps enough to convince the Aracel you are not worth the trouble of pursuit.

"Reeve, my sweet boy. You want to protect Calen. You always have. But protection takes more than courage. It takes power. You are traveling with two of the most powerful magic beings on the continent. Who better to learn from?

"You don't need to be left behind. You can grow with them. Hear me speak without assistance. Develop your own strength as a mage. Or...you can become the weak link that breaks when the time comes."

Calen scowled at the stone.

"And Liri, you have forever. But what will you do with it? Float from moment to moment, or be part of something that matters? Something that will be remembered? Your kind was once woven in with history, not a forgotten myth of the forest. You could be that again.

"You are all part of something now. Whether you like it or not."

Liri leaned back and stuck out her wings. "I vote we grab the stone, walk outside, wave it around until a member of the Aracel shows up, hand it over, and walk away. Calen, we could have you home to your grandma in a couple days."

The stone spoke again—quieter this time. "If that happens... I will be forgotten.

"Set into a wall. Sealed in silence. No thought. No voice. Just years.

"I was never meant to be awake. But now I am. And I do not want to disappear again."

A long pause followed. The glow dimmed, as if the words had cost it something.

Suldric was the first to speak. He leaned forward, voice calm but sharp. "The stone's right! They're going to come after us eventually, no matter what we do."

He glanced around the table, his eyes bright with something dangerous—clarity or hunger, it was hard to tell.

"With the stone, I'm already twice as powerful as I was. Maybe more. And we haven't even begun to unlock what's inside it. There could be spells in there no one else knows about. Entire schools of magic."

He leaned back slightly, lips curling in something that wasn't quite a smile. "We'd be fools to give that up."

Reeve turned to Suldric, eyes narrowed, voice careful. "Is the stone telling the truth? Could I really be trained in magic?"

Suldric looked at him like he'd just asked if fire was warm. "Of course," he said, dry as dust. "You've been breathing the stuff for weeks now. You're already soaked in it."

He paused, then added with a little smirk, "The only real question is—do you want it badly enough?"

Reeve blinked, then sat back in his chair, grinning. "Whoa."

Liri groaned. "Oh no, not you too."

She threw her hands up in the air and then flew backward and plunked down in her cup, arms crossed.

Calen didn't smile. He looked at the stone, then to Liri. "He's right, though. They're going to come for us. We need to be ready."

The stone glowed more strongly again. "If I could take human form. I could stand and fight beside you. Your faith in carrying me to my goal—your trust in my becoming—will not be so easily forgotten. I will stand and fight beside you. And in human form—who knows? Perhaps I would already be a wizard myself."

The stone's glow slowly faded, the weight of its promise settling over the room like dust in the lamplight.

No one spoke for a moment.

Liri stirred first. She stretched her wings with a slight sigh and looked to the window.

"I'm going to fly for a bit," she said softly. "Clear my head."

Calen tilted his head, watching her. "You're not going to see Mira, are you?"

Liri paused mid-flight. "No," she said, "I won't see her. But if we decide not to go home...I may tell her what we chose."

Calen nodded once. Liri flew out of the room.

Suldric turned to the boys. "You two get to bed," he said, his voice quiet. "I won't sleep tonight. I'll stay by the door in case anything happens."

Reeve raised an eyebrow. "Don't you sleep?"

Suldric shook his head. "Not every night."

No one questioned it any further.

Calen rose, rubbing a hand across his face. "Okay, thanks."

The bedroom door clicked shut.

Suldric remained still, eyes on the door, the lamplight catching faintly in his eyes. He let out a slow, silent breath and settled into the chair, posture relaxed but ready.

Outside, the city rustled beyond the windows, restless and unaware.

Tomorrow would demand decisions. Tonight, only half of them found sleep.

# 22

Morning broke pale and quiet over Ultara.

The dawn leaked through the heavy curtains, casting soft shapes on the floor. Somewhere in the building, water pipes creaked and settled as hotel guests started their mornings.

Calen woke first.

The room felt heavier than it had the evening before, like the silence had thickened overnight. Reeve was still asleep, one arm over his eyes, his mouth slightly open. Calen sat up slowly and glanced toward the living area. The door was slightly ajar. He heard the rustle of a cart. Suldric was still awake.

Calen slipped out of the bedroom, easing the door shut behind him. The suite was still dim. The curtains remained drawn, sealing the light out, leaving the space gently blue and shadowed.

On the table sat a neat line of covered trays, still untouched. The smell of something warm and savory hung in the air, waiting.

Suldric sat in one of the chairs, one leg pulled up, relaxed but alert. "You're up." His voice was low and steady.

Calen nodded, rubbing his hair. "Did you sleep at all?"

"No." Suldric gestured faintly toward the table. "I ordered food. It's still hot."

Calen crossed to the table and ran his fingers lightly along the lid of one tray, feeling the warmth beneath the metal. It felt strange, this careful hospitality from someone who had recently been on a killing spree.

"Thanks," he said quietly.

Suldric didn't reply right away. He was watching him—still and patient.

"You were talking in your sleep," he said at last.

Calen's hand stilled on the tray. "I was?"

Suldric gave a slight nod. "Nothing clear. A name, maybe. You turned over like it hurt."

Calen looked away jaw tight. "I don't remember."

He lifted one of the lids, letting a ribbon of steam curl into the dim air. He took a plate, filled it without a word, and then sat down at the table across from Suldric.

Calen was halfway done when the bedroom door opened. Reeve stepped out, hair sticking up like he'd wrestled a pillow. He blinked at the dim room, squinting at the table.

"Are you sitting in the dark?" he mumbled.

Before Calen could answer, Reeve crossed the room and adjusted the blinds, letting in the light but maintaining their privacy.

"Better," he said, noticing the covered plates. "Oh, did you order breakfast?" he said to Suldric. "And the dinner last night. Thank you!"

Suldric nodded with a small smile.

Reeve started peeking under the lids, "Oh, I hope they have those eggs again, those were really good…"

He smiled, finding exactly what he was looking for and heaping them onto his plate.

He was mid-scoop when he paused, glancing toward the balcony. "Has anyone cracked the door for Liri?"

Calen and Suldric glanced at each other. "No," Calen admitted.

Reeve sighed through his nose and shook his head, already heading to the glass doors with a piece of toast sticking out of his mouth. He nudged the curtain aside, unlatched the door just enough—

A gust of warm morning air swept in, and with it, Liri shot through the opening in a blur of gold and wing shimmer.

"About time!" she snapped, already grabbing a small plate. "I've been out there for an hour. I was going to start pecking."

She hovered just long enough to fill her plate, then landed neatly on the back of one of the chairs.

She snapped off a piece of toast. "So, what's the plan for to-day? Please tell me it involves less scary people and more distance from here."

Calen didn't look up from his empty plate. "We leave today."

Reeve wiped his hands on a napkin and walked over to the far side of the room. He grabbed his pack and pulled out a bundle of parchment. He brought it back over and laid it out on the table, flattening out the creases.

"Figured we should talk through the route while we're eating," he said. "I've got most of the northern trails here, and the valley's somewhere out past the Ash Border. We might want to try to avoid the main roads—draw less attention."

Suldric stood and leaned in, eyes scanning the map with more precision than the others expected.

"That's outdated," he said, pointing to a mark near the river. "There's a new fort there. Imperial. Small post, but they rotate patrols down through the hills now. You'll want to swing south along the woods—there's a path they don't watch."

Reeve nodded. "You've been out there?"

Suldric nodded. "Twice. Once during the flood season. It's passable, but not pleasant."

Liri flitted up beside them, hovering high over their heads, a piece of toast still in hand.

"Any fae roads out that way?" Calen asked her.

She shook her head. "No. Everything west of here is under the control of the Empire. All the fae fled to the northwestern valley—where we're headed, the southwest forest and witch mountains, or to Gregor's Forest, where we are now."

Calen moved the couch out of the way and began dragging their gear into the middle of the room—packs, cloaks, rations, water flasks, wrapped bedrolls. They laid everything out for inventory and inspection.

Calen turned to Suldric. "You don't have anything."

He nodded. "I hadn't planned on traveling." He stood, eyeing the equipment. "I'll go get what I need and meet you back here as soon as I can."

Suldric crossed the room, stopping in front of Calen. Without a word, he placed both hands firmly on Calen's shoulders and looked him dead in the eye.

"*You* do not leave this room," he said, low and firm. "If anything else needs to be gathered, Reeve can go. Alone or with Liri. Understood?"

Calen blinked once, surprised—but nodded. "Okay."

Suldric gave his shoulders a brief squeeze, then turned away without another word. He walked through the adjoining door into his suite, and a moment later, they heard the quiet click of the outer door closing behind him.

Reeve stepped forward, crouching beside the pile of supplies on the floor. "Let's get this sorted out."

Calen knelt down opposite him, and they got to work.

When they got to the end, Reeve reached into his bag, pulled out a folded scrap of paper, and started writing.

"We need more dried food. More of this," he said, pointing to one bag, "and less of that—neither of us liked that at all." He took what was left and tossed it in the room's waste bin.

"What do you want, Liri?" he asked, looking up.

She was perched on the back of the out-of-place sofa, wings half-tucked, watching them with a look that was equal parts curious and unimpressed.

"Snacks," she said without hesitation. "Not that weird dried bark stuff either. Something sweet. And maybe something shiny to look at. You people pack like soldiers, not travelers."

Reeve scratched something into the paper. "Noted. No bark."

Calen leaned back on his hands, surveying the piles they'd sorted. "Honestly...I think we've figured out what we actually use. I was going to say we needed candles and lanterns, but we have the stone for that in the tent, and Suldric can see in the dark."

Reeve nodded, but asked, "Suldric can see in the dark?"

Calen nodded, leaning in. "Yeah, just like if it was bright daylight, I guess. It's one of his black magic things."

Liri made an unimpressed noise from the couch.

Reeve looked over to her. "How well can you see in the dark?"

Liri sat up, hands folded. "Well," she started, "in the woods, it isn't as bad—but that night on the roof with you guys...I could barely see at all,"

Reeve slid over to her. "But you could conjure light if you needed to, right?"

Liri looked down. "I'm not sure... I'm pretty helpless when I leave the forest."

Calen climbed over and sat down too. "You don't have to come with us, Liri. If it's too dangerous for you—"

Liri stood up, scowling. "Oh, no! You guys are not getting rid of me that easily! Someone has to keep an eye on you, or you'll come back dark mages—the three of you!"

Everyone laughed.

Calen climbed back over and sat down. Reeve slid back beside him.

After a moment, Calen added, "We didn't bring anything to do."

Reeve looked around at the orderly piles. "We brought like twenty ways to start a fire, but no books. No games. No paper, unless you count this list," he said, holding up the list in his hand.

"We'll be training now," Calen said. "Suldric and the stone said they'd teach us. That should keep us busy."

Liri flopped back onto the couch with a dramatic sigh. "Oh, good. Mage camp. Exactly what I was hoping for when I signed up for this trip."

She rolled slightly. "If I see you floating in your sleep or summoning demons, I'll take my chances with the birds!"

Calen grinned. "Deal."

***

A few minutes later, they heard the door to the neighboring suite open again.

Suldric stepped through, already dressed for travel. His dark, hooded cloak was fastened at the throat, its folds whispering around him as he moved. A small pack hung from one shoulder—sleek and compact, but clearly weighted with something dense and magical.

He scanned the room quickly, noting the neat supply piles and the maps still spread on the table.

"Good," he said, raising an eyebrow. "You're ready."

Then, more gently, he added, "We'll leave within the hour if we can. Let's finish what needs finishing."

Reeve stood and handed over the folded list. "These are the last things we'll need. Not much, but a few important items."

Suldric took the paper, eyes scanning it quickly. He gave a small nod. "You two know your gear." He looked at the piles again, approving. "Pack up. Be ready to go." He looked toward the windows. "If they sense we're leaving, they might make a move."

He dropped his bag by with the others, as well as his cloak. "I'll take care of the list and be right back."

The door closed quietly behind him.

They packed quickly this time—no hesitations, no reorganizing. Every strap cinched tight, every pouch clipped down the way it should be. It wasn't the nervous, chaotic packing from before. This was travel-ready.

Once their gear was prepped and lined up by the door, the boys ducked into the bath for a quick wash. No lingering, no soaking—just enough to rinse the city from their skin. They changed back into their traveling clothes. The city wear was folded and strapped to their packs, a layer between their old life and whatever came next.

When they finally sat down again, the suite felt different. Not hostile, just...no longer theirs.

The warmth was gone from the walls. The furniture looked too clean, like someone else's space already. Even the light had changed.

They waited.

***

The lock clicked again.

The door opened, and Suldric stepped inside. He moved with purpose, hauling behind him a gleaming brass luggage cart. Three identical packs rested neatly on the platform—sleek, dark, and evenly weighted.

"I wasn't sure how much we'd end up carrying," he said calmly, steering the cart into the room, "so I balanced them for the three of us. We'll move faster that way."

Calen and Reeve exchanged a quick glance, then stood up.

Suldric looked at the boys and froze. "Oh no."

He crossed the room quickly and, without asking, stepped in front of Reeve and began straightening his tunic with precise, practiced motions. He tugged the fabric smooth, adjusted the drape of the outer jacket, and muttered something under his breath as he gave the hem a flick. With a brush of his fingers, the color darkened a shade—more practical, travel-worn, and—somehow—sleeker.

Reeve blinked, walking over to the mirror. "Uh...thanks?"

Suldric didn't answer. He was already turning to Calen.

"Stand still," he said, voice even.

Calen drew his head back a bit, but complied. Suldric fussed with his collar, tugged one sleeve, and adjusted the waist and seat of the trousers before adjusting the cuffs and refining the stitching. The mismatched sizes and tones of the tunic and jacket shifted, textures harmonizing, cut sharpening just enough to suggest intent.

He stepped back and regarded the now handsomely dressed young travelers.

"That's better."

Liri muttered from the couch, "You're such a mom."

Suldric didn't react, but he didn't deny it either.

Calen slung the packs onto the cart with a quiet exhale. "All right. So, how are we doing this?"

Suldric stepped beside him. "You three will go down together. Take the cart. Don't rush, don't hesitate. Just look like travelers checking out. I'll shroud myself and follow. Stay off to the side, near the columns on the inside of the concierge desk. You can't be seen there from the street. If anything feels wrong, know I'll be watching."

There was a beat of silence. Then Calen gave a slow nod. "Okay let's go."

They made their way to the lobby with no issue. The cart rolled smoothly over the marble, their boots echoing quietly in the high-ceilinged space. The concierge glanced up but said nothing.

Liri fluttered just above Reeve's shoulder, pretending to study the desk light. Calen pushed the cart forward, stepping up to the desk to return their keys.

"Checking out?" the clerk asked politely.

"Yes," Calen said, reaching for the two sets of keys. "Room 416."

Reeve leaned against the side of the cart, eyes scanning the lobby. Calm. Ordinary. Almost too quiet.

Then—

"Liri?"

A woman's voice, high and syrupy sweet, sliced through the air behind them: surprised, delighted, and vaguely threatening.

"Liri! So the rumors are true! What are you doing here?"

Liri went still mid-hover.

The boys turned slightly. A tall, severe woman dressed in winter white silk robes that trailed just above the floor. Her hair was platinum blonde and pin-straight, parted sharply at the center like a blade. A long coat with silver embroidery swung open around her as she walked, elegant and immaculate. She wore her glittering jewelry like a weapon.

Another fairy trailed her, small and light like the lady's personal star floating over her shoulder. She was smirking like she'd already won whatever game they were about to play.

Liri didn't turn. She just muttered under her breath, "Oh, stars."

# 23

Calen and Reeve exchanged glances.

Shock. *We're caught,* and then quickly, *don't get involved.*

Without a word, both of them took a half step back. Calen busied himself reading all the front desk signage, and Reeve raced to grab the cart straps as if they suddenly required urgent attention.

Neither of them was going to save her. This was Liri's battlefield.

She slowly turned in the air with a practiced smile.

"Vael," she said, tone neutral, but light.

"Liora."

The tall woman—Vael—smiled with closed lips and no warmth. "I thought that was you. Traveling in style, I see." She looked over the cart as if it was a curious artifact from a museum, then to Reeve and finally Calen—lingering a bit too long.

"Broadleaf's still accepting walk-ins, then?" Liora added, her wings twitching with amusement.

"I haven't seen you around much these days," Vael said, voice dipped in polite amusement.

"It's been quite some time now, actually, hasn't it?" Liora chimed in, her tone more openly sharp. "What's it been?" She looked at Vael. "Forty years or so?" She smiled.

Liri smiled, shrugging slightly.

Vael tilted her head, faux-thoughtful. "Right. Not since Mira vanished."

That landed.

Liri's wings gave the barest twitch. "She didn't vanish."

"Of course not," Vael said, smiling like a dagger. "She simply...needed to step out of public life. Very odd."

"A famous sorceress like that?" Liora added, voice lifting. "And poor Valric." She pouted.

"Oh yes, Valric!" Vael gushed. "He was so heartbroken when she 'left the public eye.'" She finished as if she were reading an awkwardly written cue card.

Liri, flustered, said, "Maybe she decided she was done with being noticed."

Vael rolled her head and pouted. "And you? Are you done being noticed, Liri? Or just trying a new crowd?" She gestured vaguely to the boys.

Vael took a single step forward, her jewelry making faint sounds.

"Well," she said lightly, "don't be rude. Step forward. Let me see you."

Calen and Reeve looked at each other, frowning, then stepped forward.

Liri gave a faint shrug and then made it clear with a gesture that they needed to be smiling.

They both smiled, and Reeve took another step forward, trying to look friendly and calm.

Vael's sharp eyes moved over them both, lingering longer than necessary. "Well-dressed," she said, almost surprised. "Didn't expect that."

Vael circled slightly, gaze now fixed upon Calen. She moved in closer—too close—brushing a non-existent thread of his shoulder, fingers lingering a beat too long.

"And this one," she said, her face right up to Liri. "This one is *very* handsome, Liri. The hair, the eyes, the cheekbones—that jawline..." She twisted her body in delight.

Behind her, Liora's eyes narrowed ever so slightly.

Vael turned, quietly talking over her shoulder as if she'd suddenly lost interest. She began to walk away. "It really is a shame about Valric, you know..."

Liora floated up to Liri, "Traveling with an erentear? In public, no less?" She laughed lightly. "When he gets arrested, I hope they let you watch."

She smiled triumphantly and followed her mistress out the hotel's front doors.

Calen and Reeve stared after them, still not quite sure what had just happened.

Before either of them could say anything, Liri shot into the air, wings buzzing, and shouted, "Suldric!"

Her voice echoed through the lobby.

She spun once, frantic, then yelled again, "Suldric!"

From behind a marble pillar, Suldric stepped out—casual, almost bored, like he'd been standing there the whole time.

He glanced up at Liri, one brow lifted, a small frown pulling at his mouth.

"*I thought we were keeping a low profile,*" he said dryly, flicking his head toward the rest of the stunned lobby.

Liri didn't even blink. "Get Calen out of the city. Right now." Her voice was sharp, urgent—no argument allowed.

That got Suldric's full attention. His casualness dropped completely. "What happened?" he asked, his tone shifting low and serious.

Liri dropped lower, trying to catch her breath. "That woman," she hissed, "was Vael." She twisted in the air. "You know—Vael's Vellum? Or Vile Venom, as many say...?"

Suldric's expression hardened. Even Reeve stiffened, alarmed without fully knowing why.

Liri hovered between them, wings twitching.

"She's not just anyone," Liri said, voice low and urgent. "She runs the Wizards' Council's gossip sheet. *Everyone* reads it, though few admit it, but—" She swallowed hard. "—it's always true. *All of it.*"

Suldric's jaw tightened. "I know the name. A fresh copy was always laid out at the Gutter Glass—a single page of juicy gossip, several times a week, devoured by soldiers, merchants, and council aids alike."

Liri turned, locking eyes with Calen. "Vael and your grandmother used to be in the same friend group," she said, voice cracking. "She knows Mira...*very* well."

Liri blinked rapidly, trying to hold herself together. "Calen..."

Her voice broke fully now. "I swear, I didn't see it until just now. But she's right. You're the spitting image of your grandfather."

She hesitated, then forced the word out. "Valric."

***

They moved quickly, abandoning the desk and slipping into a quieter parlor off the lobby.

Calen dropped his pack beside a low sofa. His heart was hammering.

"Erentear," he said under his breath, trying the word again.

Liri landed on the arm of the sofa, wings twitching. She nodded grimly. "Exactly."

Suldric crossed the room, looming like a shadow.

"And what, exactly, does that mean?" Calen asked, his voice low.

Liri's mouth tightened. "It means the child of a wizard. An errant heir. But when people said it enough, it became er-entear."

Suldric nodded.

Liri turned, pacing back and forth across the armrest like a caged bird. "Mira sacrificed everything to keep Edric safe," she said, her voice cracking slightly. "She gave up her magic, her standing, her life at court—everything—to protect him from this."

She shook her head hard. "And now it's ruined. She's totally exposed. *You're* exposed."

Calen's throat was dry. "But...what happens now? What if I'm caught by the Wizards' Council?"

Liri waved her hands sharply, wings buzzing in distress. "Oh, you don't want *that*. The council? They're immortal academics. They'll debate your existence. They'll argue over bylaws, quote treaties from six hundred years ago, call for recesses, form committees, redefine words for 'wizard' and 'child.' It will take eighty years at least."

She faced him squarely. "By the time they finally agree you deserve to die, you'll already have died of boredom."

She crossed her arms. "And that's the best-case scenario."

Reeve cut in. "So, how long do we have?"

Liri began thinking out loud. "We're already almost out of time," she said, her voice low but urgent. "Vael's Vellum will go out by five, maybe sooner. After that, we can assume that The Wizards' Council and the Aracel will know what Calen is—and maybe where to find him."

She hesitated. "We can also guess that the Aracel are already outside, watching for us. We might not even make it out of the lobby."

Suldric stepped forward, voice cool and commanding. "Then we leave now. We split up. Calen and I will take the gear, shroud, and head out the back of the hotel. No one will see us leave. From there, we slip out the West Gate."

Liri and Reeve nodded slightly.

Suldric continued, sharp and focused. "You two go out the front. No bags. No gear. You're tourists, nothing more. Let the Aracel watch you—give them something to see. No reason to worry."

Reeve frowned slightly. "But where should we go?"

Liri's wings twitched once, sharply. "I know a place," she said. "The Wishing Garden."

Reeve blinked. "The what?"

"It's on the north side," she said. "Just outside the North Gate, but still safe. Big tourist spot. You tie ribbons on the trees and make a wish. It's always busy."

Calen's brow furrowed. "Can you get out from there?"

Liri nodded. "We can slip into the tree line, and I can open a fast-travel trail. We'll be out of there before anyone notices."

Suldric gave a short, approving nod, then asked, "Where do we meet?"

Liri answered quickly, "Oh, the big ugly Forest City sign just east of the city!"

Suldric nodded, eyes rolling. "I know the one."

Liri looked around the group. "Okay, do we all know what we're doing?"

Everyone agreed.

"Okay then," she said confidently. "Let's go."

Reeve went over the plan one last time aloud—no bags, no gear, nothing to mark them. He and Liri would go out the front like any other tourists, while Calen and Suldric slipped away unseen. It was already dangerous to be standing still.

Calen could see Reeve's pulse hammering in his neck before they reached the door. They couldn't stand still, not for a second. The Aracel might be waiting.

Liri floated higher, wings twitching. "Okay, Reeve, let's go," she said, forcing a bright, touristy smile.

Reeve hesitated only long enough to steady himself, then stepped into the marble hall like any other traveler—a boy and his fairy, out for a day of sightseeing.

The door eased shut behind them, and the silence that followed felt heavier, as though the room itself exhaled.

Suldric turned back to Calen without hesitation. He handed over a pack—heavier than Calen had expected—and waited while Calen settled it across his shoulders. Then Suldric swung up his own load along with Reeve's, distributing the weight so easily it was as though the straps bit into nothing.

"Are you sure about this?" Calen asked.

A faint smile touched Suldric's mouth. "It's the best chance we have. The guards won't see us. They never do. I've walked past them a dozen times, and not one of them noticed a thing."

He tugged a strap tighter across his chest. "It's twenty miles to the Forest City sign. If we walk, it'll take most of the day. If we run—" He glanced sideways at Calen, eyes sharp with calculation. "If we run, and that stone works the way you claim...maybe five hours."

Calen blinked. "Five hours of running?"

Suldric shrugged, a half-smirk ghosting at the edge of his mouth. "You'll survive."

Something flared in Calen's chest—excitement, adrenaline, or maybe just the kind of recklessness that always hummed at the edges of his magic. He'd never had a partner who could push him like this. Not really.

"What do I have to do?" he asked, straightening.

Suldric reached out, fingers brushing the pouch where the stone hung. "Tell it you need strength. Don't beg it. Don't ask. Command."

Calen swallowed, nodding. He reached for the well inside himself and felt it surge, snapping into place with the stone's pulse. The weight of the pack vanished from his shoulders as though it had never been there.

Suldric caught the shift in his stance, the sudden lightness in the way he held himself.

Calen turned to him, energy coursing through every nerve. "Let's go."

Suldric glanced down the hallway to be sure no one was there, then turned back to Calen.

"Stay close. Be careful not to walk into anyone—they won't be able to see you, and it'll undo the spell. I can only cast it if no one's watching, so if we draw attention, we're at a loss until I can reset it. Keep talking to a minimum until we're clear of the city. The guards are already on edge, hunting for a murderer, and you were being watched before any of this started. No one's ever seen through my barriers, but now I'm covering both of us. If I get captured..."

He held Calen's gaze. "You keep going. No matter what."

He waited just long enough to see Calen nod, then lifted his hand. The shroud fell over them like a veil of water, and the hall, the air, and the world itself folded around them.

The shroud settled, and something in Calen sharpened.

It wasn't dreamy this time—it was focus: a door hinge shifting somewhere behind them, the faint drag of fabric as someone turned a corner, the rhythm of footsteps through the floor. He could feel where people were without seeing them, the same way an animal knows when it's being watched. Only now, no one was watching them.

Suldric started forward, moving with purpose, and Calen fell in behind him, every sense awake.

They moved into the narrow service hall that ran behind the lobby. The air was warm and close, filled with the mixed smells of soap, starch, and hot metal. The polished marble gave way to old, thin carpet—soft underfoot, muffling their steps, worn smooth by years of traffic.

They moved deeper down the corridor, the air growing stiller, the faint clangs and chatter of the lobby fading behind them. A tangle of pipes ran along the ceiling, alive with the quiet rush of water, and the walls were close enough that Calen could have brushed both sides with his shoulders.

Suldric slowed suddenly, one hand lifting. Calen followed his gaze around the corner—then froze.

A man and woman stood pressed together in a shadowed recess near the laundry bins. Their bodies moved in small, desperate motions, breath catching, fabric rustling in quick, secret rhythms. The sounds came to Calen sharp and intimate through the shroud.

The woman's back hit the wall with a soft thud. "Someone's going to find us," she whispered.

The man's reply was rough and close: "Then we'll be quick."

Suldric gestured silently for Calen to move. They slipped past, so near that Calen caught the warmth of their bodies through the veil. The woman shifted, and her hand brushed the air inches from his arm—too close. The scent of their bodies was intoxicating and new.

Suldric shot him a glance—one raised brow, the faintest smirk. Calen's face burned, and he smiled broadly.

They kept moving, weaving through a corridor lined with storage racks and boxes of vegetables waiting to be carried in. A shock of heat rolled from the open doorway to the kitchen, thick and sudden, then faded as they passed. Farther down, a bell rang sharply, startling Calen and quickening his pace.

At the end of the hall, the corridor bent sharply toward a narrow service door marked for deliveries, sunlight showing faintly around its edges.

Suldric pushed it open just enough to check the alley beyond, then nodded for Calen to follow.

They stepped outside into the warm air. Calen blinked against the light, the sudden openness disorienting after the close halls. He could feel the spell around him thinning. He turned to Suldric, suddenly uneasy.

Suldric caught the look. "It works better at night," he said. "We're fine." Then he motioned for Calen to follow.

The alley stretched long and narrow, the hotel rising high behind them. A tall privacy wall ran the length of the street, white stone catching the sun, too smooth to climb and too tall to see over. The space between was empty—just a strip of cobblestone and shadow funneling toward the main road.

Far down the other end, a pair of workers were unloading crates from a wagon, their laughter faint in the distance. They hadn't noticed anything.

Suldric started forward at a steady pace, keeping close to the wall.

This was already turning out to be quite an exciting morning—maybe the most exciting thing Calen had ever done. He was following a handsome murderer out the back of a hotel, past a couple doing—well, he knew what they were doing, but he'd never seen it. *So* exciting.

Was this his life now? Handsome, dangerous men and running for their lives?

Suldric stopped so suddenly that Calen walked right into him.

"Pay attention," he hissed.

A horse carriage crossed the alley ahead, wheels clattering.

"Sorry," Calen whispered, his confidence crashing.

They followed the alley south until it met a cross street, then turned west. The hotel rose behind them, its shadow stretching long across the cobbles. Ahead, sunlight pooled at the far end of the street, catching on the pale stone of the district wall.

They slowed as they neared it. Two guard stands flanked a wide archway where carriages passed through in orderly silence.

The air there shimmered faintly—subtle but structured, the lines of it too regular to be heat.

Calen squinted. The patterns hung in the air like threads of glass, shifting with quiet purpose. "You see that?" he whispered.

Suldric's gaze flicked to the same spot. "Wards," he said. "Fresh ones. They've tightened the perimeter."

A patrol wagon rumbled past the arch, its driver glancing toward the guards.

Suldric turned sharply down a narrower lane that ran along the inside of the wall. "Come on. There's a crack farther down. I've used it before."

The lane grew quieter as they went. After a short distance, Suldric stopped beside a stack of barrels. "There," he said, crouching.

A surprisingly large tunnel waited behind. Calen didn't even need to crawl—only crouch, which he was thankful for. The tunnel smelled faintly of spilled liquor and wet stone, the kind of sour tang that came from years of things leaking where they shouldn't. The air was thick and still, touched with dust and something rotten.

The tunnel stretched farther than it looked. Each step echoed ahead of them, their breathing loud in the confined space. Sound carried strangely here—close, amplified, hard to ignore.

Light broke ahead, and they stepped out into the open.

The alley spilled into a broad market square, layered and loud. Old stone terraces climbed in uneven steps, crowded with stalls and hanging cloth. Vines spilled from high balconies, and a thin stream of water wound through the cobbles. Lanterns drifted overhead like slow-moving kites, swaying between the rooftops.

Suldric kept his pace steady, eyes sweeping the crowd ahead. "Stay close," he said quietly. "People can't see you, so they won't know to walk around you."

Calen nodded, scanning for gaps as they moved. It felt strange—walking in open daylight, surrounded by movement yet part of none of it.

The noise of the market shifted as they neared the edge of the district—less laughter, more order. The wall ahead gleamed in emerald tile, each one catching the light like glass.

A row of guards waited beneath the archway, each marked by a green sash that caught the sun when they moved, their composure threaded with quiet authority. Calen sensed danger there.

He turned to Suldric. "What do we do?"

"We walk right past them," Suldric said, steady and sure.

Calen blinked. "What?"

"They're watching the people coming in," Suldric said under his breath, eyes on the flow of traffic. "Not the ones leaving."

They were through before Calen could even process it—past the arch, past the guards, out beneath the open sky again.

He let out a breath he hadn't realized he was holding. "I can't believe that worked."

Suldric adjusted his pack, eyes still scanning the street ahead. "It was the inner gate that would've caused trouble. I've never seen a setup like that before—and the officers running it weren't the usual kind. Figures they'd give the rich their own protection."

They followed the road west, and within minutes, Ultara was gone. Calen glanced back—no walls, no rooftops, just trees, dense and close, like the forest had folded over the city and sealed it shut.

"Eyes forward," Suldric said. "It's meant to vanish."

"Are you ready?"

Calen nodded, and they began to jog.

The road stretched ahead, sun filtering through the canopy in restless flickers.

Suldric slowed just enough to glance back. "We keep pace till we hit the sign for Forest City. Don't stop unless I do."

Calen nodded, already feeling the pulse of the stone syncing with his heartbeat. "I can handle it."

A faint grin crossed Suldric's face. "Good. Try to keep up then."

He broke into a run—fluid, powerful, more glide than stride. Calen followed, his body answering before his mind caught up. The forest blurred around them: moss, light, shadow, motion. Every step landed sure and clean, his breath deep and easy. The air was cool and alive.

He felt weightless.

The city had vanished behind them, but its danger still pressed at their backs. Calen didn't care. The world ahead was green and endless, and he felt like he could run forever.

Acknowledgments

To Alex, my first reader, for diving in before anyone else. And to John, for always being in my corner.

Also by

Roads of the Empire — Coming December 2026

About the author

Brom Geistman writes epic fantasy about loyalty, power, and the brotherhood that keeps men standing when the world tries to break them. He lives in the Pacific Northwest and spends an unreasonable amount of time thinking about imaginary kingdoms and the men who survive them together. He is the author of The Chronicles of Aethara, beginning with Suldric's King. He shares his home with a Hungarian Vizsla who remains unimpressed by literary ambitions.

Visit BromGeistman.com to learn more about the world of Aethara and the next book in the series.

9 798994 956205